Kaiki: Uncanny Tales from Japan

Volume 3 – Tales of the Metropolis

Kaiki:
Uncanny Tales from Japan

Volume 3 – Tales of the Metropolis

Foreword by Robert Weinberg
Introduction by Higashi Masao

Kaiki: Uncanny Tales from Japan
Volume 3 - Tales of the Metropolis

Book design by j-views, Kamakura, Japan: info@j-views.biz
FG-JP0009-L23
ISBN: 978-4-902075-10-6

KURODAHAN PRESS
Kurodahan Press is a division of Intercom Ltd.
#403 Tenjin 3-9-10, Chuo-ku, Fukuoka 810-0001 Japan
www.kurodahan.com

Dedication

This volume is dedicated to the memory of Rodger Swan (1986–2010), an aspiring translator from Battle Creek, Michigan. Rodger was a graduate in English and Japanese at Western Michigan University and had studied at Keio University in Tokyo. He was living in Iwate at the time of his death from a sudden illness. Rodger was the creator of a series of popular YouTube videos that reviewed Japanese horror films and documented his daily life in Japan. By the time of his passing, his YouTube audience had nearly six thousand online subscribers and his videos had been viewed many tens of thousands of times. Rodger was an avid reader of Japanese literature, and his tastes revolved largely around writers of kaiki fiction, such as Izumi Kyōka, Edogawa Rampo, and Yumeno Kyūsaku. His translation of Toyoshima Yoshio's "The Ghosts of the Metropolis," which appears in this volume in a co-translation with Jeffrey Angles, is his first translation project to be published.

Contents

Secrets of the Metropolis

Robert Weinberg

LET ME BEGIN by repeating a warning that I stated in the earlier books in this series. The introduction to this volume by Higashi Masao is a wonderful description of the stories in this volume and the authors who wrote them. It also offers an excellent checklist of the top horror novels and story collections published in Japan. However, the introduction, describing the effect of earthquakes, lightning and fire on the Japanese people and their fiction, is best read after reading the rest of this book. The editor is so much a fan of the fiction he selected for this book that he feels he needs to describe in great detail why he chose each particular story. And, in doing so, reveals most, if not all, of the major plot twists and surprises in the fiction. Don't skip the introduction—it is filled with fascinating details and information about the Japanese horror story. But read it after having read all the stories in the book.

According to the editor, the Japanese have always feared earthquakes, lightning, and fire. These natural disasters serve a powerful symbols of fear for today's inhabitants of Japan's densely built cities. Much of the history of modern Japan has been shaped by destructive weather and earthquakes. Higashi writes that "Fires and fights are the flowers of Edo," where Edo is the original name given Tokyo. The residents, known as the *Edokko*[1], have survived great fires that destroyed their city like a continuing cycle of religious ceremonies. From the ashes of the old, they have rebuilt the city into something new and modern, thus resulting in today's high-tech city of Tokyo.

The catastrophes that befell the nation's cultural center not only led to the rebuilding of the capital but also served as a powerful influence on the modern weird tales and ghost stories.

The period from the Taishō to early Shōwa eras was the golden age for uncanny tales, with strange and mysterious stories found

1. Literally, "child of Edo." The term typically refers to those who were born and raised in Edo (Tokyo).

in every literary genre. Authors included Akutagawa Ryūnosuke (1892–1927) and Tanizaki Junichirō, both included in this volume; the stars of Taishō literature, Edogawa Rampō (1894–1965) and Yumeno Kyūsaku (1889–1936), who wrote the immensely popular detective fiction and mysteries of the time; Kunieda Shirō (1887–1943) and Nomura Kodō (1882–1963), authors of strange weird fiction; and Miyazawa Kenji (1896–1933) and Suzuki Miekichi (1882–1936), who wrote children's stories and fantastic fiction.

Readers looking for ordinary contemporary horror fiction might find the contents of this book somewhat off-kilter. There are few ordinary tales in this collection. Stories come to an end without reaching what seems to be a logical conclusion. Other tales combine what seems to be attempts at journalism that take sudden turns to the outlandish and the bizarre. Several stories describe events that make no sense but that are complete in themselves. Horror is present in this volume. It permeates the pages of this book, but it is the horror of the spirit. It is the coldness of the city, not of the grave, that sends chills down the reader's spine. These stories are filled with the ghosts of the metropolis.

Several stories reprinted in this volume deserve special mention. "In A Cup of Tea" is very typical of the best kind of Japanese horror story. The menace is so subtle that it creeps up unaware on the reader. It defines what makes a quiet horror story. Highly recommended and not easily forgotten.

"A Bizarre Reunion" is a long story telling of a prostitute going mad in Tokyo. It appeared two years before a major earthquake hit the city and killed many thousands of people. The phrase "Tokyo will turn into a wilderness" was seen by many readers as foreshadowing the destruction of Edo. The house of the lead character was quite near the site of a uniform factory where a fire killed nearly forty thousand people!

"The Arm" by Kawabata Yasunari has one of the most unusual openings of a story in any anthology:

> "I will lend you the arm for one night." She removed her right arm at the shoulder and, using her left hand, placed it on my lap.
>
> "Thank you," I said, looking down at my knees. Her arm felt warm against my legs.

Kawabata Yasunari (1899–1972), is the most famous author in this anthology. He won Japan's first Nobel Prize in literature. "One Arm" showcases his vivid imagination and unusual view of storytelling. It is a very strange story.

"The Talisman" by Masao Yamakawa reads like prime Richard Matheson. It is a perfectly told non-supernatural horror story.

The contents of this volume present a fascinating look at the Japanese weird and horror genres. While there are similarities to the American and British horror fields, the Japanese stories follow their own rules and set their own boundaries. They are exciting and different and deserve a great deal more attention than they have so far received. The future of horror fiction is printed in this book.

Robert Weinberg
Oak Forest, Illinois
May 2012

Earthquakes, Lightning, Fire, and Father

Higashi Masao

東雅夫

Translated and with footnotes by Miri Nakamura

THE JAPANESE HAVE always feared earthquakes, lightning, fire, and fathers—listed here in order of magnitude.

With the collapse of patriarchy, the image of the *ganko oyaji* (pigheaded old man) has lost its hold on society. Earthquakes, lightning, and fire, however, remain as symbols of immanent fear for today's inhabitants of Japan's densely built cities.

The Japanese archipelago sits atop the junction of the North American, Eurasian, Pacific and Philippine tectonic plates. Japan is a narrow archipelago stretching from north to south atop a hive of seismic activity and volcanoes just waiting to explode.

In his famous epic *Japan Sinks* (日本沈没, 1973), Komatsu Sakyō (1931-2011), the "father of postwar Japanese science fiction" ("The *Kudan*'s Mother," Volume 2), depicted a future in which the Japanese archipelago is destroyed by an enormous tectonic shift and sinks into the sea. The Great East Japan Earthquake of March 11, 2011 and its aftermath have demonstrated the verisimilitude of his work, further strengthening its impact.

The images of the great tsunami that devastated the northeastern seacoast after the magnitude 9.0 earthquake—the strongest on record in Japan—have driven home with terrible clarity the ferocity of nature, a ferocity that transcends human comprehension.

THE TOKYO MEGALOPOLIS, which is situated at the juncture of the four gigantic plates—serves as the setting for the tales in this volume.

The Japanese capital (formerly Edo) has seen its share of disasters—earthquakes, fires, and air raids during World War II—throughout its four hundred-year history. Every time it has been reduced to rubble, it has been reborn like the phoenix.

About three hundred years ago, a natural disaster shook the foundations of the Tokugawa shogunate. Japan was entering the

Genroku era (1688–1704), a golden age for the nation both economically and culturally.

The Genroku Earthquake, with an estimated magnitude of 8.1, devastated the entire eastern region of Japan, including Edo, in 1703. Four years later, the Hōei Earthquake (magnitude 8.7), which affected almost the entire Pacific seacoast of western Japan, triggered the Hōei[1] Eruption of Mount Fuji forty-nine days later.

Sacred Mount Fuji, famed as the symbol of Japan, appears calm now, but in the past it was a fierce mountain that erupted many times. Its ashes and destruction even reached Edo to the east.

ONE MIGHT WELL ask: Why build the national capital in such a dangerous location?

Japan is small, and every region is susceptible to earthquakes. But setting these geographical limitations aside, one must also consider "the sense of impermanence" (無常観), the Buddhist concept that all living things must constantly live, die, and transform—that nothing is everlasting.

The medieval classic "An Account of My Hut" (方丈記, 1212) by the hermit Kamo no Chōmei (1153?–1216) is a kind of "natural disaster literature" that describes the earthquakes, fires, windstorms, and famine that plagued the capital of Kyoto. The opening passages reveal the Japanese people's fundamental outlook on natural disaster:

> Though the river's current never fails, the water passing, moment by moment, is never the same. Where the current pools, bubbles form on the surface, bursting and disappearing as others rise to replace them, none lasting long. In this world, people and their dwelling places are like that, always changing.
>
> When you see the ridgepoles of the impressive houses in Heian-kyō competing to rise above one another—dwellings of people of high status or of low—they look like they might stand

> for generations, but when you inquire you discover there are very few still standing from ages past. Some may have burned down just last year, and been rebuilt since. Or a mansion may have disappeared, to be replaced by smaller houses. Things change in the lives of the people living in those houses, too. There may be just as many people, but in places where I might have known twenty or thirty people in my youth, I may only recognize one or two now. Some die in the morning; others are born in the evening. That's the way it is with the people of this world—they are like those bubbles floating on the water.[1]

It would be a mistake to interpret these words as mere resignation in the face of nature's power. Instead of trying to oppose nature, the Japanese have learned to sense danger and avoid it, thereby keeping damage to a minimum.

This idea of impermanence is not limited to Buddhism. The national religion, Shintoism, which originated in nature worship, conducts unique rituals in which sacred monuments are periodically rebuilt. The two most famous examples are the Reconstruction Ceremony of the Grand Shrine of Ise, in which the main building of the shrine is rebuilt every twenty years thereby reinstating the deity's spiritual body, and Suwa Grand Shrine's Onbashira Festival, in which priests drag gigantic trees from a sacred mountain and use them for the four pillars that support the shrine. This ceremony is held in the spring of the year of the tiger and the year of the monkey.

As evidenced by Catholic cathedrals and the shrines of ancient Greece, the West typically strives to make its religious monuments solid and durable. In Japan, however, it seems that they were envisioned from the beginning to be "reset" periodically.

---

1. Translation by Robert N. Lawson, available on Washburn University's website, http://washburn.edu/reference/bridge24/Hojoki.html, accessed January 4, 2012.

THE SAME GOES for the myriad neighborhoods of Edo, the capital since the early modern era.

As the old saying goes, "Fires and fights are the flowers of Edo." Its residents, the *Edokko,* have survived the great fires that destroyed their city like sacred ceremonies. They have rebuilt a new city each time from its ashes, resulting in today's high-tech city of Tokyo.

These catastrophes that befell the nation's cultural center not only led to the rebuilding of the megalopolis but also powerfully influenced the evolution of modern weird tales and ghost stories.

As I mentioned in the first two volumes of this series, the culture of strange tales (*kaidan*) reached its apex in the Bunka and Bunsei eras (1804–1830) of the Edo period, beginning with the late seventeenth-century *kana* booklets (*kana zōshi*). This culture experienced a revival in the early twentieth century, when a new generation of writers took it up after a hiatus in the late nineteenth century.

The epitome of this culture was the boom in ghost storytelling circles (*hyaku monogatari*). This fervor for ghost stories only increased during the *belle époque* of Taishō Japan (1912–1926) after the end of the Meiji era (1868–1912)with its mottos of "Prosperous Nation, Strong Military" and "Production, Promotion."[2]

One of the most important of such storytelling gatherings took place on July 12, 1914, at a gallery near Tokyo's Kyōbashi. Coincidentally, that same day Tokyo's *Miyako Shimbun* newspaper started a series on ghost-storytelling circles entitled "The Festival of Ghost Stories" *(kaidan shōryō matsuri)*, pointing up the surging interest in the genre. The enthusiasm for strange tales that

2. As Richard J. Samuels explains, these two phrases were "the two pillars of the evolving ideology of the Meiji period (37)." They were part of the Meiji government's effort to centralize power and reform industrial policy to fit the capitalist model. For more, see Samuels' *Rich Nation, Strong Army: National Security and the Technological Transformation of Japan* (Ithaca: Cornell University Press, 1994), especially pp. 37-45.

had swept over the literary scene was beginning to attract widespread attention from the general public as well.

An art gallery was holding an exhibit of "monster drawings" (妖怪画; *obake-e*) that had just opened on July 10. This was no doubt the reason for the choice of the location of the storytelling gathering and reveals the potential that strange tales held for bringing together literature and the visual arts.

Participants included Izumi Kyōka ("Sea Dæmons," Volume 2), often cited as the author who launched the literary boom; his close friend, famed Shinpa actor Kitamura Rokurō (1871–1961); and about sixty others, all famous figures from literary, art, or theatrical circles. Other distinguished authors of the Taishō and Shōwa (1926–1989) eras also took part, such as Tanizaki Junichirō (1886–1965), Okamoto Kidō (1872–1939; "Here Lies a Flute," Volume 1), and Hasegawa Shigure (1879–1941).

This ghost-storytelling circle is also well known for an actual supernatural incident that occurred. Among the participants that day was a last-minute addition, a man whose face was unfamiliar to the others. The koto player Suzuki Koson (1875–1931), who was also present that day, later recalled, "There was a man who sat apart and alone from the others. He seemed lost in his own thoughts, and he sat in the corner with his head hanging down, as if he were depressed. It was evident to everyone that there was some dark shadow haunting the man."[3]

> Night began to fall, and a couple of the participants had already left. At that point, the man leaned forward and said, "It is rude for me to just listen to the others' tales, so I would like to tell a ghost story as well." He began to speak with a serious face, starting with a long preface, saying, "This is a story that is important to my family," then went on. "The story took place

3. Suzuki Koson, "Ghost Stories Born of Ghost Stories" (怪談が生む怪談)

> around the end of the Bakumatsu era, sixty to seventy years ago. It is about how my father turned the tables on his enemy and defeated him. My father's lord was an extremely short-tempered man, and because of this a chief retainer by the name of Tanaka Kawachinosuke had to commit seppuku. This is where the story begins." He then began go speak in a low voice.

Kyōka and the others were listening to him, engrossed in the story's beginning, but for some strange reason, according to Suzuki, the man would go no further, which is not to say that he stopped speaking. Once he had stated that Tanaka Kawachinosuke was forced to commit seppuku, he would return to the beginning of his tale and start over again with "This is a story that is important to my family." It was as if he had turned into a mysterious broken record.

An article called "Haunting at Ghost Storytelling," published July 21, 1919 in the *Miyako Shimbun*, refers to this incident:

> Kitamura, who was intently listening to him, at first thought that the man must have forgotten his story. However, after the words "Tanaka Kawauchisuke had to commit seppuku" were repeated five times, he began to think otherwise. Izumi poked Kitamura's knee. The two exchanged glances and were becoming fidgety, but the man would not go beyond that line. The participants began to leave one by one, and eventually, only Kitamura, Izumi, Kashio Shūkiku, and Suzuki Koson were left. Suzuki eventually slipped out, and when he went downstairs, the others were gossiping about it, dumbfounded by the entire event.

There are several versions of the conclusion of this anecdote, and it is unclear which is authentic. Some say that the man had a stroke there and died. Some say that his health rapidly deteriorated after he returned home, and he passed away. None of the newspaper articles dealing with that night's gathering mention a death, so that version seems unlikely.

Tanaka Kawauchisuke (1815–1862) was a samurai and a radical supporter of the emperor. Stories about his fate circulated up through the postwar period, and manga artist and essayist Tokugawa Musei (1894–1971), anthropologist Ikeda Yasaburō (1914–1982), and writer Tanaka Sumie (1908–2000) have all produced adaptations of his strange story.

On July 4, 1919, the *Miyako Shimbun* began to publish an anonymous column called "Ghost Storytelling Gatherings and People," which served as a witness to the ghost-storytelling boom. Here is the opening of the first column, "Ghost Story: Three Men" (怪談三人男):

> Around the time of the Obon Festival, numerous ghost-storytelling gatherings are organized. Their number increases as autumn approaches. Various people choose various places and hold them with varying intents. There may not be an official ghost-storytelling circle in the strict sense, but when someone organizes a gathering, a group of regulars always appears. Hence, these circles could be deemed as official organizations.

The popularity of ghost-storytelling circles affected the new literature that arose within Taishō literary circles. Chūōkōron, a journal that served as a gateway to success for Taishō writers and a bastion of Taishō democratic sentiment, published a special issue called "One Hundred Modern Ghost Stories" (当世百物語). It represents the epitome of this flourishing of uncanny tales.

Thirteen sensationally popular writers and prominent progressive authors—Kikuchi Kan (1888–1948), Kume Masao (1891–1952), Osanai Kaoru (1881–1928), Toyoshima Yoshio (1890–1955), Satō Haruo (1892–1964), Murō Saisei (1889–1962), Ogawa Mimei (1882–1961), Uno Kōji (1891–1961), Inagaki Taruho (1900–1977)—joined forces, each with a personal and frightening tale, to create a masterpiece.

The period from the Taishō to early Shōwa eras was the golden age for uncanny tales, with strange and mysterious stories found in every literary genre. Authors included Akutagawa Ryūnosuke (1892–1927) and Tanizaki Junichirō, both included in this volume; the stars of Taishō literature, Edogawa Rampō (1894–1965) and Yumeno Kyūsaku (1889–1936), who wrote the immensely popular detective fiction and mysteries of the time; Kunieda Shirō (1887–1943) and Nomura Kodō (1882–1963), authors of strange weird fiction; and Miyazawa Kenji (1896–1933) and Suzuki Miekichi (1882–1936), who wrote children's stories and fantastic fiction.

LESS THAN SIX months after the publication of the special issue, a magnitude 7.9 earthquake struck the Tokyo region at 11:58 a.m. on September 1, 1923. It would come to be known as the Great Kantō Earthquake.

Being lunchtime, conflagrations erupted at more than a hundred sites throughout Tokyo. The fires were fanned by the strong winds and lit up the city, centered on the Shitamachi district. More than 65,000 people died within the city limits alone. An Army uniform factory in Sumida Ward, near the Kokugikan sumo arena in Ryōgoku, was the site of an especially terrible disaster. Many residents who had taken refuge there were caught up in a firestorm, resulting in the death of 38,000 people.

AKUTAGAWA'S "A BIZARRE Reunion" is a subtle horror story published two years prior to the earthquake. The repetition of the disturbing phrase "Tokyo will turn into a wilderness" seems to foreshadow the imminent destruction of Tokyo, and the words have an eerie ring even today. Even more alarming, the house of the mistress, the scene of the story, is near the former site of the uniform factory mentioned above.

Akutagawa was a true *Edokko*, who had loved reading Izumi Kyōka's strange and fantastic literature since childhood. In high school, he adored Yanagita Kunio's *Legends of Tōno* (遠野物語, 1910, Volume 2) and recorded his own strange experiences, which were published later under the title of *Shōzu shii* 椒図志異. While at the University of Tokyo, Natsume Sōseki (1867-1916) praised Akutagawa's short story "The Nose" (鼻, 1916), and overnight, Akutagawa became the favorite child of the Taishō literati. He embodied the golden age of strange fiction in which Tokyo was imbued with a sense of the mysterious. In addition to "A Bizarre Reunion," Akutagawa wrote numerous memorable masterpieces, such as "The Old Woman" (妖婆, 1919) and "Black-Robed Maria" (黒衣聖母, 1920), which are more traditional strange tales, and the ghastly novella "Kappa" (河童, 1927), written just before he committed suicide with an overdose of sleeping pills.

Akutagawa also penned essays such as "Western Ghosts" (近頃の幽霊, 1921) that reveal his profound knowledge of Western spiritualism and fantastic fiction. His contemporaries, Buddhist philosopher Inoue Enryō (1858–1919), poet Mizuno Yōshū (1883–1947), and author Hirai Kinzō (1859–1916) also researched Western spiritualism, but Akutagawa was the first to make concrete observations and commentaries on the relationship between occultism and the literature of his time.

MURAYAMA KAITA (1896–1919) was one of the first artists seduced by modern Tokyo's mysterious powers. Versed in Fauvism, he became known as a precocious genius with his free-spirited and elegant art works and poetry, but he died young after living the life of a nomad.

His rare talent shines through in the few short stories he left behind. Among them, "The Diabolical Tongue" stands out as a harbinger of Taishō decadence. The figure of the youth who wanders the city at night, enticed by the sweet scent of cannibalism and homosexual love, foreshadows the coming of the age of *ero-guro* nonsense.[4]

SPEAKING OF TAISHŌ decadence, one unforgettable essay is "The Works of Tanizaki Junichirō" (谷崎潤一郎氏の作品, 1911), which leading author Nagai Kafū (1879–1959) published in the November issue of *Mita bungaku*, a literary journal that would eventually give rise to an aesthetic school[5].

In this essay, Kafū declares that what makes Tanizaki's literature unique is his "mysterious profundity" (*shinpi yūgen*) created through "brutality and fear experienced by the body" (*nikutaijō no zannin to kyōfu*). This superb expression can be applied to the common Japanese motif of tumorous human faces that are ubiquitous in early modern ghost tales and to Tanizaki's famous piece "The Face," which was so closely tied to the film industry that it came to represent avant-garde culture at the time, as well as to Kaita's "The Diabolical Tongue."

Strange occurrences brought on by physical change are a familiar theme in Western fantastic literature such as Nikolai Gogol's "Nose" (1835–36), Guy de Maupassant's "The Hand" (1883), W. F. Harvey's "The Beast with Five Fingers" (1928), and E. L. White's "Lukundoo"

4. *Ero-guro* (erotic, grotesque) nonsense was an esthetic that arose in the 1920s and the 1930s. Historian Miriam Silverberg defines the three terms as follows: "ero" stands for the sexual promiscuity of the female body, expressiveness and affirmation of social intimacy; "guro" is tied to the malformed and obscenely criminal, social inequities and economic hardships; "nansensu" is associated with slapstick. She associates it with political, ironic humor that took on themes as transformations wrought by a modernity dominated by Euro-American mores. See Miriam Silverberg, *Erotic Grotesque Nonsense: The Mass Culture of Japanese Modern Times* (Berkeley, Los Angeles, and London: University of California Press, 2006), p. 30.

5. The aesthetic school (*tanbi-ha*) refers to a group of writers who were opposed to Japanese Naturalism, a movement known for realistic depictions and scientific method.

(1925). The Freudian notion of a modern self and its discontent also seems to underlie these works.

"The Diabolical Tongue" and "The Face," two works rich with the mysterious beauty and glory of Taishō decadence, reveal the development of Japanese uncanny tales in the Taishō era and were on a par with modern Western works.

WHILE STUDYING FRENCH literature at the University of Tokyo, Toyoshima Yoshio (1890–1955) made a name for himself as a writer by publishing in the third issue of *New Tide of Thought* (*Shinshichō*), along with Akutagawa and Kikuchi Kan. He later became known as a talented translator of *Les Misérables* (1862) and *Jean-Christophe* (1904–1912). From the Taishō era throughout World War II he produced numerous supernatural works influenced by Western spiritualism, as did Akutagawa.

"Ghosts of the Metropolis" opens with this symbolic sentence: "In the metropolis, there is a unique type of ghostly presence that haunts the city." It is a "haunted house" story in which an inhabitant comes to recognize the vague, collective existence of senses arising from the souls and bodies of the city's countless people, a grand representation of Tokyo as a gigantic haunted mansion. Instead of using the phrase *yūki* (幽鬼; ghost-demon), Toyoshima chooses *yūki* (幽気; ghostly sense), creating an innovative work that is imbued with an unprecedented spiritual realism. The formless sense of anxiety and fear that arises from the hustle and bustle of the city, the city's underside, reveals itself throughout the story. This tendency can probably be traced back to Edgar Allan Poe's "The Man of the Crowd" (1850).

EDOGAWA RAMPŌ, WHO adopted Poe's name and became the father of Japanese detective fiction, is another author who wove fantastic and strange tales about cities. He became a wanderer of the loud quarters and alleyways of nighttime Tokyo, drawn by the alluring bustle and conflict.

"Doctor Mera's Mysterious Crimes" is an outstanding example. It is set up as a story the author himself heard from a youth he met in front of the monkey cage at Ueno Zoo while out on a stroll. It is a story of "moonlight enchantment" in which the mysterious light of the moon completely alters the face of the city as it is seen in daylight. It is the author's homage to the nighttime cityscape. (The fact that the story skips over the Great Kantō Earthquake, too, is masterful.)

Rampō's essay "Introduction to Strange Tales" (怪談入門, 1948–49), published in the mystery magazine *Hōseki* in the postwar era, was the first comprehensive introduction of the literary history of Western strange fiction and greatly influenced later writers and researchers alike. Rampō also collaborated with renowned translator of strange fiction Hirai Teiichi (1902–1976, "Midnight Encounters," Volume 2) and co-edited the second volume of *Great Stories of Horror and the Supernatural* (怪奇小説傑作集, 1957). The collection includes works ranging from Sheridan Le Fanu to H.P. Lovecraft, and it was one of the earliest anthologies of British and American strange tales. Rampō added entire chapters, not merely pages, to Japan's literary history of weird fiction, both as a researcher and as an introducer.

THUS FAR, I have introduced the works according to their publication dates, but the next work I will take up, "The Midsummer Emissary" by Minagawa Hiroko (1929–), is the most recent work in this volume.

The setting is a "sandbank" (*nakasu*) at the border of Nihonbashi in Chūō ward and Kiyosu in Kōtō Ward in Tokyo. The site is near the Sumida River that Akutagawa called the homeland of the heart of Tokyoites. A great deal of construction has been done in the area since the early modern period, which served as a pleasure quarter during the Taishō period. The river has since been filled in, leaving only endless, bland buildings.

Minagawa writes in a skillful style reminiscent of Izumi Kyōka. She brings to life the mysteriously elegant waterside utopia that is now a remnant of the distant past. Led by her sensual prose, the reader is lost among the narrow pathways of the sandbank, unable to discern if the story's characters belong to this world or the next. Minagawa has worked in a variety of genres. Her *Collection of Strange Outlooks on Noh Theater* (変相能楽集, 1988) includes works like "Semimaru" (蝉丸), "Nomori" (野守), and "The Two Shizukas" (二人静) that depict a fantastic world based on the aesthetic of fantasy Noh (*mugen nō*).[6] *Rose Mourning* (薔薇忌, 1990) is a collection of ghost stories dealing with characters from performance art such as theater and Butoh dance, and they are the products of today's "horror japonesque" aesthetic. *Annals of Ghostly Cherry Blossoms* (妖櫻記, 1993) is based on *Cherry Blossom Princess* (桜姫全伝曙草紙, 1805) by Edo-period author Santō Kyōden (1761–1816). Minagawa's insatiable appetite for writing and her sense of her own vision remain unchanged.

THE GOLDEN ERA of strange fiction that spanned the period from 1912 through 1935 came to an end with the Marco Polo Bridge Incident of 1937 that set off the Second Sino-Japanese War and led to Japan's entry into World War II. Hisao Jūran's (1902–1957) "In Thy Shadow" was published during these dark times in *New Youth* (*Shin seinen*), a bastion of modernism and detective fiction. The story surrounds a youth who works as a tutor for an ex-aristocratic family, at their Western-style mansion where a cruel beauty resides. A fantastic work soaked in Taishō decadence, its prose focuses on the interior world of the mansion, seemingly reflecting the way Japan

6. Noh plays are generally divided into two "moods." *Mugen nō* normally has ghosts and spirits that appear in the second act, and *genzai nō* (realistic Noh) normally concerns the quotidian world.

itself turned inward during the war. Jūran is known for spiritualist fiction of a different type than that written by Toyoshima. His masterpieces include "Premonition" (予言, 1947), "A Living Spirit" (生霊, 1941), "From Beyond" (黄泉から, 1946), and "Path through the Clouds" (雲の小径, 1955).

THE REST OF the works here all belong to the postwar decades.

ENDŌ SHŪSAKU (1923–1996) is known for his wide range of works, varying from religious Catholic literature to light humorous essays, but he has also been active in the field of strange fiction. His occult suspense works dealing with the demons deep within the mind of modern man could only have been written by a Catholic author. In "Demon at Noon" (真昼の悪魔, 1980)a female doctor carries out evil deeds, egged on by a demon. In "Afternoon Evil" (悪霊の午後, 1983), a widow possessed by Balinese sorceress Calong Arang releases the desires hidden deep within the hearts of her suitors, leading them to their destruction.

If one were to name the work that really made Endō's name in the field of strange fiction, it would, however, have to be the short story collection *Spider*, published by Shinchōsha. It was serialized as authentic reportage with the description "Shūsaku's Scary Tale" in the weekly *Shūkan Shinchō* magazine. Endō managed to elicit the unique value of strange fiction that keeps us wavering between truth and fiction. He thus brought the genre, which was moribund even after the war, back to life with this progressive work. "Spider," the collection's representative work, is structured like a typical *hyakumonogatari* and is thus an interesting text for considering the ghost-storytelling boom that dominated literary circles in the late Meiji and Taishō eras.

YAMAKAWA MASAO'S (1930–1965) "The Talisman" (お守り, 1960) is also a seminal work that marked a milestone in the history of postwar strange fiction. With the recommendation of Arthur Koestler (1905–1983) and the English translation of Edward Seidensticker (1921–2007), it won the honor of being published in the British magazine *Life* in 1964.

The story takes place in the large housing complex where the protagonist lives with his wife. As stated in the work itself, people aspired to live in these residential complexes, which were the symbol of the new lifestyle of postwar Japan. These complexes, public housing and the system for the recruitment of residents were established in 1956. This housing was the goal of the ever-increasing population of Tokyo, which became the first city in the world to reach a population of ten million in 1962, and served as the breeding ground for the new labor force that led Japan from postwar economic recovery to its economic peaks.

In fact, many of those under forty today grew up in such complexes and feel perfectly at home there. "The Talisman" is a dark comedy about the salaried workers who reside there. One explains, "I began to feel a strange edginess or anxiety, a vague fear that I couldn't pin down, as if I couldn't find myself." Their dark, loud laughter reverberates throughout the work, and the story is like a fable that foreshadows the future of postwar Japanese society.

KAWABATA YASUNARI (1899–1972), undoubtedly the most famous name abroad among the authors of this anthology, garnered Japan's first Nobel Prize in literature. "One Arm" showcases the author's potential as a writer versed in a supernatural aesthetic and in immorality.

Kawabata lost his parents at an early age, and he had a deep interest in the afterworld from his youth. In the 1920s especially, he became interested in spiritualism, which was at its height at the time, and he raced through translations of Nicholas Flammarion (1842–1925) and Oliver Lodge (1851–1940). The works born out of these efforts were: "White Full Moon" (白い満月, 1925), "Photos with Flowers" (花ある写真, 1930), and "Requiem" (慰霊歌, 1932) in which a young girl who has psychic ability begins to experience supernatural phenomena such as spirit photos, poltergeists, telepathy, clairvoyance, and ghostly manifestations. These works are marked by a kind of occult lyricism. The work that epitomizes this trend in his writing is the renowned "Lyric Poem" (抒情歌, 1932).

Some of Kawabata's postwar short stories also travel between this world and the other: "Chrysanthemum on the Rocks" (岩に菊, 1952), "Silence" (無言, 1953), "Meeting, and Parting, and Meeting Again" (離合, 1954), and "Yumiura" (弓浦市, 1958). These works attest to the author's words: "I do not believe postwar actualities or customs. I do not believe what exists in the real. I distance myself from the concept of mimetic depiction that lies at the bottom of modern literature."[7]

I CHOSE AKAE Baku's (1933–) "Expunged by Yakumo" to provide a fitting close to this three-volume anthology that began with Lafcadio Hearn's (1850–1904) "In a Cup of Tea." The work is a masterpiece that creates a mysterious aura that emanates from the intricate box-within-a-box construction that takes in Hearn's story in its entirety. Akae captures the love-hate relationship of the man and woman, possessed by the mysterious attraction of traditional arts, in a masterful style resembling classical literature. His fictional world is referred to as "Akae Aesthetic" by his passionate devotees. He is a representative writer of today's "horror japonesque," along with Minagawa Hiroko.

His other notable work is a collection of weird short stories, *The Parade of a Hundred Demons* (野ざらし百鬼行, 1977). Its "Beautiful Skull" (花曝れ首, 1975) takes place in Kyoto's Adashino neighborhood and captures the relationship between a woman and two young ghosts, trapped in an endless cycle of blind love, in the style of fantasy Noh theater. "Funeral of Spring" (春喪祭, 1976)

7. "Pathos"(哀愁), *Shakai*, Vol. 2, No. 10, Oct. 1947

involves a girl who is picked out by an evil young monk and wanders around the darkness of Hasegawa Temple, buried in peony flowers. Her fate is recounted through the sad twanging of a biwa. "Phantom Castle" (上空の城, 1977) is a long, mysterious love romance about a girl and a boy possessed by the ghostly shadows of a castle tower that entraps a demon in its abyss. Akae received the Izumi Kyōka Prize in 1984 for "Expunged by Yakumo" (1984) and his long essay *Strait* (海峡, 1983).

MOROHOSHI DAIJIRŌ (1949-) is a genius, deservedly recognized as an artist of fantastic manga in contemporary Japan. He won the Seventh Tezuka Osamu Prize for his speculative science fiction piece "Bio City" (生物都市, 1974), and he is still publishing "Demon Hunter" (妖怪ハンター, 1974-) and "Mud Men" (マッドメン, 1975-), fantastic, romance serials that are based on his deep knowledge of ethnography. He has also written "The Monkey King and other Chinese Legends" (西遊妖猿伝, 1983-) as well as "The Zhi Guai Mysteries" (諸怪志異, 1987-), which brings in China's *zhi guai* (ghost/demons) romances, as well as works that bring Cthulhu into our daily lives, (dubbed 'Cthulhu in the Neighborhood,' or 御近所クトゥルー神話) and the serial "Bookmarks and Paper Fish" (栞と紙魚子, 1995-).

"A Sinister Spectre" is a seminal work from early in his career. It captures the quintessentially Japanese experience of commuting in packed trains, its inhuman nature, and the inhumanity of the *thing* waiting next to the railroad tracks. It thus discloses the depth of the darkness produced by Japan's rapid postwar economic growth. The profound impact of this work remains unchanged even today.

Tokyo
December 2011

A Bizarre Reunion

奇怪な再会

(Kikei na saikai)

Akutagawa Ryūnosuke (1921)

芥川 龍之介

Translation by Steven P. Venti

IT WAS EARLY winter in the 28th year of Meiji[1] when Oren was brought to live in the Yokoami area of Tokyo's Honjo district. She was given a cramped, single-story residence that overlooked the Okurahashi Bridge as well as bamboo and trees on the far side of the river in Otakekura, where Ryōgoku Depot was later built. It was a rustic spot in a relatively remote neighborhood, with little to see except tall trees that rose up to block out constantly raining skies. And at first, on those not uncommon nights when the master of the house failed to come around, it could be a very lonely place, too.

"What's that noise, Grandma?" Oren would ask of the elderly woman who kept house for her.

"Oh, that? That would be a night heron," Grandma would tell her. Grandma didn't see too well, but she and Oren spent more than a few evenings together, having conversations like that by the light of a kerosene lamp.

The master of the house was a man named Makino, who never went more than three days at a time without showing his face. Sometimes he'd show up in the afternoon on his way home from work at the municipal offices, cutting a dashing figure in his Army uniform with its warrant officer first-class insignia. Other times, he would not arrive until after nightfall, when he crossed Umayabashi Bridge on his way from where his family lived. He had a wife and two children—a boy and a girl.

Oren soon took to wearing her hair in the *marumage* style typical of married women. By this time, Makino was showing up almost nightly, sitting at the sunken hearth and getting Oren to keep his cup full while he picked at delicacies like mullet roe or fermented sea cucumber from a table on the tatami mat in front of him.

---

1. 1895

This would remind Oren of her former life and draw forth vivid memories of a certain establishment where she had once lived and worked. Yet remembering old times and the faces of her "sisters" would also intensify the loneliness of having come to live in a country so far from home, and this sense of helplessness left a dull ache in her heart. She was also annoyed by the fact that Makino was gaining weight rather steadily and had become disgustingly corpulent.

Makino, on the other hand, loved just to sit there, sip at his sake contentedly, and gaze at Oren's face as he told some joke, after which he would inevitably burst into laughter.

"So, Oren," he would say, "life in Tokyo isn't all that bad, is it?"

Oren generally responded to questions like that by flashing him a smile and refilling his cup with more sake. Makino's duties kept him pretty busy, and he rarely spent the night in Yokoami. As soon as he noticed that the clock by his pillow was approaching midnight, he would start to snake his pudgy arms through the sleeves of his knit undershirt. Oren would crouch beside him on one knee, absentmindedly helping him get dressed for the trip home, but the look in her eyes gave away her displeasure.

"Grab my overcoat, would you?" Makino would say, sounding annoyed as he stood there with his greasy face illuminated by the lamp.

Eventually, they were playing out this little scene almost every day. Oren always felt exhausted after he was gone, yet being left on her own made her lonely. Whenever it was rainy or windy outside, the rustling of the trees and bamboo in the woods on the opposite bank of the river would tear at her heart. Oren would lie there with her chilly cheeks buried in the alcohol-tinged sleeves of her pajamas and listen intently to that sound, even as her eyes welled up with tears. Other times she would quickly lapse into an oppressive slumber that was itself a kind of nightmare.

– 2 –

One dreary, drizzly day, Oren had just poured Makino a cup of sake when she noticed a bright red welt running across the dark background of his clean-shaven right cheek.

"What happened to you?" she asked with a start.

"This? Oh, my old lady scratched me," responded Makino casually, as if it were nothing more than a joke.

"My, what a horrible woman. What brought it on this time?"

"Nothing brought it on," he said. "Just the usual jealousies. If she does this to me, imagine what she would do if she ever ran into you. She would sink her fangs into your throat in a second. She's a Manchurian bloodhound, that one."

Oren chortled delightedly.

"Hey, it's nothing to laugh at. If she were ever to learn about this place, there's no guarantee that she wouldn't come barging in and do who knows what." Surprisingly, there seemed to be an element of seriousness to what Makino was saying.

"Well, if that happens, it happens," said Oren.

"Aren't you the brave one."

"No, it's not that I'm brave. It's just that people where I was born . . ." Oren seemed deep in thought as she stared into the embers of the open hearth. "Where I was born, they know when to give up."

"Meaning, I suppose, that you aren't the jealous type?" Makino's eyes glinted guilefully as he went on. "Here in Japan, we are all quite jealous. Me more than most."

The conversation was interrupted at that point, however, by the appearance of Grandma carrying a plate of broiled eel from the kitchen—one of Makino's favorite dishes, which he had ordered to celebrate a long-awaited overnight stay at the house in Yokoami.

Not long after they had gone to bed, the rain outside turned to sleet, and Oren lay awake long after Makino fell asleep. There in the depths of her wakeful consciousness cavorted visions of a woman she had never seen: Makino's wife. And although she felt no sympathy for the woman, neither did she feel jealousy or hatred. What she actually felt was a measure of curiosity, and she tried to picture what the woman might look like. Listening to the sound of sleet splattering on the trees outside her window, she wondered what kind of relationship Makino had with his wife and what they fought about.

The clock had already chimed two when she finally began to feel sleepy. A moment passed, and she found herself with a great many other people inside the gloomy cabin of a passenger ship. Through a round porthole, she looked far into the distance across wave upon wave of black ocean to see a crimson-tinged sphere that might have been either the Moon or the Sun. For some reason, all the other passengers sat in the shadows without speaking a word. Oren became more and more frightened of the silence. Her fear continued to grow, and she could feel someone approaching her from behind. Turning around to see who it was, she came face to face with a man she had once loved. He was looking down at her with a sad smile on his face. "Kim!" she cried, calling the man by his family name.

Awakened by the sound of her own voice, Oren realized that it was nearly dawn. Makino lay next to her with his back turned, breathing quietly. Oren watched him, but couldn't tell if he was awake or not.

– 3 –

Makino apparently knew that Oren had been involved with another man but gave no indication that it made any difference to him. The man himself had disappeared about the same time

Makino had fallen head over heels in love with Oren, so you might say that there had never been any real reason for Makino to be jealous.

Oren, on the other hand, had been completely enthralled by the man, and rather than merely missing him, her sentiments were of a more vindictive nature. Unable to accept the fact that he had simply stopped coming to see her, Oren had repeatedly tried to understand the reasons behind his disappearance. In spite of the fact that nothing she could remember of the events immediately before or after he stopped calling could provide a satisfactory explanation, she refused to believe that fickleness alone was all there was to it. Even if circumstances had forced him to leave, they had been far too involved for him to do so without telling her why. And even though Oren dreaded the thought that he might have been the victim of some unforeseen misfortune, that idea did offer her some solace.

Two or three days after having dreamed of the man, Oren was on her way home from the public baths when she noticed a banner flying outside a house with a latticed door. It read: Personal Consultations—Genshō, the Fortuneteller. Oren's curiosity was piqued by the banner itself, which contained the reddish image of a coin where she would have expected to see the yarrow stalks most commonly used to divine the *I Ching*. About to pass the house on by, she impulsively turned and went through the gate to consult this fortuneteller about the man's whereabouts. She was shown into a sunlit parlor that was graciously adorned with potted orchids, books from China, and tea ceremony accoutrements, thereby giving the owner away as a man of the arts. Genshō himself was a stout old man with a shaved head, who at first glance might have been taken for a Buddhist cleric. But his gold teeth and incessant puffing on cigarettes gave him a rather worldly air. Oren looked at him earnestly and asked if he would be so kind as to divine the whereabouts of a close relative, who had suddenly disappeared sometime the previous year.

The old man went to a corner of the room and came back with a small rosewood table, which he placed between them. He then reverentially arranged an incense burner of Chinese porcelain and a gold brocade pouch on the top of the table.

"How old might this relative of yours be?" he asked, to which Oren told him the man's age. "Well then, he is still young. And you know how youth has a way of making mistakes. Easy to say, of course, for an old man like myself." Genshō cast an all-knowing gaze at Oren and laughed suggestively two or three times. "You know what year he was born? Oh, never mind. Year of the Rabbit, under the sign One White Venus."

The old man removed three coins from the gold brocade pouch, each of which was wrapped in a piece of red silk. "The style of divination I practice is called *Tekisenboku*," explained the old man. "It was first practiced during the Han Dynasty by Jing Fang, who used divination coins in place of yarrow stalks. As you undoubtedly know, the yarrow stalks yield the three variations, which in turn produce the eighteen hexagrams, but that is no easy way to divine fortune or misfortune. *Tekisenboku*, on the other hand, remedies this situation, you see. . . ." All the while he made this explanation, smoke from the incense burner wafted toward the ceiling.

– 4 –

One by one, Genshō the Fortuneteller removed the divination coins from their red silk wrappings and briefly held each in the smoke that rose from the incense burner. He then moved to the alcove and bowed his round head to the hanging scroll displayed there. The scroll was in the style of the Kanō school and depicted the four great Chinese sages: Fu Xi, first of the Three Sovereigns;

Wen Wang, King of Zhou; Zhou Gong, Duke of Zhou; and the venerable Confucius. "Omniscient lords in heaven, universal in holiness, listen now to our entreaties and honor us with thy perspicacity. Unrelieved of our burden, we ask only that the Divine Spirits cast away our restiveness and bestow mercy upon us through revelation of our fortune anon." Finishing the incantation, he returned to his seat and tossed all three of the coins on top of the rosewood table. Then, taking up a writing brush and paper scroll, proceeded to record the result as one head and two tails. Each toss of the coins revealed a bit more of the yin and yang governing the situation, and the entire process was completed with six tosses. Oren gazed pensively at the coins as they lay on the table.

"Well now," said Genshō, his eyes fixed on the paper scroll as he contemplated the meaning of what he had recorded during the silent ritual. "This hexagram is traditionally known as Taking Apart, and it is interpreted to mean that things will not work out as desired," he pronounced. Fearfully, Oren moved her gaze from the three coins to the old man's face. "I'm afraid there is little chance of you ever seeing this young relative of yours again." Even as he spoke, Genshō the Fortuneteller began replacing the divination coins one by one in the red silk wrappings from which they had emerged.

"You mean to say that he is no longer alive?" asked Oren in a shaky voice that seemed to convey both dread and relief at the same time.

"I wouldn't want to venture a guess as to that. But I would go so far as to say that there is no hope of the two of you ever meeting again."

"Not ever? No matter what happens?"

Pressed for a clear answer, Genshō closed the mouth of the gold brocade pouch and allowed just a trace of disdain to flash from his chubby face. "If some apocalyptic event were to happen—if

Tokyo were suddenly turned into a wilderness—it's not impossible that you might see him again. But what the hexagrams say is what they say."

Oren, more disheartened than ever, paid the soothsayer's not inconsiderable fee and went straight home.

That evening, she sat before the hearth with her chin planted firmly in the palm of her hands and listened intently to the sound of the kettle on the fire. The fortuneteller's prediction had left her with no clearer idea of what had happened between her and the man. Even worse, the last glimmer of hope that she had held—as infinitesimal and forlorn as it might have been—even that last glimmer of a one-in-a-million chance had vanished into thin air. Was he dead, as the fortuneteller had suggested? The area in which she had lived at the time had been the scene of some disturbing incidents, and it was certainly conceivable that he had been on his way to see her when waylaid by some misfortune. Otherwise, why would he have suddenly disappeared, as if he had never known her?

Oren could feel the glow from the hearth against the white makeup on her cheek, and found herself absentmindedly waving the tongs she held in her hand as if they were a writing brush. Once, twice, three times and more, there above the glowing coals, she traced the Chinese character for the man's name and watched the strokes disappear into empty space.

-5-

Oren was sitting there, tracing in air the man's name over and over, when she suddenly heard a soft cry from Grandma, who was no more than a few steps away on the other side of the sliding paper door that separated the living room from the kitchen.

"What's wrong, Grandma?"

"Mistress! Come here and see for yourself. I just can't believe it. . . ."

Oren hurriedly went to see. The kitchen was only slightly larger than the oven it housed, but there, where the lamp cast a dull and unwavering light against the sliding door, Oren saw Grandma crouch down to gather in her arms a whitish animal.

"A kitten?" she asked.

"No, it's a puppy."

Oren stood with her arms crossed on her chest as she gazed at the animal. Still in Grandma's arms, it looked back and forth with moist eyes as it snorted excitedly.

"It was whining down by the dump this morning when I took out the trash. How on earth did it get in here, I wonder?"

"You have no idea?"

"Of course not. And wouldn't you know, I was right here washing the crockery, when . . . Well, what can you do about it, when you don't see so well."

Grandma opened the kitchen door and was about to put the dog out into the darkness when Oren stopped her.

"Wait! Let me hold it just a bit."

"You really shouldn't, you know. It would be a shame for your clothes to get dirty. . . ."

Paying no heed to Grandma's admonishment, Oren picked up the dog and felt it shiver as she held it in her arms. In an instant, she was taken back to the days when she had had a white puppy for company on evenings when there were no visitors to that certain establishment. "Poor little thing. Maybe we should give it a home."

Grandma's eyelids fluttered, as if she had seen this coming.

"What do you think, Grandma? Let's keep it! I'll take care of it. It won't be any trouble."

Oren let the puppy down to the kitchen floor. It looked about with an innocent expression and then placed one paw up on the cupboard, unsure of whether it was safe to forage about or not.

By the next morning, the white puppy had taken its place at the house in Yokoami, wearing a red collar and roaming about at will. Grandma—a rather meticulous housekeeper by nature—was by no means pleased with this development and would spend the entire day fuming whenever the puppy tried to come inside with muddy paws. Oren, however, who had little to do during the day, thoroughly enjoyed doting on the puppy as if it were a child. The dog was never far away from her during meals and at night was sure to be found curled up next to her futon as she lay sleeping.

"The very idea of that white dog staring at the young mistress's face in the lamplight," said Grandma, describing the situation to the attending physician, Dr. K, almost a year later. "From then on, I found the whole thing very annoying. . . ."

–6–

Grandma was not the only one annoyed by the presence of the white dog. Makino, dressed in his army uniform, saw the dog lounging on the tatami mats and knitted his brow into a scornful frown. "What the . . . Get out of my way!" he said and kicked the dog aside. The dog howled hysterically, the hair on its back bristling, as Makino made his way into the sitting room. "I've had enough of your love of animals," he said, and continued to scowl at the dog disgustedly as he drank. "Didn't you used to have a dog just like this one?"

"I did. And it was white, too."

"You put yourself through quite an ordeal, not wanting to leave that dog behind, as I recall."

Oren smiled reluctantly as she petted the puppy on her knee. She had known full well that taking a dog on an extended journey by ship and train was not practical. But having just separated from the man, it would have been more than she could bear to leave the dog behind and set off for a foreign land as if she had never known the poor animal. And so it was that she spent the night before they left holding the dog in her arms and nuzzling her cheek against its nose, sniffling over and over again as she fought to hold back her tears.

"That was actually a pretty smart dog, but this one doesn't appear to be even half as clever. He's got a rather ordinary-looking nose—or muzzle, that is." Makino was by now inebriated enough that he had forgotten his initial displeasure with the dog and was throwing it pieces of sashimi.

"Really? I rather thought that they quite resembled one another. The only real difference is the color of the muzzle."

"What? The muzzle? Imagine that."

"This one has a black nose, right? The other one's nose was brown." Oren continued to fill Makino's glass even as she recalled the nose of the earlier dog as vividly as if it were there in front of her—always moist with saliva and brown speckles, as if it were the nipple on a wet nurse's breast.

"Hmm, now that you mention it, I suppose a brown nose does make for a more beautiful dog," mused Makino. "He was as handsome as can be, the other one. This black-nosed one is an ugly duckling, for sure. Both male, are they? And here I was thinking that I was the only male who ever came round here. How vain of me, eh?" Makino poked Oren's arm and fell over laughing. He was obviously in high spirits.

Eventually, Makino lost interest in the dog, and the two of them went to bed. Before long, however, the dog came to the sliding door of the room where they lay and began to whine incessantly, eventually putting his paws up on the wooden lattice and scratching at the paper covering. There in the dull glow of the night lamp, Makino sneered and then told Oren to let the dog in. She did so, and the dog walked slowly to the head of the futon, lay down like a pale shadow in the darkness, and then gazed intently at the two of them. Looking back at the dog, Oren thought there was something almost human in the way he was eyeing her.

-7-

A few days later, Makino was able to slip out for the evening and took Oren to a vaudeville performance at a local theater. There were magic acts, sword dances, a magic lantern show, and lion dances—all of which drew such a large crowd that there was barely room to move about. After a short wait, they were shown to rather cramped seats quite far from the stage. Almost as if on cue, everyone sitting around them turned to stare at Oren. You might have thought they had never seen the *marumage* hairstyle before. It made Oren the center of attention for a moment, but there was also something rather sad about it.Standing center stage in the lamplight, a man wearing a white *hachimaki* headband and wielding a long sword danced to the recitation of a poem by an accompanist: "The mists above the hills and mountains that I traverse . . ."

Oren was bored to tears, but Makino lit a cigarette, sat back, and enjoyed the show. Next came the magic lantern show, in which scenes from the Sino-Japanese War were projected onto a scrim hung over the stage. The program included the sinking of the Chinese flagship *Dingyuan,* complete with huge plumes of water, and the famous scene of Captain Higuchi directing his troops in battle even while protecting a Chinese baby held in one arm. The large crowd would cheer each time the Japanese flag appeared, and there were even a few who screamed "Banzai! Long live the Emperor!" at the top of their lungs. Makino, however, had seen combat himself and would have nothing to do with such histrionics. He sat and watched a depiction of the Battle of Yingkou with a smirk on his face. “If that were all there was to it, we would have won the war in a week,” he said to Oren but loudly enough for those around him to hear. Oren kept her eyes fixed on the screen and acknowledged the comment with only the briefest of nods.

Having only rarely seen magic lantern shows before, she quite likely would have been intrigued by even the most unremarkable images. But the scenes in the program that night—the snow-covered roof of the gate to a Chinese castle, donkeys tethered to an old willow tree, Chinese troops with their hair in queues—each was enough to call forth her deepest emotions.

The program ended at ten, and the two of them walked side by side down a lifeless street of nondescript residences with shuttered windows. In the sky above the city, the crescent moon shone down coldly on frosty rooftops. Strolling through the moonlight, Makino puffed on a cigarette and intoned snippets of old-fashioned poetry as if he were still watching the sword dance: “Oh! The furtive snapping of horsewhips as we crossed the river that night . . .”

They had just turned into a side street when Oren suddenly grabbed the sleeve of Makino’s overcoat with a start.

“What’s the matter?” asked Makino, who kept walking but turned around as he did to face Oren.

“I thought someone was calling me.” She sidled up to him with a disturbed look on her face.

“Still calling?” he asked, and stopped momentarily to listen for himself. But there was no sound to be heard in that deserted street, not even the barking of a dog. “Oh, come on. You must be hearing things. Who would be calling you out here?” he asked. “I don’t suppose that magic lantern was a bit much for you, was it?”

“I guess it was just my imagination after all,” she admitted.

– 8 –

The following morning, her toothbrush in her mouth, Oren went out to the veranda to wash her face. Just as always, a bronze basin full of hot water had been placed in front of the well. The wintry yard was lifeless, and cloudy skies reflected on the surface of the river across the garden made a dreary landscape. Gazing at these surroundings as she gargled, Oren recalled a dream that she had forgotten until that moment. In the dream, she had been wandering alone through some kind of wooded area or maybe a grove of bamboo. Following a narrow path, she thought to herself: *At last my wish has come true. Tokyo has turned into a deserted wilderness for as far as the eye can see, and I'll finally be reunited with Kim.* She continued along the path, her heart filled with that thought, when she suddenly heard the sound of a cannon firing and gunshots off in the distance. The treetops above her head gradually turned redder and redder as if bathed in the light from an inferno. War! *A war has started,* she thought and tied to run. But try as she might, her legs would not move any faster.

Not wanting to soil her clothing as she washed her face, she stripped to the waist and was about to dip her hands into the wash basin when she felt something cold and wet on her back. "Ahh!" Not particularly surprised, she turned her moist eyes around to see the puppy wagging its tail as it nuzzled her repeatedly.

– 9 –

Two or three days later, Makino arrived earlier than usual, bringing with him a companion named Tamiya, who was a manager at a well-known mercantile house and who had done quite a bit to help Makino set up Oren in Yokoami.

"Very strange, if you ask me—this *marumage* hairstyle she wears now. Doesn't look a bit like the old Oren I used to know." Sitting in lamplight, Tamiya's pockmarked face shone brightly as he poured his host another cup of sake.

"What do you think, Makino? Either a *shimada* or a *shaguma* would be appropriate enough for a young woman of her background, don't you think?"

"Hey," hissed Makino. "The housekeeper might not have the sharpest vision in the world, but there's nothing wrong with her hearing." Makino pretended to be annoyed, but he was grinning from ear to ear.

"Nothing to worry about. She wouldn't understand even if she did hear us," said Tamiya. "What do you say, Oren? Considering where you came from, you must feel like you are living a dream, eh?"

Oren averted her eyes and continued to play with the dog on her lap.

"I did what I could because Makino asked me to, and let me tell you, I had many a sleepless night pondering just what in hell I would have to do to get everything safely into Kobe if we had been discovered."

"Well, that's over and done with," said Makino, "dangerous as it might have been."

"You've got to be kidding me. Anyway, that's the last time I smuggle human cargo." Tamiya finished off what was in his cup then made a sour face, seemingly on purpose. "But it does make me happy to look around and see everything you've done for Oren," he concluded.

Makino thrust out his meaty arm, offering to fill Tamiya's cup with more sake.

"I'm glad you think so. I know it was a frightening experience for all of us, especially while we were on the ship. Why, just as we were approaching Fukuoka, the seas got frighteningly rough, didn't they, Oren?"

"I thought we were done for," she replied, "and that the ship and everything in it was going down right there." Filling Tamiya's cup herself, Oren at last began to participate in the conversation. For just the briefest moment, she also thought to herself that she might have been better off if the ship had sunk.

"But happily for us all, here we are today. You know, Makino, Oren looks wonderful with her hair done in a *marumage*, but doesn't it make you want to see her just one more time, like she used to look in the old days?"

"I sometimes think so myself, but what can you do?"

"Well, we can't turn back the clock, I guess. But she must have brought at least one old kimono with her, no?"

"Kimono? She brought everything she owned, right down to the last comb and hairpin, too. The more I told her to leave behind, the more she crammed into her luggage." Makino glanced at Oren's face across the hearth, but she appeared not to have heard the comment as she kept an eye on the hot kettle.

"This is our chance, then! How about it, Oren? How about dressing up like it was the old days and pouring us all a drink?"

"After which, you will sit back and reminisce about a certain someone you used to know?"

"If only she had been as comely as Oren. That would be worth reminiscing about." Tamiya's pockmarked face scrunched up in laughter as if someone had tickled him, while he swirled his chopsticks around in a dish of vegetables.

That night, after Tamiya had gone home, Makino broke the news to Oren that he was about to resign his army commission and take a position at a mercantile house. As soon as his resignation was accepted, he claimed, the same well-known business that employed Tamiya would immediately offer him a position at a lucrative salary.

"Once that happens," said Makino, "there's no reason for us to stay here, so why don't we move into a bigger place?" Makino appeared to be tired and lay on his side before the hearth as he puffed away on one of the Manila cigars that Tamiya had brought him that evening.

"This house is more than big enough," said Oren. "It's just Grandma and me, after all." She was feeding leftovers to the dog, who greedily scarfed the morsels down.

"I'd be living there, too, you know," said Makino casually.

"Oh? And what are you going to do with your wife in that case?"

"My old lady? I don't think she and I are going to be together much longer, actually." Judging from the way he said it and the color of his face, it didn't appear that this unexpected news was intended as a joke.

"You wouldn't do anything that you'd regret later, would you?" asked Oren.

"Like it matters? What goes around comes around, and it's not like I'm the only one at fault." Makino stared hard across the room as he puffed on his cigar, but Oren had no response save for a melancholy look on her face.

– 10 –

It was some time later that Grandma told Dr. K about what had happened to the dog. "It started to become a nuisance. Let's see . . . I would say the day after Mr. Tamiya visited. Probably food poisoning or something like that. At first, it just slept in front of the hearth. But before long, I don't know why, but it started soiling the tatami mats. Mistress treated that dog like it was her own child—ordered milk for it, gave it medicine, and took very good care of it. No mystery to that, I'd say. No reason there should be, but can you imagine? It got sicker, and Mistress started to talk to it, and then she got into the habit of conversing with it all day long. When I say conversing with it, of course, I mean that she was talking to herself the whole time. But can you imagine listening to that all night long? Sometimes I would swear that the dog was talking back to her, and that was a creepy feeling, too, let me tell you.

"And on top of that, one time—it was an especially dry and windy winter's day—I had just come home from an errand. Oh, and this errand, by the way, was to a nearby fortune-teller to ask about the dog's illness. So, I had just come home from this errand, and the sliding doors were rattling all over, but I could still hear Mistress' voice coming from the living room. At first I thought that Mr. Makino had come, but looking through the sliding doors, I saw Mistress all by herself. Well, the wind was blowing and the sun was going in and out of the clouds. Mistress was sitting there with that dog in her lap as the room grew light and then dark and then light again. Well, it was just disturbing, and even at my age I had never come across a creepier sight. Of course I felt sorry for Mistress when the dog died, but to tell the truth, I was relieved. What pleased me most was that I wouldn't have to be the one to clean up the mess when the dog soiled the floor anymore.

"When he heard the news, Mr. Makino sat there grinning like a man who just won a bet. Oh, the dog? The dog died some time before either Mistress or I awakened. We found it lying there in front of the dressing table with something green coming out of its mouth. It wasn't much more than two weeks from the time it began moping around in front of the hearth."

Oren discovered the dog lying in front of the dressing table, its cold body in a pool of green spew on the floor. Having previously left one dog behind, she had been prepared for this eventuality by past experience, yet her heart was now weighed down by quiet despair. She began to feel that perhaps she was fated never to keep a dog for very long. She stared vacantly at the body of the dog for a while, then turned and raised her eyes to look at the cold surface of the mirror. Seeing herself sitting next to where the dog lay dead on the tatami, she gazed momentarily at that image then suddenly covered her face with both hands as if she were experiencing a dizzy spell. She looked once more, and from her lips came the faintest of cries. The dog in the mirror, which until then had always had a black nose, now had a brown one.

– 11 –

The New Year holidays were far from festive at Oren's house, even though they observed traditions like decorating the front door with bamboo or ordering a plate of New Year delicacies for the sitting room. Mostly Oren sat alone in front of the hearth, chin in hand, with a preoccupied look on her face as her weary eyes watched the sunlight on the sliding doors fade away. Oren was never what you would call easygoing, but since the death of the dog at the end of the previous year, she had become even more prone to fits of depression. The death of the dog, her lack of knowledge about what had happened to Kim, and the situation with Makino's wife—a woman she had never even seen let alone met—all weighed on her mind. On top of all that, she began to suffer from hallucinations.

One evening, just as she was about to fall asleep, she felt something heavy on the sleeve of her gown. It was the exact same soft and heavy sensation she used to feel when the dog would climb onto the futon and curl up beside her. Oren lifted her head from the pillow, but saw nothing in the lamplight apart from the checkered pattern of the bedclothes.

Another time, as she sat before the dressing table, combing her hair in the mirror, she thought she saw something white dart across the room behind her. At first, she paid no attention and continued to comb her hair. A moment later, however, she saw it again, this time moving in the opposite direction. With her comb still in hand, she turned around but found neither hide nor hair of any living creature in the well-lit room. *I must be seeing things,* she thought to herself and turned back to the mirror, only to notice for a third time something white moving in the room behind her.

Yet another incident happened while she was sitting alone in front of the hearth and heard the sound of her own name amid the distant clamor of street noise. She heard it only once through the rustling of the bamboo leaves on the front door, but she was convinced that it was the voice of that man, Kim. She had never stopped thinking of him, even though it had been quite some time now since she had come to Tokyo. She sat with bated breath, listening intently for the voice. Once again, somewhere from the distant bustle of people going to and fro, came the indistinct yet familiar sound of a voice that seemed to be getting closer and closer, until at last she heard clearly the windblown howl of a dog. A little while later, after having gone to bed alone, Oren awoke to find a man asleep beside her. The narrow forehead, the long eyelashes—there in the lamplight everything seemed exactly as it was back then. At the corner of his eye was even the same mole, and once she saw that, she was certain it was him. Her heart danced with joy as she abandoned all doubt and threw her arms around his neck, clinging tightly as if she would never let go. But when the man began to grumble about being awakened, there was no mistaking Makino's voice. Coming to her senses, Oren realized whose neck she was hugging.

Each of these fantasies had an effect on the delicate balance of Oren's world. But before the New Year decorations had been taken down, something even more devastating happened: Oren received an unannounced visit from Makino's wife.

– 12 –

Oren was startled by the sound of someone calling at the front door, but Grandma was out of the house on an errand, and she had no choice except to drag her weary self into the dimly lit hallway of the house in Yokoami. Through the latticed door that barred the north entrance, Oren could see a woman waiting outside. She wore glasses and had an old, attenuated shawl draped over her shoulders, but judging from the color of her downcast face, the woman was feeling less than her best.

"May I ask who is calling?" said Oren politely. Intuiting the answer even as she spoke, she gazed intently at this homely woman, who stood there with an unraveling chignon, one hand gripping the other beneath the patterned sleeves of her over-garment.

"I am . . ." The woman hesitated briefly then continued with a mumble as she looked at her feet. "I am Makino's wife. My name is Taki."

Now it was Oren's turn to mumble. "Oh, is that right? I am . . ."

"It's alright," said the woman. "I know who you are. I'd just like to say that I appreciate all you have done for Makino." She spoke gently and without the least bit of sarcasm in her voice, which made it even more difficult for Oren to know how to respond.

"And, insofar as it's the beginning of a new year, I've come to pay my respects and to ask you something of a favor."

"Gladly, if I am able to . . ." Oren had not let her guard down and felt she more or less knew what was coming next. She also had a fair number of things to say in response, if it came to that. But when she heard what the woman had to say, spoken so quietly and with eyes downcast, she realized that she had been completely mistaken about what was about to happen.

"Well, I suppose I did say a favor, but it's nothing major at all. It's just that I've heard that before too long all of Tokyo will turn into a wilderness. And when that happens, I was hoping that—

just like Makino—I could come to live here in your home. That's the extent of it, really." She made this request, speaking just as calmly and quietly as before, yet seemed to be completely unaware that she was making no sense whatsoever.

Oren was quite taken aback and could do little for the moment except stare at this melancholy woman, who stood at the door with the sun at her back.

"Would that be possible? For me to live here?"

Oren's tongue sat there in her mouth, as if it had turned to stone. Makino's wife at last raised her head and through her glasses stared icily at Oren, who had the uncomfortable feeling that all this was just a scene in a very bad dream.

"I really don't care what happens to me," the woman said. "But if Makino should lose his livelihood, my two children would be the ones to suffer. So I would very much appreciate it if you would be kind enough to take care of them here in your home." Having said this, the woman suddenly wrapped her shawl around her face and began to sob. Oren, who had been listening in silence, was suddenly overcome with sadness. On the one hand, she had felt buoyed by the expectation that she would soon be reunited with Kim when Tokyo turned into a wilderness. But now there were tears streaming down her cheeks and onto her festive New Year's outfit. Oren then realized that her visitor must have left, because she was there all alone in the shadows on the northern side of the house.

– 13 –

January 7 is the Festival of Seven Herbs, and Makino arrived at the house that evening to be greeted by Oren with the story of how his wife had come to visit. Puffing on a Manila cigar, he remained remarkably calm as he listened patiently to the entire story.

"The woman clearly has something wrong with her," he said.

Oren, who had worked herself into a good lather telling the story, stubbornly insisted. "If you don't do something for her now, she might do something that we will all regret."

"We'll cross that bridge when we come to it," he said, gazing at her through the cigar smoke with half-open eyes. "Never mind my old lady. You need to start taking better care of yourself. Every time I come over here lately, you are laid up in bed."

"I really don't care what happens to me. . . ."

"Well, I *do* care."

Oren's face was clouded by a frown as she held her peace for the moment. Suddenly, she looked at him with tearful eyes and blurted out, "For mercy's sake, don't you ever leave your wife."

Makino sat there, dumbfounded.

"For mercy's sake, please. . . ." Then, burying her face in a sleeve of black satin, she tried to hide her tears. "Surely you must realize that you are the most important thing in the world to your wife. Only the most heartless man in the world could fail to realize that. Even where I come from, every woman feels that way about . . ."

"Alright, alright. I get your point. It's nothing you have to worry about." Makino sat there with the cigar in his hand then spoke as if he were trying to appease a child. "You know, this house can get so gloomy. I mean, the dog just died and everything. I can't blame you for getting depressed. I bet we could find someplace nicer before too long, so why don't we do just that and get out of here? Someplace sunny and cheerful. Hell, in another ten days, I'll get my discharge." Makino tried hard to get her to cheer up that evening, but no matter what he said or did, her somber expression remained unchanged.

Grandma later told Dr. K about the situation in some detail: "Why, Mr. Makino was actually quite concerned about Mistress, that I can assure you. When she got sick this time, well, it was as if we could already tell what would happen. And Mr. Makino, why, there wasn't much he could do other than accept the situation. His wife just showed up at the house in Yokoami, you know. And when I got home from my errand, why, there was Mistress, sitting at the doorway in a daze. And there was Mrs. Makino, staring at her through those glasses. She didn't even try to come in the house but just stood there, speaking to Mistress in the most spiteful sarcasm.

"I heard that Mr. Makino himself had to listen to that all the time at home. I certainly didn't want to let it go on, but it wasn't my place to say anything. That would just make the situation worse. After all, four or five years ago, I used to be in service at the Makino residence, and if Mrs. Makino were ever to find me, well, that would probably just make things worse for Mistress. And I didn't want that to happen. Mrs. Makino was already fit to be tied, so I just stayed out of sight until she went home. But after she did, Mistress . . . well, she took one look at me and says, 'Grandma, did you know that Mrs. Makino just came to call on us? She came all the way over here and was really very nice. Not a mean bone in her body, really. What a wonderful person,' she says! Well, I was about to laugh myself silly when she says, 'And she told me that, before too long, Tokyo would turn into one great wilderness!' I felt sorry for her, you know. She seemed so strange, and, well, I ask you, what was I to make of that?"

– 14 –

By February, Oren's melancholy gave no sign of clearing up, even after moving to a spacious, two-story home in Honjo Matsui-chō. She rarely spoke, not even to Grandma, and spent most of her time alone in the living room, listening to the kettle boil. Within a week of having moved to the new house, Tamiya, who had been out drinking somewhere, came calling. Makino had just sat down himself and happily proffered the cup in his hand to his drinking buddy. But before taking the cup, Tamiya reached inside his vest and withdrew a red tin can. "A gift for the missus, if you will," he said as he held his cup for Oren to fill. "This is for you, Oren."

"What's this?" asked Makino, examining the tin can while Oren was thanking Tamiya.

"Take a look at the label. It's seal meat. Canned fur seal meat. I heard that melancholy is now recognized as an illness, so I brought this for her. Works for prenatal, postnatal, and any other feminine affliction, too. That's what my friend told me it's good for, anyway. This is the very first can of this stuff that we sold." Tamiya licked his lips as he looked back and forth at his two companions for their reactions.

"Can you eat this stuff, Oren? Fur seal meat?" asked Makino. Oren briefly forced her lips into a smile.

Tamiya took that for an answer and dismissed the issue with a wave of his hand. "She'll be fine. Nothing to worry about. Say, Oren, did you know that a lone male fur seal will keep a harem of up to one hundred females? Doesn't that make you think that Makino might be part fur seal? Heck, with that face, he kind of looks like a fur seal, don't you think? But let me tell you, my friend, that's what makes you so lovable. Isn't it, Oren?"

"What the heck are you talking about," said Makino with an uneasy smirk.

"A lone male fur seal. . . . Right, Makino? You have to admit the resemblance, don't you?" Tamiya's pockmarked face was grinning from ear to ear, and he continued to chatter, without giving too much thought to what he was saying. "I was talking with my friend—the guy who sells canned goods—today, and he told me that when two male seals start to fight over a female . . . Oh, the heck with fur seals. Let me tell you something. Tonight, Oren, I want to see you the way you used to look in the old days. What do you say? We all call you 'Oren' now, but everyone knows that's just a name we use to hide the truth from prying eyes. Tonight, I want you to get top billing under your real name! Oren is none other than . . ."

"Hey!" interrupted Makino. "So what happens when they fight over a female? Let's hear about that first." Makino would have much preferred discussing fur seals to the present topic of conversation, but even that offered no guarantee that his embarrassment was over.

"Fight over a female? Well, when they do, it's a winner-take-all proposition. But they go at it head to head and strength against strength—none of the sneaky tricks you like so much, Makino. Ahh, what am I saying? All right! I'll shut up. Loose lips sink ships . . .and other things. Oren, have one on me," said Tamiya.

Makino's blanched face glowered at Tamiya, who tried to conceal his own embarrassment by attempting to pour Oren a drink. Oren, however, simply sat there looking at him without picking up her cup.

– 15 –

Oren got out of bed sometime after three that morning. She groped her way out of the bedroom, down the dark stairs, and then made her way to the dressing table. Crouching, she took out of a drawer the box that held the razors.

"That son of a bitch. Damn you, Makino." Continuing to mutter, she gently opened the box and smelled the faint yet distinct odor of a newly stropped razor. Deep within her heart there now stirred a most savage cruelty. A barbarity born of conflict with a heartless stepmother, which had brought her so low as to sell herself to men. And although the life she had been leading for the past few years had enabled her to conceal that barbarity the way fresh makeup conceals blemished skin, it was now closer than it had been in some time to breaking through that facade. "Bastard! Scum of the earth! You've seen the light of day for the last time." Oren took a razor, hid it in the sleeve of her brightly colored long underwear, and then stood before the mirror on the dressing table.

Yet, at that very moment, she heard a faint voice in her ear saying, "Stop! Don't do it!"

Oren gasped and held her breath, then realized that all she had heard was the pendulum of the clock, ticking away the seconds in the darkness. She was about to climb the stairs to the second floor, when she once again heard the voice calling to her, "No! Don't do it! Stop!"

She went back to the living room and turned on a light.

"Who's there?"

"Me. It's me!" It was the voice of one of her "sisters"—a woman who had once been one of her closest friends.

"Is that you, Kazue?"

"Yes, it's me."

"How on earth have you been? What are you doing these days?" Oren was seated in front of the hearth as if it were the middle of a perfectly ordinary day.

"Don't do it, Oren." Receiving no response, the voice exhorted repeatedly, "Don't do it!"

"Why do you have to stop me? What difference does it make whether I kill him or not?"

"Don't do it, because he's alive. He's alive!"

"Alive? Who's alive?" asked Oren. She waited but heard no reply—just the pendulum of the clock ticking away, endlessly punctuating the silence. After a moment, she asked again, "Tell me who is alive!" But this time, she heard an old, familiar name whispered in her ear.

"Kim is. Kim!"

"He is? Are you sure? Oh, that would make me so happy if it were true...." Oren sat with her chin nestled in the palm of her hand and stared pensively into space. "But, if he were alive, he'd come to see me, wouldn't he?"

"Yes, he would. And he will."

"He will? When?"

"Tomorrow. He's coming to Mirokuji Temple to see you tomorrow evening."

"You mean, he's coming to Mirokuji Bridge, right?"

"That's right. Mirokuji Bridge. Tomorrow night. He'll be there." And that was the last thing that the voice said, even though Oren sat there in the cold for the longest time, wearing nothing but her long underwear.

– 16 –

The following day, Oren did not leave the second-floor bedroom until almost evening. She finally got out of bed around four p.m. and did her makeup even more carefully than usual. Then, as if she were about to go to the theater, she began putting on her favorite kimono along with the rest of her best things.

"Well, well. And just why are you getting all decked out?" asked Makino suspiciously. Instead of going to work, he had been lying around the house all day, reading illustrated magazines.

"There's a small errand I have to run." Oren stood calmly in front of the dressing table as she finished tying her patterned obi.

"Where you going?"

"I have to go over to Mirokuji Bridge."

"Mirokuji Bridge?" Makino seemed to be more worried than suspicious at this point, which in turn, made Oren indescribably happy. "What do you need to do over at Mirokuji Bridge?"

"What do I need to do ... ?" Glancing at Makino's face, she shot a look of scorn in his direction as she finished straightening her obi. "You needn't concern yourself about me. I'm not going to throw myself off the bridge, if that's what you're worried about."

"Stop being ridiculous." Makino slammed the magazine he was reading onto the tatami mat and sat there, clucking his tongue in disgust.

They went around in circles like that for quite some time. Oren refused to listen to Makino and eventually left the house alone. Grandma, too, was quite concerned, but no matter what either of them said, Oren refused to allow anyone else to come along. Oren kept insisting that she would die if she couldn't go alone, and they eventually gave up trying to convince her otherwise. Of course, Makino wasn't about to let her go off on her own, and followed at a short distance so that he wouldn't be seen.

As it happened, it was the monthly Festival of the Medicine Buddha at Mirokuji Bridge, which meant a fair number of people were out that evening, in spite of the cold weather. This presented Makino with the perfect opportunity to follow Oren without being seen. He strolled along not too far behind her and in the end was able to avoid being seen thanks to the festival crowd. Both sides of the street were lined with the vendor stalls that you usually find on these occasions. Signboards decorated with big swirl lollipops for the candy vendors or red parasols for the bean vendors were illuminated by a variety of lamps and lanterns. Oren, however, was immersed in her own thoughts and took no notice of any of this as she nimbly threaded her way through the throng. She moved so quickly that even Makino had trouble keeping up with her.

Reaching the skirt of Mirokuji Bridge, she stopped and began to look around absentmindedly. Turning toward the river, she saw some pine and cypress trees growing in a large tree nursery. By this point, the crowd had thinned out considerably, it being just a local festival, and there was nothing in this area but a verdant expanse of young plants and shrubs.

"I guess there's nothing strange about her coming here," thought Makino, "but what on earth for?"

He was standing behind a telephone pole near the bridge as he watched Oren, who stood there, gazing absentmindedly at the lines of trees and shrubs around her. Stealthily, Makino approached her from behind and could hear her talking to herself, happily repeating the same words over and over: "A wilderness! At last, Tokyo has turned into a wilderness!"

– 17 –

Just when it looked like Oren was about to turn around and head home, a snow-white puppy happened to appear out of the crowd. Oren suddenly stretched out her arms, scooped it up, and began to talk to it excitedly.

"You did come, didn't you? And I'll bet it was quite a long journey for you, over the mountains and across the sea. There hasn't been a single day that I haven't cried since we parted. I had another dog that I found to take your place. But wouldn't you know it, he died on me, too, not so long ago."

She continued to explain her fantasy to the puppy, which must have been rather lonely because it never barked nor bit. It just snorted and kept on licking at Oren's hands and face. Makino got to the point where he couldn't wait any longer and spoke to Oren, but she steadfastly refused to leave the spot, saying that she was waiting for Kim. At this point, a crowd begun to gather, one of whom just had to say in a voice loud enough for everyone to hear, "*That woman is as crazy as she is beautiful!*"

Fortunately, since Oren was really quite fond of dogs, coming in contact with that puppy actually seemed to help calm her down. It took a bit more inveigling on Makino's part, but eventually he convinced her to come back to the house with him. Then, just as they were about to get away from the crowd, there were more catcalls, and Oren suddenly headed back in the direction of Mirokuji Bridge. Makino had all he could do to coax her into returning home, and by the time they did get back to the house in Matsui-chō, he was quite exhausted. Once inside, Oren made her way to the second-floor bedroom, still holding that white puppy in her arms. She sat down there in the dark and released the poor animal, which proceeded to prance around the room excitedly, wagging its little tail. It walked exactly like the puppy she had had before—the one that had jumped from her bedroom window all the way to the stone pavement.

"Well, well," she muttered. Oren looked around the darkened room as if she didn't really recognize her surroundings. Finally, she noticed the light from a Chinese-style lantern hung from the ceiling directly above her head and looked up. "My, what a pretty sight! Just like it was back in the old days," she said. She sat there fascinated, gazing at the shimmering light from the lantern. After a moment, she looked at herself in the mirror, and shook her head sadly but repeatedly. "No, no. No one calls me Hui-liang anymore. My name is Oren, and I am Japanese now. And there is no reason to expect that Kim would ever come to see me now, no matter how much I wish he would."

Oren's head had drooped just a bit and then she suddenly let out a cry. There beside her, where the dog had just been, now lay a Chinaman, resting his head on a square pillow and slowly puffing away on an opium pipe. And if the narrow forehead, the long eyelashes, and the mole at the corner of his left eye weren't enough to remove any doubt, there was that same a hint of a grin that he always had as he puffed on his pipe and gazed at Oren with a faraway look in his eyes.

"See for yourself," he said. "That's all that's left of Tokyo. Nothing but a wilderness now."

There was no longer any doubt about it. There outside the Chinese balustrade on the second floor was a most unusual tree. Its branches were spread wide and half a dozen songbirds chirped gaily in a scene that was vaguely reminiscent of something you might find on an embroidered cloth. Oren spent the night gazing out over that landscape as she sat enraptured beside her long-lost Kim.

A day or two later, Oren was brought to Dr. K's sanatorium. The first few days, she would not take off her cheongsam no matter what anyone said. And if the dog was out of her sight for even a moment, she would make a huge commotion, calling that man's name over and over. Dr. K eventually discovered that her real name was Meng Hui-liang and that she had been a prostitute at a brothel in Weihai during the Sino-Japanese War. Among her things, he found a very old photo of a sad-looking woman in a cheongsam, holding a small, white dog.

Dr. K later told the investigators that he came to have a lot of sympathy for Makino: "Yes, he did keep that poor woman as a mistress, but he was little more than an ordinary soldier himself when he brought her over from China at the end of the war. Who knows what he must have gone through to achieve that little feat. And although I never did find out what happened to Kim, I think we are all better off just leaving that issue alone. Personally, I'm not entirely convinced that the dogs died of natural causes, if you see what I mean."

The Diabolical Tongue

悪魔の舌

(Akuma no shita)

Murayama Kaita (1915)

村山槐多

Translation by Jeffrey Angles

IT WAS A clear day in early May. Around eleven in the evening, I was lounging in the garden and staring up at the deep blue vault of heaven when suddenly, I heard a voice outside the front gate.

"Telegram!"

I took the telegram from the carrier, but the message only contained the following few words: "*Kudanzaka 301 Kaneko.*"

"What on earth is this? 301?" A strange feeling crept over me. Kaneko was the name of one of my friends—but he was not just any old friend; he was probably the strangest of all of my acquaintances. "Well, he is a poet, so maybe this is some sort of riddle." I took the mysterious telegram in my hand and began to think. The time of the dispatch was 10:45, and he had sent it from Ōtsuka. Still, no matter how long I thought about it, the message did not make any sense to me. I decided that the best course of action was just to go to Kudanzaka and take a look around, so I changed my kimono and went out the door.

My residence was a fair distance from the railways. As I walked, I was completely absorbed in thoughts of Kaneko. I had first met him at a dinner banquet in the autumn two years ago. All of the invitees were unusual, eccentric types, and Kaneko Eikichi was among them. At the time of the banquet, he must have been a young poet of around twenty-five years old, but his face made him look considerably older. His unusually reddish face was marked with deep creases that ran across his forehead, giving him a decadent look, and his large eyes glinted with a pale, bluish light. What's more, his nose was thick and protruded prominently from his face. The main reason I got to know him, however, had to do with his lips. The dinner was hosted by a rather morbid bunch, so there were strange-looking folks on every side. To outsiders, it probably would have looked like a gathering of demons, but the young poet with the unusual features stood out even among this unusual assortment of characters, and my eyes could not help but be drawn to his lips.

He was facing my direction, so I could look him full in the face. His lips were enormous. They looked like two copper rods covered with verdigris butting up against one another. They twitched incessantly. When he ate, the spectacle was even more unbelievable. The copper rods of his lips, flushed bright red with warm blood, would open and shut, flicking up and down like lightning as they gulped down his food. I had never seen anyone with such thick, full lips. I forgot myself and just stared for a few moments, mesmerized by the sight of him as he ate.

All of the sudden, his frightening eyes turned my way. He stood up with a start and thundered, "Hey! You! Why are you staring at me like that?"

I realized what I had been doing. "Oh, I'm sorry."

He sat down again. "I don't like being stared at. I'd venture a guess you'd feel the same way." With this, he downed a large glass of beer, and looked at me with his glittering eyes.

"You're right. It's just that your face struck me as rather interesting."

"Well, I don't appreciate it. What's it to you?" He still seemed to be out of sorts.

"Hey, don't get mad. Let's have a drink together."

—And that is how Kaneko Eikichi and I got to know one another.

The more I interacted with him, the stranger I realized he was. He had a rather sizeable fortune but was all alone in the world, without parents or siblings. He had gone to a couple of different schools, but none of those experiences had ever ended satisfactorily. He did not like to talk much about his personal history, so I am not sure of the details, but I gathered he was a poet of sorts. He believed in keeping his own life private, and he hated having guests to his home, so I do not know what sorts of things he did there. I do know, however, that he spent a great deal of time walking the city streets. He would constantly show up at bars and restaurants, but then he would suddenly disappear again for two or three months. I did not know much else about his background. I was probably one of the closest people in the world to him, and he also seemed to put some trust in me, but even so, I knew little about him, other than that he was a strange character who remained very much an enigma.

– 2 –

These were the thoughts that were going through my mind as I climbed the sloping street of Kudanzaka. As I gazed around me, I saw the nighttime landscape of the capital spread below me. The light from the lanterns of Jinbo-chō overflowed into the darkness, glittering like diamonds in a hunk of ore. I looked up and down the slope, thinking Kaneko was probably waiting there somewhere for me. Still, there was nosign of him. I looked over by the bronze statue of Ōmura, but there was not a soul to be found.[1] I waited at Kudanzaka for approximately thirty minutes before deciding to go to his home, which was located near Tomizaka.[2] It was rather small but an attractive place to live.

When I reached the street in front of his home, I saw that there were policemen going in and out of the building. Surprised, I asked them what had happened. They told me that Kaneko had committed suicide. I rushed inside and saw Kaneko's corpse. He was lying on the floor in a six-mat room, surrounded by two or three friends and a group of policemen.

He had died by piercing his heart with a pair of long, metal chopsticks—the kind usually used for positioning hot coals in a hibachi. The marks on his body showed that he had stabbed

1. Near Kudanzaka, in the direction of Yasukuni Shrine, is a bronze statue of Ōmura Masujirō (1824-1869), a scholar of medicine, Western learning, and military strategy.

2. Tomizaka is about a kilometer and a half to the north of Kudanzaka.

himself not once, but two or three times. His face had turned a pale shade of purple, but apart from the discoloration, he looked like he was merely sleeping. The doctor guessed that he had been drinking heavily and had some sort of psychological disturbance that resulted in this tragic end. The corpse did reek of alcohol. At the moment he stabbed himself, some passerby outside happened to overhear someone cry out in pain, and that was what had led to all of the uproar.

He had left no suicide note, but that made the telegram I had received all the more mysterious. When I considered the time indicated on the telegram, it seemed clear that Kaneko must have committed suicide soon after sending it. I slunk back alone to Kudanzaka to think. What could the number 301 in the telegram be referring to? Was there something with that number somewhere on the sloping streets of Kudanzaka? I looked but could not find anything.

That's when it hit me. In all of Kudanzaka, there was only one thing that might run to over three hundred in number. I was thinking of the rectangular stones that covered the underground gutters that ran alongside the road. I went to the top of the hill then started down the slope, counting the gutter stones on the right side of the street. When I reached the three-hundred-and-first stone, I took a good look, but there was nothing out of the ordinary about it.

Perhaps he had been counting from the other direction. There were three hundred and ten stones in all. That meant the tenth stone from the top would correspond to the three-hundred-and-first stone from the bottom. I rushed back up the slope and took a look.

Sure enough, there was something black wedged between the tenth and eleventh stones. I pulled it out and saw that it was a thick, black envelope made of oiled paper. "This is it! I've got it!" I clutched the envelope excitedly and quickly bounded home.

Inside the envelope was a document with a black cover. As I read it, Kaneko Eikichi's true form appeared before my eyes for the first time. His true form—indeed it was terrifying, something the likes of which the world has rarely ever seen. "He was not human. He was a devil!" I shouted to myself as I read it.

Dear readers, even as I present his last testament to you now, I feel myself shudder once again. What I share with you below is the complete text of his final testament.

– 3 –

My dear friend, I have decided that I must die. I have taken a pair of metal chopsticks and sharpened them to a fine, awl-like point to stab into my heart. By the time that you read this letter, my life will already be over. As you read through this letter, you will find that the poet you took as your friend is really a terrifying criminal, the likes of which has never before been seen. You will probably be ashamed and frightened that you ever dared to befriend me. However, if I were to express one last wish, it would be that rather than looking upon my corpse with disdain, you will feel some pity for me. Truly I deserve your pity.

With this hope, I have decided to write out my entire history, hiding no details about my past. I am not originally from Tokyo. I was born in a valley in the province of Hida, and it was there that I spent my youth.[3] For generations, my family traded in lumber, and by the time of my father's generation, we had earned a reputation as one of the most wealthy and influential families in the region.

My father was an extremely simple and upstanding person, but in the prime of his life, he took in a woman from Nagoya as his mistress. She gave birth to one son. That was I. By the time I

3. Hida, the old name for the northern part of modern Gifu prefecture, is a mountainous region to the northwest of Nagoya.

was born, his wife—in other words, the woman that stepped in and acted as my stepmother—already had children of her own. I know it sounds immoral, but my father had his wife and his mistress live together. As a result, all of us children were raised alongside one another. When I was twelve, my stepmother already had four children of her own. That April, another child was born to her—her fifth. The baby soon became the subject of many rumors in the village because on the bottom of his right foot there was a golden-colored birthmark in the shape of a crescent moon.

One day, an itinerant fortune-teller came to see the baby. He predicted, "This child will die a terrible death." At least, that is how the rumors went. When I look back upon it now, I realize that this frightening prediction was entirely accurate. Even though I was young at the time, the crescent-shaped birthmark on the bottom of the baby's foot also gave me a strange feeling.

For me too, that year was impossible to forget. My father died quite suddenly in October. According to the will he created before his death, my mother and I were to receive ten thousand yen, and with that, all of our relations with the rest of the family were severed. My elder brother, who was three years older than I, inherited the family home. My father had been a kind man, and so he had planned for the happiness of me and my mother in his will by leaving us a handsome sum of money. To be honest, there had been an enmity between my mother and my stepmother that had rendered our lives intolerable. It had been clear as day that if my stepmother had been able to take the reins as head of the household, she would have made life a living hell for my mother.

As soon as my father's funeral was over, the two of us left for Tokyo. I have never again set foot in the province where I grew up, nor have I made any attempt to stay in touch with the family I left behind. We have nothing to do with one another. My mother and I were able to live off of the interest generated by the ten thousand yen. My mother was a wise and simple woman, completely unlike those women who form relations with men just for money.

My mother passed away when I was eighteen. I was left to live alone, and almost before I knew it, I began living the dissipated, licentious life of a poet. That is my life in a nutshell, but somewhere in the shadows of all of this, a series of frightening events had begun to unfold. The frightening events I am about to describe transpired one after another. Ever since I was young, I had been an unusual child. I was not at all innocent and carefree like other children. I was always quiet and preferred to be by myself. I did not play in the ways that one might expect of a little boy. I would go into the mountains and stand in the shadows of rocks or other such places while staring absentmindedly at the clouds passing through the sky.

These romantic habits grew increasingly morbid year by year, but about two years before I left Hida, I fell ill with a strange illness, which afflicted me for a full half a year. The disease made my backbone itch so much I could hardly stand it, and I was left listless and tired all the time. To top that off, I could not walk straight. Whenever I tried, I would stumble. My color was not good, and I gradually lost more and more weight. My mother was terribly worried and tried all sorts of different treatments, and in the process, my condition did eventually improve.

During my illness, however, I experienced strange feelings. I wanted to eat strange and unusual things—the sorts of things that no normal person would ever eat. First, I developed an intense craving to eat the kind of mud used to build walls. Every time I could lay my hands on some, I would hide myself from the eyes of others and gobble it down. It tasted delectable. I was especially fond of the mud from the white walls of our family storehouse. In fact, as I ate away at it, I managed to my horror to create a hole deep enough to go all the way through one of the thick walls.

After that, I developed a secret desire to try eating all sorts of things that most people would never even dream of putting into their mouths. It helped that these were the sorts of things that most people hate and would simply pass up. I don't know how many times I slurped down slugs. I was already eating frogs and snakes. These things were not especially unusual in the mountainous areas of Hida. I also pulled earthworms and grubs from the dirt in the backyard and ate them. When spring came around, I would feast on caterpillars, both the hairy kind and the hairless ones. They were golden, purple, green, and other poisonous-looking colors, and they let out a powerful stink, but they always managed to satisfy my strange appetites. There were times others from my family would discover me with my lips bright red and swollen from where the woolly caterpillars had stung me. I ate all sorts of other things too, but this unusual cuisine never made me sick. These strange habits showed no sign of abating, but their development was interrupted by my move to Tokyo with my mother. As I grew accustomed to life in the city, my strange habits naturally came to an end.

– 4 –

During the winter of my eighteenth year, my mother passed away. My grief was so intense that I hardly knew what to do with myself. I was constantly bursting into tears. My body, which was weak to begin with, grew even worse as I developed a severe case of neurasthenia. I grew so weak that I looked like little more than a ghost. I had a recurrence of the spinal disease that had afflicted me during my childhood. Fearing for my health, I dropped out of school and moved to Kamakura to recuperate. I was twenty at the time. I spent some time relaxing in Kamakura and alongside the seashores of Shichirigahama and Enoshima, where my life consisted of taking walks and taking dips in the sea.

Meanwhile, a gradual transformation took place in my body. My old self, which had spent so much time in the hustle and bustle of the big city, came to occupy a new body there on the beautiful seashore. My mind, as well as my body, grew increasingly healthy. I returned to my natural state. The spirit of the young boy who had enjoyed spending time alone back in the mountains of Hida had once again returned to its natural state.

One evening, I got to thinking, and I realized that all of the food I had consumed over the course of the last month had tasted dreadful. It did not make sense that the fine food they served there in the inn would so taste bad, especially when I was hungry from spending all day swimming in the sea. I took a look at myself in a little hand-held mirror. The countenance that had once been so pale was now a rosy red. The eyes that had once been so distant and unfocused now sparkled with the light of vitality. Why would things taste so bad, even as I was regaining my health?

I stuck out my tongue and turned toward the mirror once again. Right then, I instinctively dropped the mirror. My tongue was terrifically long! It was probably ten centimeters or so. When had it grown so long? And what a frightening shape! Had my tongue been like this all along? No, no, that couldn't be!

But as I picked up the mirror and looked again, sure enough, I saw the same huge lump of flesh, dripping with saliva, slide from between my lips. Its entire surface was covered with pointed warts in purple and a brocade of other shades. Upon closer inspection, I was astonished to realize that what I had initially thought to be warts were little spines. The entire surface of my tongue had grown spines like the tongue of a cat. I tried touching them with my finger, and realized that they were indeed hard spines, sharp enough to make anything that touched them smart. Could such a bizarre thing really happen? What astonished me most of all was the realization that right there, smack in the middle of the mirror, was the brilliant red face of a devil. My face was suddenly terrifying. Its big eyes shone back at me with a ferocious glare.

The shock of this discovery left me flabbergasted for several moments, but just then, I heard the voice of the devil in the mirror screaming at me, "Your tongue is the tongue of a devil! A diabolical tongue cannot be satisfied with anything but food fit for a devil. Eat! Eat everything! Go find diabolical food for yourself! If you fail to do this, your tastes will never be satisfied!"

I thought for a few moments before coming to a realization. "Fine, I'm desperate! I will taste all sorts of diabolical things with this terrible tongue of mine. I'll find out what food really is worthy of the devil!" I threw the mirror aside and jumped up. "That must be it . . . It was during this month that my tongue transformed into this diabolical tongue. That's the reason that everything tasted so awful."

A new world—a completely new world—lay before me. I immediately moved out of the inn where I had been staying. I left Kamakura and rented an empty house in an all-but-deserted village at the tip of the Izu Peninsula. It was there that I began my strange, new culinary life.

Indeed, ordinary foods cannot provide the right sort of stimulation for a tongue covered with spines. I had to find food that would satisfy my own peculiar tastes. Over the course of the next two months I spent living in that house, I ate dirt, paper, rats, lizards, toads, leeches, newts, snakes, and even jellyfish and blowfish. I let all my vegetables become soggy and rotten before I would eat them. When I stuffed the sloppy, rotten vegetables into my mouth, their scent, color, and flavor were irresistibly wonderful to me. These foods provided me a great deal of satisfaction.

After two months, my already reddish coloring took on a strange green-and-red tinge. I felt my entire body undergo a gradual transformation, as if I were becoming some mystical ascetic. It was during all of this that I began wondering what it would be like to eat human flesh. When this thought first occurred to me, a shudder ran through my body, but at that same moment, the following words began to burn within me with a ferocious intensity: *I want to eat human flesh!* That was January of last year.

-5-

After that I could not get to sleep. When I did, I dreamed of human flesh. My lips would begin to tremble, and my bright red tongue would slither around the inside of my mouth like a snake. Even I could not help but be afraid of the strength of the desires welling up inside of me. I decided that I must forcibly suppress them, but the devil that dwelled within my tongue shouted at me, "Look! You've come to appreciate the greatest, most delectable taste on earth! Pluck up your courage, and eat human flesh! Eat it!" I would look in the mirror and see a terrifying smile spread across my demonic face. My tongue had swollen even bigger, and the spines covering its surface glittered even more sharply in the light.

I shut my eyes. "No! I will not eat human flesh! I am not some savage from the Congo. I am one of the virtuous people of Japan!" But inside my mouth, that demon was smiling derisively at me. I was assailed by a fear that was almost impossible to bear. In order to deal with it, I had no choice but to stay constantly drunk. I was always going to bars, hoping that I might somehow escape these desires for even a single moment, but as pitiful as my plight might have been, fate did not take pity on me.

I will never forget what happened last year on the fifth of February. I was on my way home from Asakusa after getting completely drunk. The sky was clouded over, covering the world with such blackness that one could barely see what was right before one's eyes. I was trying to make my way home, relying on what few lights happened to be there, but I took a wrong turn. It was only when I heard the roar of a steam engine that I realized I had arrived at the railroad tracks by Nippori Station. I crossed the tracks, then climbed the hill to where the Nippori graveyard is located. I walked inside and collapsed onto the ground.

When I opened my eyes, it was still the middle of the night. I struck a match and looked at my watch to find it was one o'clock in the morning. I wandered among the graves, my drunkenness having abated a good deal. All of a sudden, one of my feet sank into the earth. Surprised, I struck another match only to see that my foot had plunged through the fresh dirt piled on top of a fresh grave.

At that moment, a terrifying thought seized my consciousness. I barely knew what I was doing as I grabbed a stick and immediately began digging away at the mound of dirt. I dug frantically. I dug like a madman. Before I knew it, I was clawing at the dirt with my fingers. Almost an hour later, my hands struck wood. "A coffin!" I scooped the dirt away and pried the lid open. Then, striking another match, I looked inside.

I have never experienced a feeling more horrifying than I did at that moment. Everything I had ever experienced before, and everything that I experienced afterward paled in comparison. The small flicker of the match illuminated the deathly white countenance of a woman. Her eyes were shut and her teeth were clenched in death. She had been a young, beautiful woman of only nineteen years old. Her hair was black and lustrous, shining in the light of my match. Upon closer inspection, there were clumps of black blood congealed along her neck. I realized that her head had been torn off. Her arms and legs too had been ripped from her torso, but the undertakers had just placed them alongside her in the coffin. My entire body began to tremble. When I realized that this was a makeshift burial for some unidentified woman who had committed suicide by throwing herself on the railroad tracks, my trembling subsided a little.

I took a jackknife from my pocket and stuck it into the woman's breast. The appealing stench of decay assailed my nose. First, I set to work cutting off her breasts. A foul liquid oozed out of her body and covered my hands. Next, I cut off part of her cheeks. Once I finished that, I began to be frightened by what I had done. I could hear my conscience screaming at me, "What on earth do you think you are doing?" Still, I wrapped the lumps of flesh I had severed tightly in my handkerchief, then closed the lid of the coffin. I mounded the dirt up like before and quickly dashed out of the graveyard. I hired a rickshaw and returned to my home in Tomizaka.

As soon I was indoors, I bolted the door and took the lumps of flesh out of my handkerchief. I started by roasting the flesh that I had cut from her cheeks over an open flame. Before long, the meat began to release a delicious aroma. I was beside myself with ecstasy. The meat started to sizzle over the flame. My diabolical tongue danced delightedly, as if it had taken on a life of its own. My mouth watered until I was drooling.

Unable to stand it any longer, I crammed the half-cooked lump of meat into my mouth. At that moment, I was plunged into raptures of ecstasy. It was as if I had been caught up in some opium-induced dream. It was truly a miracle that something here in this world should taste so magnificent! How could I go on living without it? I had finally found "food fit for a devil." This is what my tongue had been wanting all this time! It had been hungering after the flesh of a human being. Ah, finally I had discovered what it craved! Next I bit into the flesh I had carved from the breast of the corpse. I danced about the room as if an electrical current were running through me. When I finally finished eating everything, my stomach was full. I was satisfied—in fact, it was the first time in my life I had ever been so thoroughly satiated by a meal.

–6–

The following day, I spent the entire day pulling up my floor and digging a huge hole in the ground. When done, I lined the inside of the hole with wooden boards. I had built a pit in which I could store an entire human body. "Ah, I will be bringing my precious food here!" My eyes sparkled with the thought. Even as I walked through the city streets, the drool oozed from my mouth. Every single person I encountered just whetted my appetite all the more. The most delicious looking of them all were the adolescent boys and girls of around fourteen or fifteen years old. Each time I passed one of them, I had such a ferocious desire to bite right into them that I could barely restrain myself. But I had been thinking about the best way to capture my prey, so I had prepared some anesthetic and a handkerchief, which I kept in my pocket. I had decided that it would be best to knock my victim out, then drag him or her straight back to my place.

What I am about to describe took place on April 25, exactly ten days ago. I got on the train to go from Tabata to Ueno.[4] I had no sooner looked up when I saw a young man sitting across from me, with his knees almost touching mine. He had a rather countrified look about him, but still, he was a truly beautiful, young man. My mouth grew wet with saliva. Drool began to overflow my lips. Upon closer inspection, he seemed to be traveling alone. Finally, the train stopped at Ueno. After leaving the station, the young man lingered absentmindedly for a few moments before beginning to walk in the direction of Ueno Park. Eventually, he sat down on a bench, and began to gaze with a forlorn expression at the reflections of the lights on the surface of Shinobazu Pond.

4. Tabata is on the northeast side of the loop-line that now encircles central Tokyo. Ueno is a few stops away. Murayama Kaita lived in Tabata toward the end of his life.

Looking around, I saw that there was no one else about. I furtively slipped the bottle of anesthesia from my pocket and put it against the handkerchief until the cloth was soaked in it. The young man continued to gaze absentmindedly at the pond. All of the sudden, I wrapped my arms around him and pressed the handkerchief against his nose. He kicked two or three times, but the anesthesia did its trick, and he fell limp in my arms. I carried him right away to the bottom of the stone staircase, called for a rickshaw, then ordered the driver to take us all the way to Tomizaka.

Once inside, I locked the door securely. In the light, I could clearly see he was indeed very attractive. I took out the large, sharp knife that I had prepared, and with all my might, I rammed it into the back of his head. Until that point, the young man had been knocked out, but when I stabbed him, his eyes suddenly flew wide open. A moment later, the light in the dark centers of his eyes faded away, and his face quickly grew pale. I lifted up the young man, so pale from death, in my arms, and I placed him into the underground pit.

-7-

Having decided that I would eat every part of this young man's body that I possibly could, I came up with a plan of action. I started by completely eating away his brain, cheeks, tongue, and nose, roasting the individual hunks of meat one by one. The incredible taste of his body drove me wild. The savory flavor of the brain was especially mysterious and hard to fathom. I fell asleep, thoroughly satisfied, and when I woke up the following morning at nine, I ate my fill of flesh cut from his midsection.

Ah, the next evening was indeed even more terrifying than the last! It was that evening that I accomplished the aim for which I had decided to commit murder. That night was terribly cruel! I crawled down into the pit beneath the floor, my eyes sparkling like those of a wild beast as I thought about how I would turn to the arms and legs for my evil repast. I stood over him for a few moments with a saw in my hand, thinking how I would slice off his limbs. I pulled on the young man's left leg. Just then, his body flipped over. When I saw the mark on the sole of his right foot, I jumped up as if I had been struck square in my chest. *Look! There is a birthmark the shape of a crescent moon on the sole of his right foot!*

You no doubt remember the description of my younger brother's birth at the beginning of this letter. I realized that the baby I had known must now be around fifteen or sixteen years old. Have you ever heard such a terrifying tale? I had consumed my own brother. When I came to my senses, I opened the bag the young man had been carrying. Inside were four or five notebooks in which he had written his name as plain as day—Kaneko Gorō. That was my younger brother's name. When I read further, I learned that he had left Hida out of a yearning to come to Tokyo—he had heard about me and dreamed of coming to find me.

There is no way that I can go on living! My friend, this is all that I have to tell you. Please, take pity on my poor, wretched soul!

***

That is the end of Kaneko's long, final testament. I could not help but question his sanity. The penmanship and the content both led me to wonder if he had been in his right mind when he wrote it. When the body was inspected, the police indeed found spines on his tongue like the letter describes, but his description of his own face as that of a devil was probably nothing more than the wild imaginings of a poet.

The drawings are by Murayama Kaita himself, for the original 1915 publication of his story in the magazine *Bukyō sekai* (*World of Heroism*). From the collection of the translator.

The Face

人面疽

(Jinmensō)

Tanizaki Jun'ichirō (1918)

谷崎 潤一郎

Translation by Kathleen Taji

UTAGAWA YURIE STARTED hearing rumors about a film that was making the rounds in little-known silent movie theaters around Shinjuku and Shibuya on the outskirts of Tokyo. A very eerie drama, and supposedly one of the many films she'd played in when she was still living in America and under contract to Globe Studios in Los Angeles. The cast was a mix of American and Japanese actors. The Japanese title was "Obsession," but the English title was "The Tumor with a Human Face." It was a long film consisting of five reels; and it was creating something of a stir as an artistic, gloomy, and extremely bizarre masterpiece.

This was not the first time that a film of Yurie's that had been produced in America showed up at a moving picture theater in Japan. Before her return to her homeland, she was seen from time to time in different films imported from Globe Studios. Her curvaceous figure and sleek legs along with her Western-style seductiveness and refined Asian beauty quickly made her popular among the fraternity of moving-picture connoisseurs.

The personality she exuded on film was exceptionally vivacious for a Japanese woman. Endowed with pluck and a lack of reserve, she happily plunged into her roles in some very avant-garde films. Her fortes were the gun moll, *femme fatale*, and female detective, roles in which her mesmerizing beauty and physical agility came into full play. This was especially true in "The Samurai's Daughter," a film that had played at the Shikishima Moving Picture Theater in Asakusa not long before.

The story was about a young Japanese girl, Kikuko, who became a spy in Europe where she assumed the guise of geisha, noblewoman, and circus stunt rider. Yurie's accomplished performance as the heroine boosted her popularity among the silent cinema audience at the time. She had returned to Japan the year before after a five-year absence at the invitation of Tokyo's Nitto Moving Picture Company, which was paying her an unheard-of salary—the result of having won the enormous acclaim of her fellow countrymen thanks to that film.

But Yurie didn't recall acting in a drama called "The Tumor with a Human Face." Those who saw the film described the story and the scenes in detail, yet she had no recollection of ever having made the picture.

The story had its beginnings in a charming Japanese port town, like those seen in Hiroshige's prints, that bordered the ocean of a southern prefecture—probably a town like Nagasaki. It was a tale about an *oiran*, a high-class courtesan, named Ayamedayu, who lived in the red-light district along the main road that ran along the bay. Touted as the most beautiful woman in town, she would appear at dusk leaning against the third-floor balustrade of the brothel, Aozakura, which overlooked the bay, and listen to the sound of a shakuhachi played somewhere in the distance.

The shakuhachi player was a lowly, young beggar, who was smitten with the *oiran*. He desired her favors for just one night—after which he was willing to quietly disappear. The beggar enjoyed catching glimpses of her by playing his shakuhachi while wandering in the shadows of the wharf, always under the cover of dusk, ashamed of his ugliness and pitiful lot in life. Many had fallen in love with the *oiran*, but only one man had succeeded in winning her heart: an American sailor on a U.S. merchant vessel that had dropped anchor there last spring, a sailor with whom promises were exchanged. She was unable to forget him and waited for the promised reunion that was to take place in the fall of that year. As she listened to the beggar's shakuhachi, she would gaze at the sails offshore, lost in reverie.

This was the opening scene of the movie.

When the American sailor returned, he did not have the enormous amount of money needed to release her from bondage. Desperate, he devised a plan to smuggle her away in the hold of his ship, and he convinced the young beggar to help him.

The plan was for the *oiran* to go quietly to the back exit of the brothel, where the waiting sailor would place her inside a large trunk loaded on a cart. He would return to his ship and the beggar would take the cart to an old, abandoned Buddhist temple on a cliff fronting an isolated beach. The trunk would be unloaded and placed next to the dais in the temple. The American would bring a boat to the beach at the bottom of the cliff to claim the *oiran* around midnight the next day. He would then take the trunk from the beggar, and stow it aboard the merchant vessel.

The beggar was only too happy to help. But he asked to be paid with something other than money.

"I would do anything for the *oiran* even if it means losing my life because she loves you. This is the least that I can do for her. But if you have any thought for this wretched beggar, even a smidgen of pity, please let me have my way with her while she is hidden there for the night. This is all I ask."

With his forehead pressed against the ground and tears streaming down his face, the beggar pleaded, groveling.

"Last spring, when your ship left this port, it was I who played the shakuhachi and consoled her, day after day. As a beggar, I dare to overreach, and I know that what I ask is unseemly coming from one so wretched. But if you grant me this one wish, I will willingly take the blame for this trickery and help the two of you to the very end," he said.

The sailor found it hard to refuse. True, the *oiran* was his precious love, but she was a courtesan, who had given herself to many others. He thought it reasonable to reward the beggar's kindness with her favors.

But Ayamedayu, who had seen the beggar only once through the latticework of the brothel window, shuddered. Ever proud and pampered, she would rather have died than let that grimy, ugly youth touch the sleeve of her kimono, much less her body. So she and her lover plotted to deceive him.

Parting from the beggar, the sailor returned to his ship. The beggar pulled the cart into the old temple and tried to open the lid. But it was securely locked. Clinging to the trunk, he vented his anguish and bitterness at the sailor's betrayal to the *oiran* hidden inside.

"My lover did not do this to deceive you. In his haste, he simply forgot to give you the key. When he arrives, he will open this trunk and the promise will be kept," she said anxiously, trying to pacify him.

The sailor rushed to the temple at dawn. He apologized to the beggar for having forgotten the key and then said, "My ship is raising anchor and will be leaving port soon. There's no time to keep my promise to you, so please make do with this."

With that, the young man threw the beggar a purse filled with money. The beggar was dejected.

"I cannot live in a world where I will not be able to gaze on the *oiran*. My life will have no meaning. I will drown myself in the sea. If the *oiran* detests me that much, I will not force myself on her, but grant the last wish of one about to die and let me have one last look at her. Allow me one kiss on the hem of her beautiful gold-embroidered kimono."

Despite his repeated pleas, the *oiran* would not agree.

"No matter what he says, don't open the lid of this trunk. Hurry and put me on the ship," she cried out to her lover.

"I'm sorry, but I cannot force her. Besides, I didn't bring the key to the trunk today," the American sailor explained, seemingly at a loss.

"Then so be it. Even in death, I will not rest without seeing the *oiran*. And when I see her, I will voice my anger and bitterness," the beggar said.

"If you wish to die, go ahead and die," cried the *oiran* once again from the trunk.

"When I am dead, this ugly visage will invade the *oiran*'s body and torment her forever. Once that happens, no amount of remorse and penance will undo the deed."

No sooner were these words spoken, than the beggar jumped off the cliff in front of the temple and into the sea. For a few moments, the American stood there, seemingly relieved, then hurriedly took the key from his pocket and unlocked the lid of the trunk. He comforted the *oiran*, and the two of them rejoiced at their success.

The story up to this point was contained in the first and second reels.

From the third reel on, the story takes place on board the ship and in America. In the first scene, the trunk is in the ship's hold along with the other cargo, and its interior is shown from the side.

The *oiran* survived on bread and water placed inside the trunk. She sat cramped, her forehead resting on her drawn-up knees. Three days had passed when a strange boil erupted on her right knee and began to swell. Four tiny growths began to emerge on its soft pulpy surface. Strangely, the boil was painless, and she slapped and pushed down on it. So harshly and repeatedly did she do this that its soft surface became harder with each passing day, and the contours of the four tiny growths began to stand out. The two at the top became circular; the one in the center became vertically elongated; and the lowermost one stretched sinuously sideways and was eerily reminiscent of a crawling caterpillar.

From the small openings created to allow air into the trunk, a dim luminescence lit up the normally pitch-dark interior of the trunk, and a circle of light outlined her right kneecap.

As she stared intently at the afflicted knee, the two protuberances at the top appeared like the eyes of a creature. The elongated growth in the center began to look like a nose, and the lower one shaped like a caterpillar appeared like lips. She suddenly realized that the entire swollen surface looked like a human face.

"I'm just being neurotic," she thought.

But, it was clearly a human face—eerily reminiscent of the beggar's visage, though it was like a child's drawing with just a few simple lines. Assailed by indescribable terror, she fainted.

The unconscious *oiran* sat with her head drooping, covering the afflicted knee. Meanwhile the protuberances continued to grow. The eyes, nose, and mouth that had been mere lines gradually became more distinct until they formed the image of the beggar's face. The vindictive expression of the beggar emerged silently, as if carved by the hand of a master sculptor.

From then on, the face took its revenge on the *oiran* in many ways through the grisly events that unfold.

After the ship arrived in America, she kept the face on her knee a closely guarded secret from her lover. The two eventually settled in the outskirts of San Francisco. The sailor gave up the seaman's life and went to work for a company. Suspicious of her very depressed state, he quietly observed her until one evening, he discovered her terrible secret and tried to flee. A violent struggle ensued as the *oiran* desperately tried to stop him. Possessed by the vengeful spirit and having gained enormous physical strength, she strangled him. She saw the Face looking down on the body of her lover through a tear in her clothing. Moving its formerly immobile facial muscles for the first time, it smiled and gave an unearthly chuckle. After this, the Face began to show emotion. It would roll its eyes with anger and stick out its tongue. Sometimes it wept bitterly, with tears coursing down its face, or contorted its lips and drooled.

The *oiran* became a wanton vamp. Her beauty grew even more breathtaking, and she became even more seductive. She deceived men and robbed them of their wealth and even their lives. Haunted by her crimes, she would resolve to turn over a new leaf, but the Face always interfered, jeering at her for being craven and inciting her to commit more crimes. Her life gradually became a cycle of abasement and repentance.

As she grew richer, the setting moved from San Francisco to New York. Many prominent and wealthy men fell under her spell only to be destroyed. She lived in a beautiful mansion and was thought to be a great heiress.

But, when alone, her conscience plagued her, and the more she suffered, the more her body grew luscious and ripe, her appearance more radiant than ever.

She fell in love with a European aristocrat and married him. One night, the newlywed couple hosted a dinner party with many guests at which her Face was revealed to everyone. The tumor was always covered in gauze over which a tight stocking was fitted snugly; and she made it a point never to expose her knees. But, that evening as she danced, a bright red stream of blood suddenly stained the pure white silk of her stocking and left droplets of blood on the dance floor. Unaware, she continued to dance. Her husband, who had always wondered why his wife kept her knee wrapped in bandages, approached and examined her wound.

The Face had torn the stocking with its teeth, and, sticking out its long tongue, it was laughing crazily while bleeding from its eyes and nose.

Mad with fear and shame, the *oiran* ran to her bedroom, fell on her dagger and took her own life. The Face continued to laugh.

This was the story of "The Tumor with a Human Face." The film ended with a close-up shot of the Face.

The names of the actors and director did not appear anywhere in the film, only the name of Utagawa Yurie in the role of Ayame-dayu. At the premiere, she alone, dressed as the *oiran* appeared bowing and smiling to the audience. But the Japanese actor who played an even more important role as the shakuhachi-playing beggar received no mention. No one knew who he was or where he came from.

Yurie had absolutely no recollection of having played that role. Unlike stage acting, the scenes weren't always filmed in sequence, and several scenes from completely different dramas were occasionally filmed simultaneously. In many cases, the actors didn't know the story line of the drama they were performing.

This was especially true of Globe Studios where Yurie was under contract. The director made it a point never to tell the actors the plot. They weren't required to read a script or rehearse their lines. They took their acting cues from the director. They laughed and cried, and performed from one cut to another. This was the method generally adopted by American film companies.

During the four or five years she worked for Globe Company, Yurie had been filmed in countless scenes, but she never knew what scene of what drama she was playing in or what types of dramas were being put together. She was like a factory worker working in a small section of a large machinery plant.

But she did remember some of the roles she played. Since her acting talent ran to gun molls and female detectives, she had played countless scenes hiding in trunks, playing fast and loose with men, and murdering them. So it was only natural she didn't know which scenes had been used for "The Tumor with a Human Face." To top it off, film tricks by an experienced technician such as burning and overlaying the beggar's face on her knee had been used in the picture. That may have been why she didn't remember the film.

At Globe, there had been a highly skilled technician named Jefferson, who specialized in burn overlay and trick photography. "The Tumor with a Human Face" had probably been the just the film he had been waiting for to demonstrate his expertise. Remembering Jefferson's cheerful, funny personality, she thought he must have wanted to surprise her.

Along with the tumor, he had used subtle techniques in unexpected places throughout the film. But he would have shown the film to her. She also had questions about the beggar. Only three Japanese actors had been employed at Globe. Not one of them had stood in front of the camera with her and played the role of a beggar in a port town like Nagasaki. Who was the Japanese whose ugly visage was burned for eternity on her white satin-smooth knee? The longer and harder she thought about it, the more Yurie began to feel she was cursed by someone she didn't know.

She suddenly recalled a long-time, top-ranking manager at Nitto Moving Picture Company who was in charge of corresponding with foreign companies and translating moving picture magazines and scripts. He knew what year the American films brought into Japan were made, who imported them, and who the actors were.

One day, she visited Mr. H's second-story office near the studio in Nippori.

"Ah, yes. That film. Well, I do know something about it," Mr. H said in answer to her question. He kept blinking and seemed to be very uncomfortable. Looking anxious, he stood up and walked over to close the door that Yurie had left open.

"So, you don't remember making that picture either—which makes it a strange and weird film. What I know is a bit eerie, so I've hesitated to bring up the subject. Please don't be too unnerved by what I'm about to tell you."

"Don't worry. If it's that's frightening, that's all the more reason for me to hear it," Yurie said as she laughed nervously.

"That film belongs to us, and until a short time ago it had been loaned out to a small-town movie theater. The company bought the film one month before your return to Japan. We didn't buy it directly from Globe but from a Frenchman in Yokohama who offered to sell it to us. Apparently, he had purchased it in Shanghai along with many other films for his own personal collection. But before that it had been shown quite a bit in the colonies in Southeast Asia and in China. It was badly scratched and damaged. Your popularity had been skyrocketing ever since "The Samurai's Daughter" came out, and you had just signed a contract with us. Besides, the images in the film were still good despite the damage. So we bought it for an outrageous sum of money.

"Shortly after we got it, a queer rumor started to go around. It was said that if you watched the film alone late at night, something so terrifying would happen that you would not be able to watch it to the end. That was what happened to M, one of the technicians who used to work for us. He was repairing the film's emulsion late one night in one of the rooms downstairs and viewing the film while checking it for scratches.

"Nobody believed him at first. Out of curiosity, several of the other guys took turns watching it. Later they also said it was bizarre and haunted. But what was strange was that it didn't end there. M, the technician who had been scared witless, slowly became mentally unhinged, and not long after that he left the company. The others who saw the film after him, started having nightmares every night and came down with some kind of sickness that made them dizzy and unsteady on their feet. A lot of unexplainable things happened. Even the boss tried to watch it alone, and about two weeks later he too came down with some unknown fever and his health deteriorated.

"As you know, the boss is a superstitious, nervous person. He immediately held a secret meeting where he insisted on two things—that the company sell the film to another firm as soon as possible and that the employment contract that we'd just signed with you be cancelled. But, there was a lot of opposition to the boss's demands. As we'd paid a lot for the film, some thought it was a mistake to sell it so quickly. Others opposed the idea of canceling your contract, and we'd already paid you an exorbitant advance. The discussion got really heated until a compromise was finally reached. Since the eerie phenomenon occurred only in the dead of night when there was only one viewer, they figured nobody would find out about it because nothing happened when the film was seen by many people at the same time. But, the boss was insistent about not wanting that film on the company's premises, so it was leased to other firms for a while until someone was willing to buy it from us at a high price.

"As for your contract, it was decided that it was completely unnecessary to cancel it. If that were to become known it would affect your reputation as well as the film's value, so the consensus was to keep it strictly under wraps. It was also unanimously agreed to keep the employees in the dark about this as much as possible. Everyone who'd experienced this terrifying ordeal is gone, so there's no one here who knows this secret.

"At first, the executives who attended this secret meeting wanted to lease the film out to a large company, but because of tough competition and friction between rival companies, that didn't pan out. The company was forced to lease it out to small moving picture theaters around Kyoto, Osaka, and Nagoya. But there was no full-blown advertising in the newspapers, which kept it from attracting the attention of well-known critics. That's how such a masterpiece managed to get by without getting any reviews.

"Personally, I've never experienced this weird, late-night phenomenon. I'm just repeating what I heard from those who did. But I was one of the few who watched the film to the end at its preview shortly after the company bought it. What struck me as odd at the time was the Japanese actor playing the beggar. I know the names of all of the main actors in that film, but I've never laid eyes on that actor. If I'm not mistaken, S, K, and C were the only actors who could have been in that film with you, right? But none of them played that beggar. Do you know who it might have been?"

And with that Mr. H ended his long monologue.

"No, I don't. But could someone have burned and overlaid the image of someone I don't know?"

"I thought of that. I've also heard about Jefferson, that wizard of trick photography. But no matter how good the technician is, there're usually one or two places where the work is too good to be true. If that is a completely burned-in image, then he's using some secret technique that we're unaware of. About six months ago, the company put all their questions together in a letter and sent it off to Globe Studios. They eventually sent a reply that was a complete disappointment. According to them, they've never produced a film called "The Tumor with a Human Face." But they did produce a piece with a similar story line in which some of the scenes from this film appear to have been used.

"So either somebody mixed in parts of that film or parts of it were modified and the images were burned and overlaid to produce images not captured by the camera. Globe said it was hard to believe that some of their exclusively contracted actors could have produced such a film in secret. They were busy every day making films at the studio and didn't have that kind of time. They said that only three Japanese actors, S, K, and C, were employed at Globe when you were there. Several others had been hired and released before your time.

"As far as they're concerned, it's possible that an image of a Japanese actor that you didn't know was burned and overlaid in the film. But, although Globe Studios was able to carry out a very difficult, highly technical burn, to what extent and how they did it are trade secrets; and they couldn't provide details. If the film was really doctored, Globe couldn't let that go unnoticed. They wanted Nitto Moving Picture Company to sell it to them so they could take a look at it. And they were willing to pay a high price for it. It's just as Globe said: Somebody took a film with a similar story line and spliced it with different parts of another film, skillfully modified it, and burned and overlaid images to make another film. That is the most plausible theory. If they're right, then the person who did it has to be even more skilled than Jefferson.

"This may be a strange question, but did you do anything in America to make someone hate you? No matter how you look at it, this must have something to do with someone who was very taken with you but was terribly disliked or deceived, and that film's been cursed by his obsession for revenge."

"I can't recall having done anything to trigger such obsessive hatred. Tell me, exactly what does the face on that tumor look like? I hear it's really ugly."

"Yes, it's frighteningly ugly. The face looks like a tumor—fat and round. He's around thirty, and in the film he looks about ten years older than you. It's a face you can't forget once you've seen it. You can't help but think that the actor is someone who doesn't exist. He's just a phantom who lives in that film. Not one person who has experienced that weird phenomenon in the film believes that he's a real person. They all say he's evil, that he's not an actor, or that he's demonic."

"That's what I want to find out—what this weird phenomenon is all about. You've told me everything except what I want to know."

"Well, I've purposely avoided talking about this for fear it might make you more nervous, but since I've told you this much, I might as well tell you everything. I later heard from M, the technician who went insane, exactly what happened to him. That weird phenomenon appears to be caused by the face of that phantom. Based on M's many years of technical experience, what gives moving pictures their appeal and sense of excitement is being able to watch them while listening to live music and the voice of the narrator in a moving picture theater. But when this film is seen late at night, alone, in a darkened room without the narrator or the live music, you get a frightening and ominous feeling. This would be understandable if the story was about stillness and desolation, but the scenes in this film are filled with people and depict splendid banquets and a lot of action. Yet the viewer begins to feel uncomfortable, as if they're going to disappear into the film. The creepiest part is the close-up of that smirking face. When that face appears, it's so chilling the operator forgets to keep the projector turning. It's not the angry face that's so frightening but the smiling face. That's what M said. 'It's nothing to me,' he said, 'because I'm just the technician, but if that actor saw his image in that film when he was operating the projector all alone, he'd probably get this strange sensation that the image in the film was his real self and the person watching the film was his shadow.'

"From the moment the shakuhachi-playing beggar appears in the first reel, certain strange thoughts begin to enter your mind. The terribly scratched condition of the film and its slightly blurry images don't interfere with the experience; they seem to add to the weirdness of it all. Somehow you're able to get through the first four reels, but everyone seems to blank out for a while when they get to the final scenes in reel 5 when Ayamedayu kills herself. The scene is a close-up your right leg from the knee to the toes. The face or tumor growing from the knee looks very serious. It twists its lips and lets out a strange, tearful laugh, seemingly satisfied that it's had its revenge. It's a sudden laugh that's barely audible yet undeniably heard. M thought it must be noise coming from outside. The sound was very slight, and you had to be listening very intently. Maybe it was there when the movie was being shown to the general public and nobody's noticed it until now.

"Well, what do you think? Oh yes, I forgot to mention that that film is going to be turned over to Globe Studios. A few days ago, it was picked up from a moving picture theater in Sugamo, and it's on that shelf in this office right now. The boss gave strict orders that it wasn't to be shown while it was here, but there's no rule against looking at the film itself. What do you think? Do you want to take a look at it? You might find a clue to solving this mystery."

Yurie nodded, her eyes shining with excitement. Mr. H pulled the metal canisters containing reels one and five from among the canisters stacked on a nearby shelf. Removing the lids and placing them on his desk, he pulled out a long ribbon of film and, stretching it out vertically against the light from the window, he showed it to Yurie.

"See, look. That's the beggar."

Then he showed her the face of the tumor burned on her knee in the fifth reel.

"This is when he's the tumor. Even I can tell that the face has been burned onto the knee. Have you ever seen this man before?"

"No, I've never seen him in my life," she said. "But, Mr. H, this face has clearly been burned on, which means that he must exist somewhere. He can't be a ghost."

"But there's one place where it's impossible to do this. Look here. This is in the middle of reel five. When the *oiran* tries to hit the face, it bites her wrist and the skin at the base of her right thumb is between its teeth. Your fingers are writhing in pain, and you're struggling to pull away. There's no way that a burn-on is possible here."

So saying, Mr. H put the film in Yurie's hand, lit a cigarette, and began walking around the room, talking to himself.

"I wonder what will happen when this film is sent to Globe Studios. That company's never one to pass up a chance to make money. They'll make several copies and sell them outright. I bet that's what they're going to do."

Ghosts of the Metropolis

都会の幽気

(Tokai no yūki)

Toyoshima Yoshio (1924)

豊島与 志雄

Translation by Rodger Swan and Jeffrey Angles

IN THE METROPOLIS, there is a unique type of ghostly presence that haunts the city. When the rain is falling heavily and the wind is blowing outside, these ghostly presences flit aimlessly through the urban streets then disappear, rarely showing themselves. But when the air begins to grow still—more often during the evening than in the daytime—they begin to show their dim outlines in a shadowy form and swirl unsteadily, wandering through the back alleys.

Ghostly presences are not only found in the city. In the country, there are rural ghosts, and in the mountains, forests, rice paddies, and fields there are ghosts that belong to each of those places. Those ghosts, however, carry with them a whiff of inhuman strangeness. But when it comes right down to it, it is only the ghostly presences which dwell in the city that have something human about them; they are the ones that carry the scent of humanity.

What I am describing is a kind of a spirit, not some sort of demon. That much is clear. Leaving the question of whether it has a form or not aside, let me say that what I am describing is something that does not make a sound, something that does not speak, something that only makes its presence felt. It floats about in a vague form, but you only have to come into contact with it once and a cold shudder will pass through you, spreading its terrifying poison through your body.

Where do these ghostly presences come from? Probably what happens is that the breath of the countless people in the city, the desires in their hearts, and the scents of their flesh all congeal and come alive in some vague way. Indeed, there are countless people huddled together, living in the city. There is not a single corner of the city that human feet have not trodden, not even in the deepest back streets of the city. There is not a single crack that human eyes have not yet spotted, not even on the walls of the deepest alleys. The air that is inhaled into our lungs and that touches our skin has been in the lungs and on the skin of countless other people. Everything in the city has been touched by human hands and possesses a hint of humanity. In the city, the breath of the inhabitants thickens and becomes a kind of vapor that veils the place, just like the stinking, moist vapor that lingers in theaters, playhouses, cinemas, and other such places.

Moreover, countless different shapes, ambitions, and even scents leave their traces in this vaporous fog. Young men must have waited for their lovers at the corners of these alleys. Thieves certainly have lurked with bated breath in those dark shadows. Detectives surely have searched for devious criminals in the shadows of these utility poles. Ailing beggars must have welcomed the coming of morning underneath those eaves. The dead bodies of children run over by cars must have lain on the flagstones of these roads. Drunks must have stumbled on these pointed rocks as they were walking home well past the usual hour. Young couples must have gone for a stroll hand in hand in those quiet back streets. Old people with diseased lungs must have spit up blood into these very hedges. Beggars blessed with gifts of charity have surely choked up with tears of gratitude under those very gates. Unemployed people living hand to mouth must have shaken their fists in indignation under the shadows of these very trees. Violent men have surely flashed their daggers in these street crossings. Cackling madmen must have spit upon these stone walls. People have done many different things here at different times and places, and all of them have left their traces in the fog of the city. The traces of these people swirl, collect, and gather together, forming ghostly presences which take on a dim spark of life and float through the city.

When these ghostly presences encounter the fierce rain of a howling storm, they are blown about by the storm, but on days when the air slowly grows still, the vapor is likely to stagnate and grow thick. Then, from this strange vapor, the ghostly presences take on vague forms and float about aimlessly. On days when the sun's bright light falls upon them, they dissolve and disappear, but when the sky darkens ever so slightly and casts a chill, or when evening begins to fall, the vague outlines of the presences appear once again to haunt the city.

There once was a time when I developed a habit of going out at night and staying out very late. I say I had a "habit," but perhaps it's more accurate to say that I had a *desire* to stay out late. I had failed to win the heart of the one I loved, and everything had lost its meaning. Nothing excited me. I was able to get by during the day, but when night fell, I found I couldn't stay all alone in my apartment. To allay my boredom, I would go and spend a rowdy couple of hours in the home of a married friend, at a billiard parlor, a *go* parlor, or even some seedy restaurant or bar.[1] I would not feel the urge to go home until after midnight—in other words, unless I was completely drained and dying to get some sleep. It was not uncommon for me to stay out past two or three in the morning.

One night, I experienced a strange turn of events. No, it would be more accurate to say I experienced a strange *feeling*. I had been at a friend's house playing *hana-awase* late into the night.[2] It must have been around 1:30 a.m. when I set out for my apartment, which was not too far away. The night was quiet, the sky was slightly overcast, and the cool evening air had settled. The evening air felt pleasant on my cheeks, still flushed with excitement from the card game. With a hat pulled down low over my brow and my hands shoved into my overcoat pockets, I walked

1. *Go* (also called *igo*) is an ancient Chinese board game in which two players place stones in strategic formations on a checkered board, attempting to occupy as much of the board as possible while invading and destabilizing the other player's formations.

2. *Hana-awase* is a traditional Japanese card game that involves players competing to get as many cards as possible of high value. The cards feature flowers, poems (*tanzaku*), and other images.

along unsteadily. Meanwhile, my mind was full of images of the card game I had just been playing: I saw the round red moon of the flower cards, the image of *Ono no Tōfū* holding his umbrella, the long poem card inscribed with the word *akayoroshi.* I was still thinking about the cards as I walked down the road. My surroundings were so familiar that nothing attracted my attention, and my eyes did not stop on anything in particular. I left the streets where the trolley ran, and veered into a lonely side street. I turned right and approached the stone walls of a spacious mansion. I was recalling how unpleasant it was to have my chrysanthemum cup and poetry card exposed, leaving me with a poor hand, when I realized someone was trailing me. Actually, I had noticed someone behind me earlier, but it was then I realized whoever it was actually following me. I wondered to myself who it could be so late at night. I turned around to cast a glance over my shoulder, but no one was there. The gloomy darkness filled the street all the way to the intersection behind me. The lonely street was punctuated only by the glow of the occasional streetlamp.

A few moments later, I once again felt certain that someone was following me. I turned to look over my shoulder again, but again, no one was there. This happened two or three more times, and I felt a cold chill go through my body. I quickened my pace, but whoever was following me also quickened their pace to equal mine. I say that, but in actuality, I could not hear a voice or the sound of any footsteps. Whoever was following me was as silent as the wind. It crossed my mind that I was just being silly, but the more I thought about it, the stranger it all seemed. It was pointless to keep looking back, so I just quickened my pace and kept going. When I reached my building, a sense of relief washed over me. The presence had completely disappeared. With a strange feeling, I looked back at the silent, slumbering street then approached the front glass door. The door was always shut but never locked. I pulled the door open, still slightly flustered, and stepped inside. Once there, I calmed down somewhat. I closed the door quietly and quietly, pulled aside the white curtain that lead inside, and went in. Straight ahead, there was a large wall clock like the kind you see at railway stations, and as I entered, I saw its pendulum swinging gently, just like always. When I saw that familiar sight, the creepy feeling finally melted away.

But that was not the last time something like that happened. I had encounters like that over and over again. They never happened during the day in well-lit places, such as near the trolley tracks. It would be when I was walking the lonely back alleys late at night—no specific time or place in particular—that I would suddenly realize someone was following me. Just like before, I would turn around, but no one would be there. As I started to walk on, I would again feel the presence of somebody following me like the wind. On nights when there was a drizzle, I would feel the presence crowd in under my umbrella, pressing so close I could practically feel it against the back of my neck. A cold shiver would run down my spine, but I would do my best to suppress these feelings. If I lit a cigarette, they would vanish.

The more this happened, the more I became accustomed to the strange presences, and I began to guess why they might be following me. As I thought about it, I realized that I encountered them whenever I was engrossed in something, when my mind was focused on a single thought, and I had forgotten all else. They would appear when I was tired but calm—when I was lost in thought yet still in a state of heightened sensitivity. Meanwhile, I would stroll through the late-night streets where the air was quiet and still, stirring up waves in the air behind me like the wake of a boat on the surface of the sea. Maybe it was these waves that gave me the impression something was following me. When this explanation occurred to me, I felt a sense of relief at having been so silly. I decided that the next time I sensed one of the presences

I would not let it upset me. For a while, I was able to get away with thinking, *Oh, there they are again. . . .*

But the situation got worse. The feeling that somebody was following me gradually developed into something else. I know it sounds strange, but whatever it was took on a much clearer form.

One night at about one o'clock in the morning, I got off the trolley and was returning home. I was quite drunk. I had been out fooling around with several friends, and on our return home we dropped into a coffee shop. I was a mess, drunk in that particular way you get when you mix Japanese and Western-style alcohol, and my head was spinning. I could see the world around me, but that was about it. All sorts of scenes one might expect to see at night crowded their way into my brain—the wild, seemingly frightened countenances of passengers racing for their train, the cold faces of passengers lost deep in thought, the faces of the four or five train conductors who were sitting together and dozing off, the red lettering on the advertisements hanging from the ceiling, and the ashen flecks of dirt on the windows—all of these things were illuminated by the dim red lights of the train.[3] Even though these images forced their way into my head, something was still lacking. That was when I realized something was about to come after me. That feeling made me focus my eyes intently as I walked through the lonely back streets, looking at my surroundings. As soon as I became aware of this feeling I thought, *There it is again*—whoever it was that was following me.

At that instant, I caught a glimpse of something like a human face peering at me from amid the darkness. *Oh my*! I thought, but when I turned to look straight at it, all traces of it had vanished. All I could see were the pitch black shadows cast by the single branch of an oak tree hanging over a hedge. I took four or five steps forward as if to say, "*Don't you threaten me!*" but just then,

3. Trolleys changed the color of their lights from white to red to indicate the last run of the evening.

under the eaves of a house on the other side of the street I saw the faint silhouette of a crouching figure. But I was drunk and rather used to seeing such things, so I just thought that the man I had seen earlier had managed to get ahead of me. I walked along without giving it much thought, until I glanced back and realized no one was there anymore.

I came to a building that had a small window just under the eaves. It seemed to belong to a maid's room and was six or seven *shaku* above the ground.[4] As I peered at the house in the dead of night, I saw that the storm shutters were not shut, and the sooty paper on the wooden lattice of the *shōji* was illuminated by the pale light of an electric lamp.[5] I stopped briefly and looked. Just then, the silhouette of a woman's head unexpectedly appeared upon the *shōji* for a moment, then vanished just as quickly. The woman's hair had come somewhat undone. As soon as the silhouette disappeared, I felt a cold chill pass through my body. Lewd visions filled my mind: a voluptuous maid in a disheveled state was standing there expectantly, casting her shadow against the *shōji*, while someone else stood there burning with lust. I imagined myself in that vision. My mind ran wild with bawdy thoughts, so I quickly walked away.

A few moments later, from a spot in the shadow of a utility pole, I took another casual glance over my shoulder. The only thing coming from the window was a vague, pale light. No one was visible anymore. I remained there peering from behind the pole, and then the shadow of a detective appeared, lying in wait for somebody in a similar hiding place and standing in same posture as I was. He seemed to be trying to get into the position where

4. A *shaku* is a traditional Japanese unit for measuring length. One *shaku* is approximately one foot.

5. *Shōji* are windows or doors constructed by affixing paper to a wooden lattice. The paper allows light to pass through during the day, but it still maintains a degree of privacy for the people inside the room

I was standing, and surprised by his behavior, I began to walk away. As I did so, the shadow of a foolish, drunken man returning home at a late hour just like I was began to trail me at close quarters.

I did not feel I could keep going, but I did not feel I could stop either. Something strange was happening. I was seeing the shadows of people who had once walked and stood in these very same spots. They had shown up at exactly the same places in exactly the same postures and with exactly the same timing as before, but now they were following me. They were only vague shadows whose shapes were hard to make out, but although they seemed very familiar, there was something completely alien about them as well.

As I walked through the alleys to my building, which was only four or five blocks away, I saw countless more silhouettes of people roaming the streets. No, these were not just shadows. What I was seeing were the *spirits* of people. There were spirits at the end of stone walls, beneath the branches of the plantings, beside the hedges, underneath the eaves at the entrances to buildings, beside the telephone poles at the three-way intersection, on the stone markers beside the gutter, in the windows looking out onto the street—almost everywhere a person might go. There were people with clenched teeth; people looking for something; people furrowing their brows; people laughing with white, protruding teeth; people with wild hair; people doing all sorts of things that people had done there in the past. I was not able to make out their expressions clearly, but I could sense what these vague ghostly presences were doing as they hovered about, as lightly as if floating on air. As I walked by them, they floated closer as if trying to follow me.

I found myself unable either to run or stand still, so I attempted to drag myself along, but my legs had grown heavy. When I tried to scream, my voice caught in my throat. Hardly able to catch my breath, I just looked up at the sky. It had gone black, and there was not a single star anywhere. The streetlights of the bustling town in the distance shone an uncanny pale red in the cloudy atmosphere. Oh, what a massive metropolis! It seemed to stretch on and on! What an eerie, confused town! And what a suffocating, murky atmosphere all these countless people create as they swarm on top of one another and carry out their everyday activities! And at night, while everyone sleeps in their safe little nests, the forms that they created earlier appear as shadowy presences, divorced from their bodies, and wander the streets in countless numbers!

At last I arrived at my building. It was not until I opened the glass door and passed through the curtain hanging inside that I finally felt safe. I fixed my gaze, which had now lost the panic of a moment before, on the large clock and saw its pendulum swinging slowly. As I watched the pendulum swing back and forth, I let out a sigh of relief as if I had arrived in the safety of a fortress.

Although those experiences were frightening, they paled in comparison with what happened next. One strangely chilly, cloudy afternoon around 3:30, I was heading home, hands shoved in my pockets. I had been playing billiards since that morning, and had grown tired. When I came within sight of my building, I saw a young man standing abstractedly in front of the gate. As I thought to myself, *How strange*, he suddenly began walking in my direction. Had he noticed me as well? When we passed each other on the street a minute or two later, a cold shiver ran through me. The instant we passed each other, I realized that, strangely enough, that I could not recall a single detail of the man's appearance or clothing. Not a single footfall had sounded in my ears. He passed me like the wind. I looked back over my shoulder, but the man was nowhere to be seen. I had a clear view of the quiet street, but it was empty as far as the eye could see—the only thing in the road was the bright, pale light of afternoon. This surprised me, and I quickened my pace, my nerves still rattled. I dashed into my building just as the clock on the wall struck the half hour with a loud gong. None of the maids came to greet me. Even the manager, who was always around, failed to show her face. It was as if the place had been abandoned. I was standing there thinking how strange it was when I realized I could feel him behind me. The man must have turned around and followed me, probably just as we passed each other in the street. I shuddered and ran up to my room.

The encounter bothered me all the more because it had happened in the afternoon. If the mysterious figure had ventured into the building during the day, who knew what it might have done if it were nighttime? I found myself descending into a state of complete paranoia and decided I would shut myself up in my room as much as possible. I am not sure if it was my imagination or something in the air, but the thought of hiding in my room was not enough to put me at ease. If it were merely a man tailing me, well, I could deal with that, but it seemed all sorts of shadowy forms were floating up and coming at me from every direction. No matter how much I thought about it, I could not figure out what was going on. I was not just imagining things. No doubt about it, there were spirits rising up like smoke and flitting about around me.

I shut myself up in my room, wondering what I should do next. I felt like I was in a living nightmare. I decided I would try not to go outside on cloudy days, even when it was light outside, and I would go to bed as early as possible. I would call my friends on the telephone and have them come over to play *go*, *shogi*, and *hana-awase*, and that way, I could amuse myself as much as possible, even while staying cooped up. When I was alone, however, I quickly grew depressed, as something was haunting me. The light from the electric bulb in my room would dim, and the vague outlines of the spirits would appear in the nooks and crannies of the room. An irrational sense of uneasiness would overcome me. When that happened, I would hunch over my desk and try to lose myself in a good book. An interesting story would pull me in, and by the time I had read for an hour, my mind would let go of a little of its usual stress, but then I would see something out of the corner of my right eye. Something vague and amorphous was hanging up there, floating lightly in the air. Each time I looked up, however, there was nothing there. The only thing I could see was the *otoshigake* with its whitish grain.[6] It was about one *shaku* above the lintel over the *shōji*, and looked newer than the ceiling boards, the pillars, and the lintel. My eyes would slide across the grain, then for a few moments I would gaze at the painting of bamboo hanging in the alcove before returning to my book. After a little while, the spot above me would begin to bother me again. It seemed there was some vague shape hanging up there to the right. I would look up again, but still there was nothing there.

This happened over and over, and before long, I could no longer relax even in the comfort of my own room. To make matters worse, I had a strange dream. It started off with a jumble of different things, none of which had a recognizable form, but gradually, a young man emerged from them. I could not make out a single thing about him—not his hairstyle, his facial features, his expressions, nor the pattern on his kimono—but I could tell he was a young student. He had placed a desk in the alcove and was standing on top of it and using a pair of the kind of metal chopsticks ordinarily used for picking up hot coals to poke a hole through the wall just above the *otoshigake*. I watched him, thinking how bizarre his actions were. Eventually, he made a

6. In traditional Japanese rooms, there is often a recessed alcove (*tokonoma*) in which people place flower arrangements, hanging scrolls, or other decorations. The alcove is open to the room in all places but the top, where there is usually a horizontal plaster or stucco barrier that extends a foot or two downward from the ceiling and runs across the front of the alcove. An *otoshigake* is a horizontal piece of wood that runs along the bottom of this barrier.

hole big enough to stick his finger through. Before I knew it, he had strung more than two *shaku* of rope through the hole, tied it in a loop, and stuck his head through it. *He's going to kill himself!* The instant this thought flashed through my mind, he kicked the desk away, leaving his body swinging there as the life passed out of it. He hung there, a corpse, not moving in the slightest. But the most horrifying thing about it was that I realized he was *me*. I looked on in a state of shock, thinking that was impossible, but, sure enough, his features were identical to mine.

My God! I awoke just as I was about to scream, but I am not sure if any sound escaped my lips or not. My room was illuminated by the dim light from the lamp, which was still on. As I looked around, I saw everything was just as it always had been. The scroll with the painting of the bamboo was hanging in the alcove, and the *otoshigake* above still had its whitish grain. Rather than putting me at ease, however, the fact that everything was just as usual struck me as unsettling, and I pulled my bedcovers over my head. I tossed and turned in my futon many times as I tried in vain to go back to sleep.

I woke up late the next morning to find sunlight already bursting into my room. I had forgotten about the dream and proceeded to have breakfast as usual. Thinking I would go out while the sunlight was still shining through the clear skies, I decided to take a walk and just go wherever my fancy would take me. I played billiards for a while, and in the afternoon I walked through the bustling streets of the city. On the way home, I stopped by a friend's house, played some *go*, and was even served a nice dinner. I was beginning to become a bit anxious about going home, so I went back home through the busy streets soon after sunset. I did not encounter any strange, ghostly presences, and I made my way back to my own room without incident. Feeling relieved, I blew out a puff of cigarette smoke, but what happened next shocked me so much that I nearly leapt out of my chair.

The smoke from my cigarette wafted up toward the ceiling. Just as the curls of smoke were about to disappear, they took on the contours of a person hanging from the *otoshigake.* Looking up in surprise, I recalled the dream from the previous night in vivid detail. As I looked around carefully, I realized the desk I was leaning on and the metal chopsticks in the brazier looked exactly like the ones I had seen in my dream. The only difference was that the hemp rope was nowhere to be found. But it was not long before I began to realize I had seen it hanging outside; it was the weather-beaten rope on the railing outside the window. I could not muster up the courage to open the storm doors and determine if I was right or not.

Still, that was the least of my worries. There was a corpse swinging from the *otoshigake* above my head. When I peered directly at it, it would disappear, but when I shifted my gaze away for a moment, it would reappear. A strange feeling rose within me. I stared at the *otoshigake,* which was newer then the rest of the wood around it. As I stared, I imagined myself standing up unsteadily, boring a hole through the wall, fashioning a noose in the hemp rope, standing on the desk, then dropping. These thoughts sent a shudder through me. It was as if some impulse was driving me to do these things, but instead I froze completely as if tangled in a spider's web. If I moved a single muscle, I might end up dangling there with my neck in a noose. As I fixated on this possibility, the tragic sight of the figure hanging from the *otoshigake* seemed to grow gradually clearer.

I could not stand it another second, so I burst out of my room and ran down the staircase. I was wondering what to do when the manager's chubby, expressionless face peeked out from behind the sliding latticed door by the entrance. I approached her, and unable to think straight, I simply blurted out the question that was on my mind. "That room . . . my room . . . something strange happened there, didn't it?"

Perhaps it was because I was acting so oddly, but the manager grew pale. "What's wrong? Did something happen?"

"Something weird. Maybe it's my imagination but . . ."

"No doubt you imagined it. I'm sure of that. Nothing strange has happened since. . . ."

There was some nervousness in her tone of voice, and when she slipped and said "since," my suspicions grew. Something had happened there. I could not stand it any longer, and I suddenly burst out, "The truth is . . . Well, I saw a young man hanging from the beam in the alcove!"

"What? Are you serious?" gasped the manager. I also grew tense. Our glances met for a moment, and then she heaved a sigh of resignation. She invited me into her room, and, making me promise not to tell anyone else, she told me the whole story in a hushed whisper.

Exactly five years ago at this time of year, a young student had hanged himself in that room. He was an extremely studious, quiet young man, but he failed his high school entrance exams, and had lived there for a year while commuting to prep school as he prepared to take the exams again.[7] Even so, he failed the exams again the following year, and after that, he began to unravel. To make matters worse, he was seduced by a middle-aged maid who was working there. He was already of a weak disposition, but when he found out the maid was pregnant, he became so depressed that he decided to kill himself. Later, the authorities discovered a final letter he had sent to his parents in his hometown, but it contained only an apology for the unfilial act of preceding his mother and father to the grave. He did not explain any of the details. The young man had stood on the desk in the alcove, used a pair of metal chopsticks to poke a hole in the wall, then hanged himself with a hemp rope. He had died in precisely the way I

7. High schools in pre-World War II Japan, were the equivalent of modern-day colleges. The student would have been in his late teens.

had seen in my dream. For the next six months, the room was nailed shut and kept off limits, but the fact that the room was shut up only attracted more attention. The *otoshigake* with the hole above it was replaced, and the wall was re-plastered. The room was refurbished so boarders could live there again. The manager told me that before I moved in, two other people had rented it, but nothing weird had ever happened to them.

After hearing her story, I knew I could never go back to that room. It would have been different had I heard the story first and then had the dream, but I had had the dream before ever hearing a word about this. The dream was not a product of my wild imagination. My nightmare had played out exactly as it had in real life, and it had all been so vivid! I promised the manager I would not tell a soul about what she had said. In exchange, I requested that she allow me to move to another room, but the only room available was a tiny four-and-a-half-mat room at the rear of the building, behind the stairs.[8] The room got very little sun, and it was gloomy and somewhat grimy. Still, I did not feel like quibbling over such details. I made light of my move by joking to the maids that I had to live more frugally now, but I was still on edge. I had them help me move my belongings that very evening.

It was past midnight by the time I had put my things away. Thinking how cramped the new room was, I crawled into my futon, but could not sleep. Either people did not know what had happened in my original room, or they knew and were just pretending not to. In any case, if something so terrible had happened in that room, then who knew what horrible things might have transpired in the new room as well? As this thought raced through my mind, I found myself all the more wide awake.

8. Japanese often measure the size of a room by the number of straw *tatami* mats that fit into the floor. A four-and-a-half-mat room would be approximately nine feet square.

Once again, I saw all sorts of visions. One after another, I imagined all kinds of things that might have happened in the spot where I was lying: a poor student suffering from tuberculosis writhing in agony as he coughed up blood, a drunken good-for-nothing pulling a beautiful maid into the room and forcing her to submit to his beastly desires, an armed burglar prying open the window and peering inside. . . . These images and those of other people rose before me, becoming vague presences in the damp, musty air of the room. They stared at me from every direction and attempted to latch onto me. I curled up in a ball inside the futon, but I was too frightened to sleep. As I waited for dawn, I tried to lull myself to sleep with my own breathing.

When the next day came, I waited for what seemed an eternity, but no sunlight found its way into my room. What little light did seep in from the cracks in the storm doors seemed to be that of a gloomy, leaden, overcast day, but no matter how long I waited, the light remained hazy. I finally resolved to get up. Much to my astonishment, it was already past ten. I washed my face and ate my cold breakfast, but dark shadows seemed to be floating around the nooks and crannies of the room, which had windows only on the north side. I began to feel as if there was some sort of vague presence there with me. Unable to remain there any longer, I left, even though I had no particular destination in mind. The manager came outside as if she were about to ask how the new room was. I avoided her gaze and rushed out the front door.

The sky was covered by a low-hanging layer of something that seemed more like mist than fog. The gloomy air was still and heavy. These were exactly the right weather conditions for the ghostly presences to come floating out of the shadows of the lonely back alleys. I felt a shiver run through my body as I wondered where to go.

At times like that, the best way to distract myself was to have a drink, but it was too early in the day for that, and my mind was already full of terrifying memories. One night, a while back, after the spirits had started to tail me, I had decided to put up a bold front and go out for a stiff drink. I slipped into a house with a round window where I had been once or twice before. The prostitute I slept with there was a complete stranger, but as I lay next to her, the silhouettes of the men the woman had previously slept with came floating up on either side of me. I felt my spine tingle, and had a sudden impulse to put my hands around the woman's neck and strangle her. When I realized what I was doing, I became even more frightened. I bolted out of the place even though it was around two-thirty in the morning. There was no way I could go back. I supposed I could go to a pool hall, a *go* parlor, or a friend's house, but that would only kill a little time. And when night fell, where could I go to rest? I was stuck. I could not go home, nor anywhere else.

Oh, what a large metropolis this is! How many people there are here! Too many to count! The sky hangs low, and the air is clouded with dust. There are so many people thronging the city that the atmosphere is stifling. Everyone in the crowds puts on calm expressions as they wriggle about, going here and there, but in the smothering haze they leave countless traces, countless human shapes—human shapes that have formed out of their ardent desires, human shapes left everywhere from each and every moment, from ancient times to the present. They swirl, approach one another, and gather together, becoming vague ghostly presences which come alive, taking on their own indistinct, horrible forms. On leaden afternoons like that day and during the night, their shapes appear and wander through the city. What could they possibly want?

I know the answer. They are trying to get close to the living people who are passing them by. They are trying to possess them. Many people become their prey. People lose their freedom, are manipulated to act in accordance to the wills of the spirits; they become fixated on the spirits' desires, and unconsciously perform the same actions the ghostly presences once acted out. Oh, what a dark spell hangs over the city!

On that overcast afternoon, not knowing what else to do, I just stood there in a daze, surrounded by the people coming and going around me.

Doctor Mera's Mysterious Crimes
目羅博士の不思議な犯罪
(Mera hakase no fushigi na hanzai)

Edogawa Rampo (1932)
江戸川 乱歩

Translation by Seth Jacobowitz

IN ORDER TO develop ideas for detective novels I often travel to different places, but when I am in Tokyo, I always return to the same spots—Asakusa Park and the Flower Palace, the Ueno Museum and Zoo, the steam ferry over the Sumida River, and the Ryōgoku Kokugikan (I'm drawn to its round roof, which reminds me of the former Panorama Building).[1] In fact I just returned home from attending a "Ghost Convention" at the Kokugikan. For old times' sake I meandered through the labyrinth of the convention, indulging in fond memories of childhood.

In any event, some time ago the pressure to produce a manuscript became so intense that I couldn't bear to remain cooped up in the house any longer. For about a week I aimlessly roamed the streets of Tokyo. Then, one day I unexpectedly met a strange character at the Ueno Zoo. That is where this story begins.

It was already evening and the zoo was near closing time. Most of the sightseers had already left, and a deep tranquility settled over the grounds.

The same thing always happens in the theaters and *yose*[2] halls. Their entrances inevitably become crowded with people taking their leave well before the final curtain draws to a close. I've never cared much for this tendency on the part of the Edokko.[3]

It was no different that day at the zoo. For some reason, Tokyo people are always in a hurry to get home. It's not like they are going to be locked in, but a place empties out until there isn't a single person left.

I was standing absent-mindedly in front of the monkey cages, enjoying the abnormal quiet that had replaced the customary bustle.

---

1. The Panorama Building, which was destroyed in the Great Kantō Earthquake of 1923, was among the first permanent places for cinema and other new media visual spectacles.

2. *Yose* were popular variety theaters similar to vaudeville.

3. A "child of Edo" - by extension, those born and bred in Tokyo.

The monkeys also looked forlorn without anyone to play with them.

It was very peaceful for a while and then suddenly I felt the presence of another person behind me.

A young man with long hair and a pale complexion was standing there. He wore shapeless clothes and bore the appearance of a so-called "lumpen,"[4] but his expression was lively. He began to tease the monkeys in the cage.

He seemed to be a frequent visitor to the zoo, as he was quite adept at sporting with the monkeys. He made them do all kinds of tricks for a treat. When he tired of his games, he would finally toss them the treat. His antics were extremely amusing, and I watched with a grin on my face.

"What puzzles me about monkeys is, why do they imitate what they see people do?" The young man asked me out of the blue. At that moment he was tossing a tangerine peel up into the air and catching it. A monkey in the cage was doing exactly the same thing, throwing the peel of a tangerine and then catching it.

I laughed and he spoke again.

"When you think about it, mimicry is a scary business. That God gave monkeys that instinct, I mean."

I decided this fellow must be a lumpen philosopher.

"It's strange to see a monkey imitate, but there's nothing unusual about human imitation. God gave human beings lots of the same instincts as monkeys. That's scary when you think about it. Do you know the story about the traveler who met a big monkey in the mountains?"

The man seemed to like telling stories, and gradually became more talkative. I am shy and don't particularly like being spoken to by strangers, but I was curious about this fellow. I guess I was

---

4. Slang for the homeless or beggars derived from "lumpen proletariat."

attracted by his pale complexion and tousled hair. Or maybe it was his philosophic way of talking which struck a chord with me.

"I never heard that one before. Did the big monkey do something?"

I indicated for him to continue his story.

"It was deep in the mountains far away from any human settlement, and a man traveling alone happened upon a big monkey. Before he could react, the monkey stole his sword: pulled the sword out of its scabbard and waved it around just for the hell of it. The traveler was a townsman, not a samurai, so when his blade was taken away he had no other. His life was in danger."

I greatly enjoyed the unique scene of standing before the monkey cage at sunset, listening to the pale man's weird tale. "Yes, I see," I nodded in appreciation.

"He tried to get his sword back, but the monkey was skillful at climbing trees, and put itself beyond his reach. However, the traveler had his wits about him, and devised an ingenious plan. He picked up a branch that had fallen from a tree nearby and, fashioning it in the likeness of a sword, tried out different moves. To the monkey's misfortune, God gave monkeys the instinct to imitate human beings and it began to mimic every gesture the traveler made. Before the monkey knew it, it had committed suicide. You see, the traveler waited until he'd caught the monkey's interest, and then made a display of hacking at his neck with the tree branch. The monkey copied this by stabbing itself in the throat with the drawn blade. It couldn't stop. Blood spilled out, but as though it couldn't believe that was its own blood, it kept slicing its throat until it expired. In the end the man not only got his sword back, he also won himself a big monkey for a souvenir. That's the story!"

The man laughed as he finished his tale, but it was a strangely unsettling laugh.

"You don't say."

I laughed back, the man abruptly became serious.

"No, it's true. The thing about monkeys is they have this sad and fearsome destiny. You want me to prove it?"

He threw a branch that had fallen nearby to one of the monkeys. He faked cutting his own throat with the walking-stick he had at his side.

It was unbelievable what happened next. The young man was such a genius at manipulation that the monkey actually picked up the branch and started jabbing at its own neck.

"What did I tell you, if that branch was a real sword, that little monkey would be on his way to heaven by now."

The expansive grounds of the park were utterly deserted. The darkness of night had already cast deep shadowy circles under the leafy trees. I shivered despite myself. I imagined that the pale-faced youth standing before me was no ordinary man, but a sorcerer.

"Now do you understand the frightfulness of mimicry? It is the same with human beings. Man can't avoid imitation, either. We, too, are born with a sad and fearsome destiny. Didn't the sociologist Tarde pretty much sum up human life with the word 'imitation?'"[5]

I can no longer remember everything he said, but the young man proceeded to explain the horrors of "imitation." Then he told me about his abnormal fear of mirrors.

"Isn't it a bit scary when you stare too long into a mirror? I can't think of anything worse. Why? Because there is another version of yourself in the mirror, which imitates you just like a monkey."

I recall him saying something to this effect.

It came time for the zoo to close its gates, and a zookeeper escorted us out. We walked out, but we didn't say our goodbyes just

---

5. Gabriel Tarde's (1843–1904) theory of imitation in *The Laws of Imitation* (1903) stressed the role of interpersonal relations and social environment in the formation of individual and group psychology.

yet. In the inky darkness under the trees in the park we walked side by side and continued our conversation.

"I know who you are. You're Mr. Edogawa, aren't you? The one who writes detective novels?"

We were walking under the dark trees when he unexpectedly confronted me like this. I was caught off guard again. He was a strange, disturbing individual. Yet, at the same time it increased my interest in him.

"I love your work. To be honest, though, I haven't enjoyed your more recent efforts. Maybe it was because your earlier works were harder to come by, but I really cherished reading them."

He was very outspoken. This, too, impressed me.

"Oh look, the moon's come out."

The young man jumped from one subject to the next in the blink of an eye. It made me half wonder if he wasn't a bit mad.

"Today is the fourteenth, isn't it? It's nearly a full moon tonight. Now that's what I call brilliant moonlight. The light of the moon is really mysterious. I read somewhere the light of the moon has the power to bewitch, and it's true. The same thing appears totally different by night than it does by day, right? Even your face has changed. You almost look like a different person now than you did just a moment ago standing in front of the monkey cage."

Seeing him stare intently at my face as he said it really did make me feel queer. With both his eyes lined with dark rings and his lips hidden in shadow, the young man's face took on a frightful appearance of its own.

"The moon is a kind of mirror. The 'moon-in-the-water,'[6] and the saying 'the moon is bright as a mirror' are proof that there is something to it. Go ahead and see for yourself."

His gaze pointed toward the smoky silver surface of the Shinobazu Pond, which looked twice as big as it did in the daytime.

6. In Buddhism, the image of the moon reflected in water is used as a didactic illustration of the illusory nature of reality.

"If what you see by day is real, then don't you think what is illuminated at night by the light of the moon must be an image of that daytime reality, reflected by the mirror of the moon?"

With his shapeless figure and ghost-white face, the young man looked like a reflection in a mirror himself.

"I bet you're gathering material for a novel. I have a story that would be perfect for you. It's a true story based on my own experiences. Maybe you'd be interested in hearing it. Do you want me to tell it to you?"

I was, in fact, gathering material for a novel. But aside from that, I was eager to hear this strange fellow's story. From what I had already heard, I couldn't imagine it would be just another run-of-the-mill yarn. "By all means, let's hear it. Would you care to join me for a bite to eat somewhere? Let's find a quiet place where we can talk undisturbed."

He shook his head and replied, "I don't want to refuse your kind offer. I never stand on ceremony. It's just that my story isn't suited to bright electric lights. If you don't mind, I'd prefer to recount it right here. We can bask in the bewitching moonlight on this sitting stone and gaze out at Shinobazu Pond, reflected by that giant mirror above us. Besides, my story isn't long in the telling."

I was happy to oblige his request. I sat down beside him on a flat rock under the trees. There, perched on a hill overlooking the pond, I listened to his extraordinary tale.

– 2 –

"As you know, there's a novel by Doyle called *The Valley of Fear*."

The young man wasted no time launching into his story.

"It was a canyon carved out between two steep mountains somewhere. But the valley of fear doesn't have to be just a natural gorge. Right here in the middle of Tokyo, even in Marunouchi, you can find a valley of fear.

"A narrow street hemmed in between two towering buildings is far steeper and more perilous than any ordinary canyon. A haunted valley made by civilization, a canyon built by science. From the street at the bottom of the canyon, the six- or seven-storey concrete buildings on both sides swallow up any hope of a view. Like natural cliffs, they have no greenery, no seasonal flowers, no protrusions to catch the eye; just two giant slabs of gray cleaved in half by an ax. The sky above is narrow as a belt. For only a few precious minutes a day they receive a decent bit of light from the sun and moon. From the bottom the noonday sun is no closer than a distant star. A weird, chilly wind is constantly whipping about.

"Before the great earthquake, I lived in one of those canyons. The front entrance of the building faced S—— Avenue in the Marunouchi. It was bright and lively. But when you went around back, you came right up against another building. The buildings presented one another with a bleak expanse of concrete: cliffs with windows facing one another across an alley scarcely two meters across. When I talk about a haunted valley in the city, this is exactly what I have in mind.

"The buildings had a few rooms which served as apartments, but for the most part they were only used in the daytime, as offices, and people would go home after dark. Bustling by day, at night they were the picture of solitude. In the heart of the Marunouchi, it was as alarming as the hoot of an owl. It felt like I was lost deep in the mountains. After nightfall, the alley behind the building truly became a canyon.

"During the day I worked at the front desk, and at night I slept in a room in the basement. There were four or five of us who lived there, but I liked art, so whenever I had a free moment I would paint my canvases in seclusion. Naturally there were many days when I didn't even speak to my companions.

"The incident I am going to tell you about occurred in the canyon around back, so I had better explain a few things. It was truly incredible how the buildings matched. What I mean is that they mirrored each other perfectly. I often wonder if the architect who designed them wasn't playing at some kind of mischief.

"Both buildings were of roughly the same height, five storeys apiece. While the color and ornamentation on the front and sides were quite different, the sides facing one another in the canyon were exactly alike. From the shape of the roof to their gray color and the arrangement of four windows per floor, they were as identical as photographs. It's possible that even the cracks and flaws in the concrete were the same.

"The rooms looking out onto the canyon scarcely received more than a few minutes of sunlight a day—well, yes, that's a bit of an exaggeration; but it didn't amount to much at all. Needless to say, no one wanted to use those rooms, especially the most inconvenient ones on the fifth floor, which always remained empty. In my free time I would frequently sneak up there with my canvases and brushes. Sure enough, whenever I looked out the window, the building across the way looked just like a photograph of the one I was in. They so resembled one another that it gave you the creeps. There was a tangible sense of foreboding that a terrible incident was waiting to happen.

"Well, it wasn't long before my premonitions proved right on the mark. There was a suicide by hanging from the northernmost window on the fifth floor. And then, before we knew it, there were two more deaths.

"The first victim was a middle-aged spice broker. From the moment he walked in to rent the office, he came across as an impressive character. He may have been a tradesman, but he sure didn't look like one. He was dark and brooding, the type that is always thinking of something. When I heard about his suicide, I wondered if he had rented one of the sunless rooms in the back that faced the canyon . Just as I suspected, the one he chose, the northernmost apartment on the fifth floor, was the furthest from human contact (it might sound strange to use an expression like this in a building, but the apartment had that kind of feeling about it). It was also the darkest one, and so naturally the rent was the cheapest for those two adjoining rooms.

"I believe he was only there for about a week after he moved in. It wasn't long at all.

"The spice broker was a bachelor, so he brought in a shoddy-looking bed and used the inner room as a bedroom. At night he would sleep alone there—a desolate cave in the steep cliffs overlooking a ghost valley. Then, on a night of bright moonlight, he flung a rope out the window onto the small crossbar of a telephone pole, and committed suicide by hanging himself.

"In the morning a laborer assigned to sweep the streets in the vicinity discovered the hanged man swinging from the cliffs high overhead, and caused a great stir.

"In the end we never learned why the man committed suicide. His business wasn't doing particularly badly, and he didn't have any worries about debt. On top of that he was a bachelor, so it couldn't have been prompted by a domestic problem. Nor was there any indication that he'd done it in a fit of passion, say, committing suicide because of a broken heart.

"'He was possessed by the devil. From the moment he arrived, he was strangely withdrawn. I knew there was something wrong with him.' That's the sort of conclusion people drew. When it happened the first time, they could dismiss it like that. But soon another renter came along who took the same room. He never slept there, but one day he said he needed to stay overnight to get some work done. We figured he must have shut himself up in that room for the night, because the next morning there was bedlam when another swinging body was discovered. He died the exact same way, suicide by hanging.

"Of course no one had the slightest idea about the cause. Unlike the spice broker, the second man had an exceedingly sunny disposition, and even his choice of that gloomy room was simply due to the fact that the rent was low.

"The window that opened onto the valley of fear was cursed. A rumor like a ghost story spread in whispers that whoever entered that room would start to crave a solitary death for no reason at all.

"The third victim was no ordinary renter. One of the office workers in the building was a brave fellow who announced he was going to give it a try. He was as adventurous as someone who explores a haunted house."

By this point in his narration, I had grown a trifle weary of the young man's story and interrupted him.

"So this brave fellow also hung himself in the same fashion?"

The young man looked at me, slightly surprised.

"That's right," he replied ominously.

"After one man hangs himself, countless others hang themselves in the same place. In other words, this horror boils down to a copycat instinct?"

"Ah, now I see why you're impatient. That's not it at all. I wouldn't waste your time with such a dull story."

With a look of relief, the young man corrected my misguided assumption.

"It's not one of those dime-a-dozen stories where people keep dying at an 'accursed' train crossing."

"Forgive my rudeness. Please continue."

I politely apologized for misunderstanding him.

– 3 –

"The office worker spent three nights alone in that demonic room. But nothing happened. He was beaming with self-satisfaction at having beaten the devil. But I set him straight. 'All three nights you slept there were overcast, right? The moon didn't come out, did it?'"

"Oh-ho, was the moon somehow related to those suicides?" I interjected, a bit excited.

"Yes, it was. I'd realized that the spice broker and the renter after him died on nights when the moon was clear. If the moon hadn't come out, the suicides wouldn't have happened. For only a few minutes a night, ghostly silver-white light flooded the narrow canyon. That's when the suicides occurred. It was the witchcraft of moonlight. I was convinced of it."

As the young man spoke, he raised his wan face and gazed down at the Shinobazu Pond bathed in moonlight.

Reflected in what the young man had called a giant mirror was the scenery surrounding the pond, silver-white and ethereal.

"This is what I am talking about: the bewitching power of moonlight. Moonlight incites dark passions like a cold flame, making hearts burn with the intensity of phosphorus. Mysterious passions that give rise, for example, to 'songs to the moon.' You don't have to be a poet to learn about the transience of life from the moon. If you'll forgive the expression 'artistic madness,' isn't that how the moon influences us?"

I was slowly becoming annoyed by the young man's manner of storytelling.

"Are you suggesting that moonlight was responsible for those men's deaths?"

"That's right. Half the blame goes to the moonlight. But moonlight alone doesn't make people take their own lives. If that were so, don't you think the two of us soaking up the radiance of the moon would be slipping nooses around our necks by now?"

The young man smirked, his face pale as a reflection in a mirror. I couldn't help feeling like a child listening to a bone-chilling ghost story.

"The brave office worker slept in that accursed room for a fourth night. Unfortunately, the moon was out that night.

"In the middle of the night I suddenly awoke in my bed in the basement and saw the light of the moon streaming in through the tall window above. I don't know why, but unthinkingly I got up. Still in my pajamas, I raced up the narrow staircase next to the elevator. You can't imagine the incredible solitude in that building that replaced the activity of the daylight hours. It was a massive graveyard with hundreds of tiny rooms. Take my word for it, it was like the catacombs in Rome. It wasn't pitch-black—there were electric lights at key places in the corridors—but those faint lights made it even scarier.

"When at last I reached the dreaded room on the fifth floor, I felt afraid for myself wandering through a deserted building like a sleepwalker. I banged madly on the door and called out the name of the office worker.

"There was no answer within. My own voice merely echoed down the corridor until it disappeared into the solitude.

"I turned the knob and the door readily swung open. On a table in the corner was an electric desk lamp with a green shade that despondently illuminated the room. By its light I could see there was no one inside. The bed was empty. And then I saw that the dreaded window was wide open.

"Outside the window, the building across the way caught the last fleeting rays of faint silvery light from the middle of the fifth floor to the roof. Directly opposite this window was another of the exact same shape, and it, too, had been flung open to form a gaping black hole. The two were identical in every way. Under the mysterious luminosity of the moon, they looked even more alike.

"I was spooked by my fearful premonitions, but I had to make certain, so I poked my head out the window. I didn't immediately have the courage to look in the direction of the telephone pole, so first I glanced at the distant bottom of the canyon. The moonlight only shone upon the uppermost portions of the building across the way. The gap created by the buildings was pitch-black, which made it appear that it plunged to bottomless depths.

"And then I forcefully twisted my neck all the way to the right. The side of the building was lost in shadows, but thanks to the moonlight reflected from the building across the way I could make out a shape of some kind there. Sure enough, as I directed my gaze that way, what I had anticipated came into view. The legs of a man in black clothes. Wrists dangling limply. Upper body stretched to the limit. A tightly constricted neck. His head drooped until his neck was almost bent in two. The fearless office worker had been caught in the witchcraft of the moon and hung himself from the crossbar of the telephone pole.

"In a panic I yanked my head back in from the window. I suppose I was worried that I, too, would be caught in the same spell. But that's when I noticed it. No sooner had I begun to pull my head out of the window, what did I spy through the jet-black square hole of the open window across the way but a man's face staring back! Only the face was immersed in the moonlight, its features standing out in sharp profile. Especially by the light of the moon, it looked yellow and withered, a deformed and despicable face. And I'll be damned if he wasn't looking in my direction the whole time!

"In that instant, I stood back and shrunk away from the window. It was altogether too astonishing. I should have explained earlier, but a lawsuit had been filed against the owner of the building across the way by the bank that served as the guarantor, with the result that the building was completely vacant. Not a soul was living there.

"But someone was in that vacant building in the dead of night. Not only that, he had a yellow face like an evil spirit that leered from the window directly across from the dreaded window where the hangings took place. There was nothing ordinary about it. Had I seen a ghost? And was that yellow-faced man with his witchcraft plotting still more hangings?

I went cold with fear, but I didn't take my eyes off that yellow face across the way. On closer inspection, I could make out he was a scrawny, small-boned man in his fifties. He continued looking in my direction, only to finally laugh broadly as if to signify something. He then abruptly vanished into the darkness of the window. His cackling visage was revolting to behold. When he smiled, his entire face crumpled up, leaving only a mouth stretched fit to bursting."

– 4 –

"The next day I asked my co-workers and the janitors about the building across the canyon, but since it was completely vacant, not even a night watchman had been there. Had it been a figment of my imagination?

"The police opened tentative investigations into the inexplicable multiple suicides: now three in a row with no rationale whatsoever. However, since there wasn't a shadow of a doubt that these were suicides, the investigations went no further. But I wasn't afraid to believe in an unconventional cause. I wasn't satisfied with the absurd explanation, which held that anyone who slept in that room went crazy. That yellow-faced man was the mastermind. He murdered all three. On each night that a hanging occurred, he was peeping through the identical window directly across the canyon. And he had laughed knowingly. There was something terrible hidden behind that laugh. I was positive of it.

"A week went by uneventfully, and then I made an astonishing discovery.

"One day as I was returning from an errand, I crossed the wide avenue where the entrance of the vacant building was located. Immediately adjacent to it was one of the Mitsubishi buildings, a modest, old-fashioned brick building with tenement-like rental offices. A gentleman bounding lightly up the stone staircase caught my attention.

"He was a delicate-boned older gentleman, with a slight stoop, dressed in a morning coat. From his profile I could swear I'd seen him somewhere before, so I paused to get a better look. He stopped at the entrance to an office, dusted off his shoes and suddenly glanced back in my direction. Shock stopped me right in my tracks. The smartly dressed gentleman was a dead ringer for the yellow-faced monster I'd seen leering through the window of the vacant building a few nights earlier.

"After he disappeared into the office, I noticed a sign written in gold letters by the door: Mera Ophthalmology, Dr. Mera Ryōsai.[7] I caught hold of a passing messenger boy and confirmed that the man who had just gone inside was Dr. Mera himself.

"It was beyond comprehension that a medical doctor would sneak into a vacant building in the middle of night, and, what's more, laugh aloud at the sight of a hanged man. I couldn't hold back a powerful burst of curiosity. Still, I tried not to let it show as I set about asking as many people as I could about Mera Ryōsai's past and daily activities.

"Despite his advanced age, Dr. Mera was not very well known, nor did he seem particularly adept at making money, considering that he was working out of a rented office. He was extremely unusual and the way he treated patients was disagreeably rough. Sometimes he even seemed to be touched with madness. He had

---

7. The doctor's last name translates into something like "eyelet." His first name seems to be a playful reference to the *Ryōsai Shi'i*, an anthology in sixteen volumes of premodern Chinese ghost stories compiled by Hoshō Rei (1640–1715).

neither a wife nor children, but had been a bachelor his whole life. His office doubled as his apartment. That's how I learned that he slept there at night. In addition, I heard rumors he was an extremely avid reader, with a sizable collection of books outside his field of expertise, such as long-forgotten works of philosophy, psychology and criminology.

"'In the private quarters connected to the examination room there's a glass case filled with fake eyes of every conceivable shape. Hundreds of glass eyes staring back at you. Fake or not, they really give you the creeps. But never mind that—what's an ophthalmologist doing with a bunch of skeletons and life-sized mannequins?' That's what a businessman in my building told me about the hair-raising experience of being examined by Dr. Mera.

"I never failed to observe the doctor's comings and goings whenever I could. I also spent some time watching the fifth floor window of the empty building, but there was nothing in particular to see. That yellow face never once materialized.

"Any way you looked at it, Dr. Mera was suspicious. The yellow face I saw glaring back from the window across the way that night was undeniably his. But the question was, how was he involved? If those three hangings weren't suicides, then even supposing Dr. Mera somehow planned those murders, how and why did he pull them off? That was the sticking point. Still, I couldn't help but remain convinced he was the killer.

"For days it obsessed me. Once I scaled the brick fence behind the doctor's office, went to the window and stole a peep at the doctor's private room. Sure enough, the skeletons, mannequin and glass eye case were there.

"One thing I couldn't figure out was how someone in the building on the other side of the canyon could freely affect a person in my building. Hypnosis? No, that was impossible. I'd heard that a life-threatening order like a command to die wouldn't work.

"About half a year passed after the last hanging when at last an opportunity arose for me to test my suspicions. Someone rented the cursed room. The renter was a man from Osaka, so he hadn't the faintest inkling about the ghastly rumors. From the perspective of the building's managers, the extra money would increase profits, so they kept their mouths shut and rented it to him. I guess no one was ready to believe that now, six months later, the same thing would happen again.

"I for one was solidly convinced that the man was going to hang himself. Somehow it was up to me to prevent it from happening.

"From that day I neglected my work and devoted myself to observing Dr. Mera's comings and goings. At long last my work paid off. I uncovered the doctor's secret."

– 5 –

"On the evening of the third night after the man from Osaka moved in, I watched the doctor's office and spotted him furtively slip out on foot without his bag for house-calls. Of course I tailed him. Contrary to my expectations, he went into a reputable clothing store in a large building nearby. He selected an off-the-rack suit from their large inventory, paid for it, and brought it straight back to his office.

"Regardless of how indigent a physician he was, Dr. Mera wasn't the type to wear a ready-made suit. But if the suit was intended for an assistant, why did he buy it himself, and try to avoid being seen doing it? The man was out of his mind. What on earth was that suit for? I stood for a while gazing remorsefully at the entrance to the office into which the doctor had disappeared when I suddenly remembered the fence around back where I could spy into the doctor's private room. I knew it was a long shot, but maybe I could catch a glimpse of him doing something in there. I quickly ran around to the back of the office.

"I scrambled over the fence and cautiously peered in. The doctor was there all right. It was obvious that he was up to something truly bizarre.

"You would never guess what that yellow-faced doctor was up to. He took the mannequin, the life-sized one I told you about a minute ago, and put the suit on it. Hundreds of glass eyes bore silent witness.

"A detective novel writer such as yourself probably has a good idea by now what I am about to say. But at the time, I was stunned. The doctor's evil plans took my breath away.

"I'll be damned if the suit which the mannequin wore wasn't an exact duplicate of the one worn by the new renter, right down to the color and striped pattern! The doctor had picked out the same off-the-rack suit and brought it home.

"I knew I had to act soon. It was supposed to be a moonlit night, so another terrible accident might occur. I had to do something, anything. I was at an utter loss, and racked my brains for a solution. Then, I amazed myself by coming up with an ingenious plan. When I tell it to you, you'll want to shake my hand and congratulate me.

"I made my preparations and waited for night, then carried a large bundle wrapped in a *furoshiki* cloth up to the cursed room. The new renter had gone home for the night, so the door was locked, but I used the spare key to open the door and enter the room. I put on clothes suitable for the night's work. I turned on the desk lamp with the green shade, shining it on myself as though I were the room's true occupant. I wore a suit I borrowed from a co-worker that closely resembled the same striped pattern. I also took care to part my hair in the same fashion to make myself look like the man from Osaka. I sat with my back to the window and patiently waited.

"Needless to say, I took these steps to alert the yellow-faced man across the way to my presence, but I was careful never to look behind me and give him the chance he was waiting for.

"I must have sat there for about three hours. Were my suspicions on target? And would my plans come to fruition? I was very impatient and spent three hours with my heart pounding. At my wit's end, I wondered if I should turn around. I don't know how many times I twisted my neck left and right.

"My watch indicated that it was ten minutes past ten o'clock. I heard the *hoot-hoot* cry of an owl. *A-ha*, that was the signal. He used an owl call to get his victims to look out the window. Who wouldn't go for a look if they heard an owl cry in the middle of the Marunouchi? When I realized what was afoot, I hesitated a moment longer, then got up from my seat, walked over to the window frame and opened the glass.

"Bathed in moonlight, the building across the way shimmered silvery gray. As I said before, the building was of identical construction to the one I was in. It was queer to look at them. I've tried to convey a sense of it, but there's really no way for you to understand that crazy feeling. It was as if an absurdly large mirrored wall suddenly sprang up before your eyes, and the building you were in was reflected back down to the last detail. Add some seductive moonlight to that physical double and you start to get the idea.

"The window where I stood was directly opposite me. It was open, too. And there I was . . . No, there was something wrong with the mirror. The only thing that didn't fit was me. Why wouldn't it reflect me, too? Thoughts like this raced through my head. I couldn't bear it. It was a trap deadly enough to make my hair stand on end.

"The next thing I knew, I had disappeared somewhere. Only a moment ago I could have sworn I was standing right by the window. I restlessly scanned the other window. I couldn't help myself.

"And then, with a start, I found my reflection. Only it wasn't in the window. It was on the wall. I was hanging from the crossbar of the telephone pole by a length of rope.

"'Ah, that's where I went. I'm over there.'

"It must sound ridiculous to hear me talk like this. But I can't express that feeling in words. It was a nightmare. . . . Yes, that's right, a nightmare in which, try as you might, you still do something against your will. Let's say you looked in the mirror and even though your own eyes were open, the image reflected back to you had its eyes shut. What would you do? Would you be able to resist shutting your eyes, too?

"Well, I was forced to imitate my reflection in the mirror and hang myself. Across the way I had hanged myself. The real me couldn't just stand there and watch.

"My hanged body didn't look the least bit frightening or repulsive. It looked beautiful. Like a picture. I felt the urge to make myself become that beautiful picture.

"It's possible that without the magic of moonlight, Dr. Mera's weird trick would have been completely useless.

"Of course you must have figured it out by now, but the doctor's trick was to dress the mannequin in the same clothes as the occupant of the room and to show it hanging itself from a length of rope attached to the same block of wood on the telephone crossbar. It was actually a very simple affair.

"He used the buildings of perfectly identical construction and seductive moonlight to brilliant effect.

"Even though I knew his trick in advance, I had almost carelessly thrown one leg over the side of the window before I came to my senses and stopped myself.

"I fought against that fearsome compulsion as if I were shaking off the effects of anesthesia. I unraveled the *furoshiki* cloth which I'd prepared, and unblinkingly watched the opposite window.

"Seconds slowly ticked by... and then my intuition proved correct. That yellow face which belonged to none other than Dr. Mera, appeared suddenly in the window to watch me die.

"I was waiting for him. What would happen if I didn't snare him in that instant?

"Grasping the object in the *furoshiki* and holding it up with both hands, I quietly rested it on the edge of the window sill.

"Can you guess what it was? Naturally, it was a mannequin. I borrowed one from the same clothing store and put a morning coat on it similar to the kind Dr. Mera always wore.

"Just then the moonlight was shining close to the bottom of the canyon, and by its pearly-white reflection my window was clearly visible.

"I felt as though I were locked in a duel as I stared at the devil across the way. 'Come on, you bastard!' I cursed in my head.

"Would you believe it? God endowed man with the same fate as monkeys, after all. Dr. Mera was caught in the same trap he had devised for others.

"The little old man pathetically straddled the window frame and did just what my mannequin did—he sat right down.

"I was the puppet master.

"I stood behind the mannequin. If I raised its arms, the doctor raised his.

"If I shook its legs, the doctor shook his.

"And what do you think I did next?

"I killed him.

"I gave the mannequin sitting on the windowsill a good shove with all my might. It gave out a hollow clatter and disappeared from view.

"Almost instantaneously, the old man in his morning coat opposite me followed suit. Imitating his reflection, he silently leapt into the night air and plunged to the bottom of the canyon!

"And then, I faintly heard a sound like something had smashed. . . . Dr. Mera was dead.

"As on the previous nights when that yellow face laughed its hideous laugh, I reeled in the string I held in my right hand—the borrowed mannequin I sent over the windowsill rose nimbly and I brought it back inside the room.

"If I had left it lying around, I would have been a prime suspect for murder, don't you agree?"

His story finished, the young man eerily laughed as I imagine the yellow-faced doctor did. He observed me closely.

"What was Dr. Mera's motive for murder? I don't need to tell that to a writer of detective novels such as yourself. You know well enough yourself that even without a motive, a murderer lives to kill."

The young man got up with an expression that would not countenance a response and quickly walked away.

Moonlight mercilessly flooded over me as I watched him disappear into the misty night. For a while I remained motionless on the sitting stone.

My encounter with the young man, his story, and yes, even the young man himself—were these not created by what he called the "bewitching power" of moonlight? It might have been nothing but an illusion; but then again, who knows?

The Midsummer Emissary
文月の使者
(Fumizuki no shisha)

Minigawa Hiroko (1918)
皆川博子

Translation by Ginny Tapley Takemori

I gave you my finger, you know.

The wavering voice had come from behind him.

He must be hearing things. Or maybe he had misheard.

He had been descending the stairs to the ferry landing at the foot of the collapsed Onnabashi bridge and was just three or four steps above the river. The well-worn stone was like a sponge, oozing water with each step. As he turned, his foot slipped, and he barely managed to stay upright. Meanwhile, the voice's owner had disappeared—not by any mysterious trick but most likely into the shadows round a bend in the alley.

He imagined her in fresh summer clothes, light and diaphanous, possibly Akashi crepe. He had the impression she was twirling a parasol. No, she wasn't carrying a parasol, or anything else. Her coiffure left the nape of her neck refreshingly exposed. And her light summer kimono had a design of irises in indigo on a white background. On her bare feet she wore geta. The straps were black, like those worn by men . . . Her toes and heels were white against the muddy path.

But nobody had been there when he turned around, so he must have imagined the voice. It was a little hoarse, but seductive nonetheless . . .

It wasn't only the owner of the voice who was out of sight; there was no sign of anybody else, either. Had the torrential rain from last night's storm washed away all the residents of Nakasu once and for all?[1]

Both the Otokobashi and Onnabashi bridges had collapsed.[2] Otokobashi appeared to have been struck by lightning, his broken girders burned black. Onnabashi looked as though she had

1. Nakasu was a popular entertainment district built on a sandbank supplemented by landfill in the Sumida River that flourished briefly from 1771 until 1790.

2. Literally, "Man Bridge" and "Woman Bridge" respectively.

followed her lover in death, her rotten girders all twisted and boards bent over at an angle, one side submerged under water.

He had first crossed over Onnabashi to visit Nakasu three years earlier. It had already been dangerous then, with crumbling handrails and holes in the boards. That time too had been just after a heavy downpour. With both the bridges down, Nakasu would be isolated and helpless, a boat cut loose and set adrift. It had been Yumimura who had said that, hadn't it?

Last night, as he crossed over Onnabashi to Nakasu, it had never occurred to him that it might fall down.

There was a small boat moored at the ferry landing.

Turbid water lapped at the landing. The wood here was rotten too, with blackish blotches, a mix of mildew and moss. Trash drifted on the surface of the swollen river, catching on posts like the floating nests of grebes.

Perhaps the ferryman was resting somewhere waiting for customers to gather, for he was nowhere to be seen. The moored boat was half full of bilge water that made him feel sick. It looked as though it would sink the moment anyone got in it.

Last night's rain had soaked into the ground and was now rising once more in the heat of the day to make the air terribly sultry. Even the sun beating down became part of the overhead mesh of hot mist that rained down. Everything before him seemed to shimmer.

I gave you my finger. Either he had been hearing things, or he had misheard, he told himself again. He groped around in the wide sleeve of his kimono that served as a pocket and found a half-crushed cigarette box. He opened it up and found it full not of cigarettes, but of severed fingers . . .

Laughing at himself for being so silly, he opened the box again. Time for a smoke, he thought. It was empty, except for the crumpled silver paper. He crushed it in his hand and threw it into the water.

Just then he saw something. Mixed in with the trash caught on a post, bobbing on the waves of the river, was a woman's pillow.

It was one of those wooden box pillows shaped like the hull of a ship, to which a small cushion was fastened. The wood was coated with an alluring vermilion lacquer that had worn away here and there over the years. The cushion was quite sodden with water. The piece of paper placed over it to keep it clean had writing on it—an unsent letter, perhaps—and the black ink was blurred.

Flowing... he read, but he was unable to make out the characters that followed it.

He strained his eyes.

Black hair... That's what it said.

Hair...

Previously he would have shuddered with horror at the sight of that word alone, but now there was no longer anything to be afraid of.

Even so, that did not mean he was over his fixation with hair, and out of curiosity he reached out his hand for the pillow. It felt slimy, as if the water had dissolved the glue on it. He scooped it up in one hand. Along with the pillow, bits of straw or something like it clung to his hand. The rotten plank beneath his feet suddenly gave way, and he stumbled forward. Yet even then he hung onto the pillow and was on the point of falling in when someone caught hold of him and a voice said, "Watch out!" He hadn't noticed anyone approaching from behind.

"Such an inconvenient thing to have dropped!"

It was a middle-aged woman. Her voice was rough, quite unlike the beguiling voice that had called to him earlier. Her "praying mantis"-style chignon was secured not with an elegant coral hairpin but with a coarse black pin, and the striped weave and black satin collar of her robe looked uncomfortably hot. Her bare feet were slipped into worn geta, her toes muddy. Something black peeped out of a folded old newspaper in her bamboo handbasket and meowed.

"You take care now," she said, turning to leave.

"Oh, but . . . is the ferryboat running?" he queried, casting a doubtful glance at the dilapidated boat and wondering whether there even was a boatman.

"I suppose so," she answered vaguely. "Perhaps you should ask the boatman."

"There doesn't appear to be one."

"Are you in such a hurry to cross the river?"

"It's not that . . . it's just that I was visiting an acquaintance and was forced to stay over by last night's rain."

"Nakasu is no place for such a good-looking student, is it?" she said, gazing lasciviously at his skin. "Did you quarrel with your companion?"

"Why do you ask?"

"That thing's dripping wet, isn't it? Throwing someone's pillow into the river isn't exactly amicable."

"It was already in the river. I just saw it and fished it out."

"On a whim, I suppose." She laughed, but apparently disinclined to inquire further, said teasingly, "A fortuitous rain, perhaps," as she took her leave. Her black cat stretched its head out of the basket and meowed disdainfully. Once she had disappeared around the bend in the alley, the place was again deserted, as if all life had died out.

The paper cover over the pillow was sodden and looked as though it would rip at the slightest touch.

Flowing black hair spreading over the water.

He could barely make out the elegantly inscribed characters.

There were more words, but the paper was wrinkled from where it was tied with cords to the pillow and it was hard to read. He would have to wait until it was dry before he could smooth it out.

He cradled the pillow gently in one hand. It felt heavier than he'd imagined. A pillow used by some unknown person, and discarded in the river to boot.

The ferryboat did not appear to be about to depart any time soon. He climbed back up the stone staircase and scanned the row of houses for a tobacconist's sign.

His feet sank in deep sludge. A black boarded fence. A storehouse, its doors closed. There was what looked like some kind of store, but a scrap of yellowish cloth—it hardly qualified as a curtain—hung behind the glass door as if to indicate it was closed. Pasted onto the fence was a handbill for a movie, or perhaps it was a play. The colors were faded and the border torn, revealing the edges of older flyers beneath. Red and blue and white: even the continuous upward spiral of the candy-striped barber's pole had come to a standstill.

He peered further along the alley and finally, amidst the darkened eaves, his eyes alighted on a sign advertising tobacco and salt. He headed for it, sidestepping the puddles formed by putrid water overflowing the rotting boards over the gutter.

The glass door of the tobacconist's stood open. Household goods from toilet paper to scrubbing brushes and disposable chopsticks were arranged on a stand, and in a glass case on the left, just as the sign had said, there were several boxes of cigarettes. Behind a lattice screen on the raised tatami floor was seated an old man, his skinny body wrapped in a washed-out, threadbare summer robe that appeared held together by starch alone. In his hand was a round, flat fan with which he directed a cool breeze to his neck, but upon noticing he had a customer he stopped fanning himself and lightly raised the rim of his reading glasses. His close-cropped hair was white and his throat scrawny, yet his eyes revealed a strength that belied old age.

"Have you any Golden Bat?"

The glass case was out of the old man's reach from where he sat behind the screen, so he stood up. He was tall, the bare shins peeping from beneath the hem of his robe so fleshless they seemed barely able to support him. Nevertheless, he moved with surprisingly agility over to the case, took out a packet of Bats, and wordlessly placed them before the student.

"Some matches, too," said the student, trying unsuccessfully to open the packet with one hand. Conscious of the drips, he placed the pillow on the edge of the raised wooden floor.

The interior of the store was dark, untouched by sunlight, yet it felt sultrier within than it did outside.

"How much?" A disagreeable voice.

"What?"

"How much?" asked the old man again.

Had he mistaken the order for salt or sugar? His hearing was evidently rather poor.

"Some matches," said the student, a little louder.

The old man reached for a bamboo basket on top of the glass case. Inside were loose matchsticks the size of toothpicks, their tips painted with red phosphorous.

"How much?" The same question again.

Next to a bundle of tissue paper was a weighing scale with a small basket placed on top of it.

The old man dropped a few matchsticks into the basket.

"You sell them by weight? Don't you have any boxes?"

"Here. On the house."

The old man took a matchstick from the basket on the scale and handed it to him. Without the striking surface on the side of the matchbox, however, it would not ignite.

The old man went inside. Visible through the open door was a small tatami room with a kitchen to the right. The alcove was decorated with what appeared to be a chest for storing armor, touches of vermilion visible on the lid. The same color ornamented a spear hanging up on the crossbeam.

The old man came right back and slid the door closed behind him, cutting off the view of the interior. He had with him an economy-sized box of matches, the sort used in kitchens. He thrust this at his customer and then took out a tobacco tray from behind the latticed screen and filled the bowl of his pipe with shredded tobacco.

He wanted someone to talk to, the student thought. The old man indicated the raised floor, as if telling him to sit down for a smoke. Not that there was anything piteous about him; on the contrary, he had the haughty air of an old-time samurai.

The old man's eyes were drawn to the writing on the sodden pillow. He adjusted his spectacles and stared at the words. "Flowing black hair . . . consume . . ." he murmured.

The student could not catch *what* was consumed but missed his chance to ask. He was about to correct the old man—"spreading over water"—when he realized it did appear to say "consume," just as the old man had said.

Flowing black hair . . . He had pictured a cascade of loosened black hair, but read another way it could mean "melting black hair." He was briefly seized with the vision of the words in ink on the pillow paper as numerous black strands of hair, tangled and flowing, welling up out of the paper, sidling up to him.

"It was in the river," he said needlessly. This did not explain why he had fished it out.

Really, why had he gone to such lengths? Looking at it now, it was just a filthy pillow used by goodness only knew who and permeated with female body grease and hair oil.

It had been because of that single word, "hair." That was why he had wanted it . . .

Such a gold- and silver-decorated red -lacquered object could only belong to a professional. There were brothels in Nakasu, too—a lustful woman, sleeping with different partners every night, probably diseased.

It wasn't Tamae's pillow, surely . . .?

It wasn't possible! *But what if . . .?* The thought weighed on him. Even though he had tried to erase all memory of the very name Tamae from his mind . . .

He heard a cat's meow followed by the sound of claws scratching, and the door slid open a crack. A black paw stretched through the gap, forced the door open, and was followed by the cat's body squeezing through.

Was it the same cat as that middle-aged woman had been holding? Had that woman been from this household? He caught a fleeting glimpse of a human figure pass behind the narrow gap. Young, dressed in a white robe . . .

As he sat there in confusion, the cat meowed again and came sidling up to him, knocking the pillow to the ground. Just as he bent down to pick it up, the door clattered wide open and bare feet peeking out from beneath the hem of a wavy-striped kimono strode through it.

"Well, well, if it isn't the student! We meet again."

"You're the mistress of this house?"

The figure he had glimpsed a moment ago was not this woman. It had been more suited to the voice that had called to him about the finger, an unspoiled young . . .

The middle-aged woman seemed to like chatting even more than the old man, for she came and sat down beside him.

"I'm his daughter-in-law."

So she was the wife of the old man's son. It had clearly been many years since she had set down roots in this house. Her husband must be working elsewhere. As though reading his thoughts, she said, "My husband has another woman across the river and no longer comes home. I'm lumped with the old man."

Having let slip such unnecessary personal details, she asked, "So didn't the ferryboat leave?"

"I don't know."

"That must be a very precious pillow for you to hold onto it for dear life like that."

"No, it's not that, but—"

"Would you like something cold? Eh, young man?"

"Yes, please, I would. I'm boiling."

The woman withdrew inside and reemerged carrying a tray upon which had been placed three cups of cold barley tea.

Kuzu zakura . . .

Immediately, his thought was turned into words.

"Would you like a *kuzu zakura* sweet?"

"No, no," he added hastily, afraid of being thought impudent.

"I just remembered the first time I came to Nakasu, a while ago. On my way to visit a friend in hospital, I was caught in a sudden downpour and took shelter beneath the eaves of a stranger's house. It was only a passing shower, but I was invited into the house to wait it out. I was cheeky enough to accept the invitation and was treated to cold barley tea and *kuzu zakura* sweets."

"How unfortunate. We're all out of sweets."

"No matter."

"Weren't there some candies in that can over there?" put in the old man, but the woman cut him short. "Those are cough sweets for old people. They're not fit to offer to a student."

She went on, "As for a hospital in Nakasu, there's only the one."

"Yes, that's the one."

"It's filthy, you know."

"It's enough to make even those of us in good health sick," he said, before realizing this was disrespectful to local people. Flustered, he said without being asked, "The sick person I went to see was called Yumimura."

The student was from Kanazawa but since passing the entrance examination into a Tokyo university he had moved to the capital and was lodging in Nezu Katamachi. He had already lost both his parents, and, lacking the money to pay for his studies, he worked during the day at a printer's so that he could attend classes in the evening.

Yumimura had lodged in the room next to his. It had been immediately obvious that this was a man with no friends. He was the sort of fellow who took pride in having a good brain and thought everyone else was stupid, and people shunned him because of this stubbornly arrogant attitude. Yet his utter aloofness was rooted in loneliness and a desperate need for attention.

Whenever he talked, he would immediately become boastful. Anything, however trivial, would be a feather in his cap, such as having managed to knock the price down even further when buying something cheap at a night stall or having argued with the local policeman. Letting Yumimura talk on and on without so much as contradicting him, the student had found himself treated as a close friend.

There came a time when Yumimura began whining about having a slight fever and a heavy feeling in his head. The student had been unable to ignore this and recommended seeing a doctor. He was diagnosed with a reoccurrence of an earlier pulmonitis, for which he needed to be hospitalized, and so the doctor referred him to the hospital in Nakasu. Packing his wicker trunk and preparing to leave the lodging house, Yumimura told him reproachfully, "It's all because you told me to see a doctor," as if he were to blame for the illness itself.

Yumimura had told him not to visit, and the student had taken him at his word and left him alone, but then a postcard arrived asking him to send a book he had left behind at the lodging house. This was just an excuse disguising the fact that Yumimura was desperate for him to visit.

For the first time in his life, the student visited Nakasu. In fact, it was the first time in his life that he had been anywhere in Tokyo outside the little triangle between his lodgings, workplace, and university, and the occasional stroll around nearby Ueno.

Little by little his story came out. The woman asked him, "And the sick man, did he get better?"

"No."

"He's been hospitalized these three years?"

"Yes."

"That's terrible. So have you come to visit him again this time?"

"Yes, well . . ."

"When you came, was the bridge still intact?"

"Yes, I came yesterday before the downpour."

"So you got caught in the rain and stayed over? The bridge is down, and the ferryboat isn't running. You're in trouble, aren't you?"

"No, I'm not particularly bothered."

"You're rather irresolute for someone so young! Put a little more energy and spirit into your conversation, can't you?"

"Um . . ." he said vaguely, raising his hand to his head.

"Don't do that!" she continued relentlessly. "It's uncouth to scratch your head. It looks cheap. You're a fine-looking student, so show some backbone."

"Have you always lived here?"

The old man nodded at his question.

"You grew up in Honjo, didn't you, Father?" said his aging daughter-in-law. "Even so, he's from a samurai family, you know. This old man's father was from a family of shogunal vassals that lived by the Honjo canal. Come the Meiji Restoration, he fell on hard times, and as no lucky break presented itself, he ended up running this general store in Nakasu, although he was already dead by the time I came to this house as a bride."

"Were you born in Nakasu?"

"Do I look like I was born on such a miserable patch of floating weeds? I'm a daughter of Fukugawa, I'll have you know. My parents were fishmongers hawking their wares on the streets, quite different from a samurai's pedigree. My mother-in-law was really hard on me, I can tell you. She's in the grave too, now."

"Do you have children?" He asked not so much out of interest as to keep the conversation flowing.

"Just this one," she said, stroking the cat's head.

"Do you know Nakasu well?"

"Well, yes, in such a small place . . . I get to hear which wives have been unfaithful and with who, what sort of guy such-and-such prostitute has for her lover and even which stray cat gave birth to how many kittens. I see things for myself, too."

"Do you know who the owner of this pillow is?"

"However big my ears are," she said with a wry smile, "how could they possibly reach the owner of an old pillow?"

"In that case, do you know of a woman with cropped hair who used to go from door to door playing the moon zither? In her house, there was an extraordinarily beautiful . . . woman," he began, but then found himself lost for words to explain it had actually been a man. "He sold himself as a woman, even in this day and age,[3] like one of those boy actor-prostitutes from the Edo period . . . so pretty . . ."

Well now! The old man and his daughter-in-law exchanged a look. He also had the impression that they were looking searchingly at each other.

"The woman with cropped hair was the lady of that house where three years ago I sheltered from the rain.

"I was sheltering from the rain under the eaves of the house when a voice came from behind the latticework inviting me,

3. The story is set in the Taishō period (1912–26)

'Come and shelter inside.' I hesitated, saying it would be too presumptuous, but pressed further, I accepted the kind offer."

"Was the cropped hair one there?"

"She looked like Hōkaibō.[4] And, the young maiden . . . The truth is that I did think he was a maiden to begin with. And a bit of a flirt at that. With a name like Tamae, how could I have thought he was anything but a woman?"

Having told the student, "Come and make yourself comfortable," the woman left him with Tamae and went out.

"It was really as though she was telling us to get on with it."

Left alone with the young woman, he found it hard to breathe. He was still a virgin and hardly knew what to do with himself.

"Tamae suddenly laughed. 'I'm a man, you know!' he said casually. 'I make a living looking like this,' he went on. 'But I won't eat you, so just relax, won't you? Eh, young man?'"

In a corner of the room was a moon zither. Tamae told him that his aunt sometimes went around the streets performing.

"'Whenever that aunt of mine takes a fancy to a man her hair is in the habit of growing and winding itself around his neck. That's why she cut her hair, you know,' he explained. Then he told me his aunt was a cook at the hospital."

"That's the hospital your friend was in, I suppose."

"Yes."

Tamae's hair was long and raven black. Once the rain had stopped the student took his leave, but behind him he heard the sound of hair being hacked off with a knife.

"Yumimura had a large six-bed room to himself. There weren't many patients."

He had handed over the book as requested.

---

4. The name of a rogue disguised as a monk, the leading character of the bawdy Kabuki play *Sumidagawa gonichi no omokage* (also commonly known as Hōkaibō).

"But then Yumimura pulled a face. 'There it is again,' he said. 'The rasping sound of a boat's scull as it passes beneath the window. It hurts my ears.' I myself couldn't hear anything, and when I said so, Yumimura replied, 'That's why I hate it.'"

Beneath the window was a narrow alley with no sign of any river.

"'As long as I hear that scull, I can't leave hospital.' Yumimura had been admitted to hospital with pneumonia, but it seemed he'd also gone a bit strange in the head."

"The poor thing," put in the woman.

"Suddenly I felt some hair winding itself around my shoulders and chest."

The hair was long, and the more he had tugged at it the longer it had grown.

"'What are you doing?'

"'The hair . . .'

"Yumimura said he couldn't see any hair, and then he laughed merrily. But I knew what it was. Tamae's hair had come after me. If I could find out about the woman Tamae called aunt, I would be able to clarify which of us was mistaken. I asked Yumimura whether there was a cook with cropped hair working at this hospital, but he answered, 'There's no one like that.' Just then, I heard a rasping sound loud and clear. My flesh broke out in goose bumps. After all, I'd seen with my own eyes that there was no river beneath the window. Seeing me shudder, Yumimura again roared with laughter. 'That's the sound of the cook pushing the trolley with the evening meals!'"

"So you met the cropped-haired cook?"

The woman prompted him to continue his story, but the old man remained silent. The only sound he made was the occasional tap of his pipe against the bamboo ash receptacle.

"Yes. When I went out into the corridor to collect Yumimura's tray, there she was, pushing the trolley, although she had a towel tied around her head.

"And?" The woman urged him to continue.

"I too found myself hospitalized without further ado."

"That's terrible!" The woman frowned. "What was wrong with you?"

"Apparently there was no such thing as a cropped-haired cook at the hospital."

"There wasn't?"

"Just as Yumimura had to remain in hospital until he could no longer hear the sound of the scull, I too was hospitalized until I could no longer see the cropped-haired cook."

"What an awful thing to happen!"

"I could have died of boredom. The two of us were there side by side, felled in action. Yumimura would trace with his finger the patterns on the wall made by stains and mildew from the leaking roof."

We're surrounded by women, so we're all right, he had said. This here was Okyō's face, this was Harube. That over there was Omin. He would idle away the hours giving them all women's names.

They're all acquaintances from the whorehouse. Hey, I'm joking. It's not that I really believe anything so silly as women's faces floating up out of the wall, he'd insisted senselessly. *Don't go telling the doctor, now. He'll say they're delusions or something and delay my release even longer. The doctor doesn't understand my jokes.*

Yumimura had mentioned numerous women but not a single one came to visit him in Nakasu, and not a single postcard came for him.

"'Meeting people is such a bother,' that's what Yumimura said. 'Before coming into hospital, I told everyone not to come and visit and not to write to me either.'"

"The bluff of a vain person," the woman put in.

"Indeed."

Amongst the stains on the wall, he could see Tamae's face.

"Of course, it was just an impression I had."

Theirs had been just a passing acquaintance. It was not as though their hands had even touched, much less their lips. Tamae may even have been merely teasing him with the story about the aunt who cut her hair short to stop it from growing and winding itself about any man she was attracted to.

However hard he tried, though, the fact was he could not rid himself of the long hair entwined around his shoulders, and it was abundantly clear to him that their meals were regularly brought to them on a trolley by the cropped-haired cook, her head covered with a hand towel. Yet Yumimura insisted that there was no hair wound about him and that the cook did not have cropped hair. The doctor agreed and told the student that as long as he saw things that did not exist, he could not allow him to leave the hospital.

"Surely all you had to do was say that you no longer saw them and you could have left the hospital right away."

"But I *could* see them."

"Honest as the day is long, aren't you?" The woman became contemplative. "What if the doctor was lying? He'd have wanted to keep you in hospital as long as he could."

"I did have my suspicions."

"The hospital fees must have been no small matter."

"You see, as a self-supporting student, there was no way I could pay a doctor's fees myself, but in the case of nervous disorders, the authorities—the government or state, I'm not sure—will pay the hospital some amount for any patient unable to meet the costs of their own treatment. If the hospital has too few admissions it would have to close, and so it welcomes such patients too. And so, perhaps . . . well, I did have my suspicions, but then it's also possible I really was ill . . . If it had been any other illness, I would have had no option but to stay in bed in my lodgings, but since I could get free treatment, well, perhaps it was a blessing in disguise."

"There you go sounding wishy-washy again. You should know yourself whether you were sick or not."

"Well, it made no difference to me either way. That in itself is perhaps an illness."

"Auntie," he had tried calling the cook who brought around the meal trolley. The woman, the towel covering her head, raised the corners of her mouth in a broad smile. "Tamae's hair has wrapped itself around me. I'm in a right fix."

"He's my nephew, after all. Whenever he falls in love, his hair kicks up a fuss. Tamae and I, we're the same. There's nothing we can do about it," whispered the aunt, her cropped hair concealed beneath the towel. "If he would only cut his hair, like I did . . . but then he's young. The poor thing shouldn't have to look like a monk."

"He doesn't even come to see me."

"Do you want him to come?"

The student was stuck for an answer. Even if Tamae did come to visit, what if Yumimura and the doctor said they couldn't see him? It would give them another excuse to keep him in hospital longer.

"Perhaps you're not in love?"

"With Tamae? Not particularly . . ."

"Really! Is that all you said? Not particularly?" said the middle-aged woman reproachfully as she lightly stroked the throat of the cat on her lap.

"Yes. I do think he's beautiful, but I can't say I'm especially in love with him."

"How calm you are, saying something so cruel!"

"Cruel?" he repeated, blankly.

"Failing to reciprocate an evil spirit's love is not exactly cruel," put in the old man.

"An . . . evil spirit?"

"Ah," was the old man's curt reply.

"That figures, I suppose. Could the pair of them have been demons?"

"There are all kinds here in Nakasu," said the woman. "I know the people here inside out, but my contacts don't extend to spirits."

"I had actually wondered about it myself. If it's true, then I feel even worse . . ."

"It's nothing to get depressed about, though."

"If someone's in love with you, better a flesh-and-blood woman."

"There shouldn't be anything dubious about a flesh-and-blood man and woman, you know." The woman batted her eyelashes. Her gaze was not directed at him, however, but at the old man.

The old man was sitting with his back straight as a rod, and his expression never so much as flickered, but the student suddenly found him comical and had to suppress a smile.

"You've been released from hospital," the old man nonchalantly changed the subject, "so congratulations are in order."

The cat turned its eyes to the boy, its large black pupils thinly bordered by golden irises.

"When did you get out?"

"It'll be over a year ago now . . ."

"So you no longer see that hair, or the cropped-haired aunt?"

"No . . ."

The words written on the pillow started drifting into his vision.

Flowing black hair . . . .

Yesterday evening . . .

"I'll come again," he said, preparing to leave the hospital as dazzling flashes of lightning raged continuously. "Are you leaving?" Yumimura twisted his fingers around the student's hand. "You shouldn't go out in this terrible storm."

"It doesn't bother me."

"I suppose not."

Lying on the bed as always, Yumimura toyed with the student's hand.

"Its all the same to you whether you get wet or not now, isn't it?"

The student nodded.

"I feel so lonely," Yumimura said. "I suppose you do, too."

"I'm used to it."

"Lucky you. Is it something you can get used to? Will I, too?"

"If you do, you do."

He hadn't intended to be funny, but Yumimura burst out laughing, a little too loudly, although he sounded forlorn and fearful as he said, "But I don't want to."

"So don't," the student soothed him. "It seems that not everyone has to." He changed the subject. "This room is as awful as ever."

"There are more women than before," Yumimura said, touching the stains on the wall.

The student sat on the edge of Yumimura's bed.

"I really envy you," Yumimura said. "How did you manage it?"

"It's not difficult."

"But thanks to you, things are worse now. They won't allow me to use anything resembling a rope. As for the toilet, they removed the door. I can't do anything."

"If you're set on doing it, you can tear up the bedclothes to make a rope."

"Don't be so glib! But then, you're brave."

"You don't need to be brave. It was just that I got fed up with everything. That's why I did it."

"And what about now? Do you feel better?"

"Nothing's really changed. I'm still fed up with everything, just as before, only now there's no more recourse so I guess it's worse than before."

"It's worse than being alive? So maybe there's no point in dying."

"If you get weary of living, you can always die, but once you're dead, you can't die again however sick of it you are."

Eight o'clock was lights out in the sickroom.

"It's stopped raining."

"But you'll stay with me, won't you? At least until morning?"

"Sure. I'm not in any particular hurry."

"Was it because of being hounded by that Tamae?"

"Was what?"

"The reason you hanged yourself."

"Not really."

"It must have been annoying."

"Well, a little."

"So you remained a virgin, after all. That's such a pity."

"It's probably better that way. That way I won't feel any regrets."

"But still," Yumimura persisted.

"Is that so? You were still a virgin when you hanged yourself?" put in the woman as she tickled the cat's neck. "That was a bit hasty, wasn't it? If you'd played around a bit, you'd have been bound to change your mind."

"Yumimura was a womanizer, but he still got depressed, so it doesn't make any difference either way."

"But he won't hang himself. That's the difference, isn't it?"

"But . . . " He flinched at the woman's forceful tone.

"Why don't you try it now? You'll regret it if you don't."

"It's already too late. I'm not bothered anyway."

"Don't be shy. Come on, get that obi off. Listen. You're just a dead man. How presumptuous of you to put on adult airs, wearing that Hakata obi. Didn't you say you had to work to pay your college fees? But if you die, you can wear a Satsuma weave with Hakata obi. How pompous. Father, it's all right if I show him what it's like to be with a woman, isn't it?"

"You're obscene," scolded the old man, but the woman paid him no heed.

"But I'm *dead*!" The student shrank away from her.

"I don't mind, I'm telling you." Her hand reached for the knot of his obi.

"But it's the middle of the day..."

"Since when did the time of day make any difference to a dead person?"

"But *he's* here."

"Don't bother about him. Father sometimes gets the urge during the day, too, but he never lets it stop him. Isn't that right, Father?"

The old man scowled and busied himself filling his pipe.

"It's because you're such a wimp that an evil spirit took advantage of you, you know."

"I *can't* let you get away with that!" The inner door slid open to reveal a young woman standing there. Oh, but her black hair was cut short!

"Tamae..." murmured the student. It had been three years.

"I've been quietly listening for some time, but you've just been going on and on about evil spirits this and evil spirits that."

"So you're the demon called Tamae, are you?" demanded the middle-aged woman. "Such impudence. You go around Nakasu acting as if you own the place, barging into people's houses without so much as a by-your-leave. When did you come in?"

"You're not the only ones in Nakasu, you know. I've been living here longer than you have," retorted Tamae. "As for this young man, I've had my eye on him from the start. Hmm, I don't suppose you even know him, let alone his name. He's called Tokio,[5] you know." He snuggled his cheek against the student. "I was waiting for you, Toki. I kept sending you tidings of my hair, but you didn't understand. I wasn't annoyed, though. After all, you're in the realm of the dead. Even my hair can't get to the bottom of that realm."

"Don't demons and ghosts get along?" sneered the woman, still hugging her cat.

Tamae picked up the pillow and opened a little drawer in the wooden box support.

Black water spilled out.

"I put my hair in the drawer to stop it from making trouble. And I even gave you my finger, Toki, but you're just so heartless."

Nestled in the melting black hair was a single white finger.

"Is that a demon's version of a love suicide? But even cutting off your finger, you don't bleed."

"And what about you? Let's find out!" Tamae took a hairpin from the breast of his kimono. Its tip was sharp.

"Tamae, stop it, please!"

"You're dead, so stay out of it."

"What a way to speak to your lover! No wonder Toki gave you the cold shoulder."

"You only just learned his name from me a few moments ago, so don't be using it so familiarly now. How imposing of you. Toki, if you're of a mind to loosen your obi, come and do it with me."

"But that thing dangling between your legs will just get in the way of doing it with a man!"

"It's a lot better than an old hag's ugly mug when it comes to servicing customers in bed. Eh, Toki?"

Tamae leaned against the student, fending the woman off with the hairpin clutched in his hand.

---

5. Written with the characters for "time" and "man."

"Damn you!" exclaimed the woman. She kicked open the door and went inside then reappeared clutching a big kitchen knife.

"Oh, please stop it," begged the student.

"I've been in love with Toki for three years, but you've only just met him!"

"A demon spurned for three years has no business barging in now. Get out!"

"Toki, you believed that it was because you were sick that you could see my hair and my aunt, didn't you? It's not that you hated me. Now that you're no longer human yourself, there's no need to keep on being so stubborn, is there?"

"Go on, get lost!" The woman thrust her knife at Tamae, who nimbly dodged it.

"If I go, it'll be together with Toki. You can't leave this world—just try it."

"In that case, I'll be a ghost too," said the woman, pointing the knife at her own throat. Instantly the old man leaped nimbly up and plucked the knife from the woman's hand and then wrested the hairpin from Tamae's grip.

"You randy old goat. You're jealous, aren't you?" cried the woman.

"You fool!"

"I have my pride too, don't I? Father, think about it. Some demon comes to Nakasu to steal my customers, and I'm to sit back and let him get away with it, am I?"

"Um, it's not that I'm your customer, or anything. I'm only a ghost," said the student nervously.

"Enough! Don't disparage yourself like that," the old man reproved him. "Young man, which of them are you in love with?"

"Neither in particular . . ."

"You're not in love? Right, as you wish." The old man strode into the inner room, opened the lid of the armor chest, and took out the suit of armor. Setting it down beside the chest, he reached up and took the spear from its place on the beam and unsheathed it. The vermilion-lacquered hilt glinted brightly in the darkened room.

Tokio, Tamae, and the woman all had their eyes glued on the old man, scarcely able to breathe.

The old man came back out and pointed the spear at Tamae. "Get in there!" he told him, chasing him into the room.

"That'll show you!" crowed the woman happily.

"You too!" The spear was turned unflinchingly on her.

"In there," the old man told the pair cowering before the spear, indicating the armor chest.

They tried to refuse, but the old man showed himself quite prepared to skewer the pair of them. Left with no choice, they stepped over the edge of the chest and crouched side-by-side inside.

The old man closed the lid and plumped himself down on top of it. "That's better!" He smiled faintly at the boy. "Those women don't half yak on."

"But one of them isn't a woman."

"Something of the sort, though."

"How long are you going to keep them locked up?"

"Nakasu's going to be filled in before long."

"I heard a rumor to that effect."

"And my time is nearly up. What little that's left to me, I want to enjoy in peace and quiet. There's some sake in the kitchen. Could I possibly trouble you to bring it to me, along with a cup?" Only a samurai descendant could use such a courteous turn of phrase.

Tokio brought the large bottle and a pair of cups.

"Oh, you'll have a drink too?"

"I'll keep you company."

The cat meowed.

"I forgot about that one," said the old man wryly. "So do you intend to stay here drinking with me until they come to fill the place in?"

"I'm afraid I'll have to be getting back."

"To the realm of the dead? No need to rush back to such a gloomy place."

"There's something I have to do. I'll be coming back to Nakasu soon for Yumimura."

"Is that the role you'll be playing from now on?"

"Yes. It's not one that everyone can get used to, but it suits me. I'll come for you too, when your turn comes."

"I'd be most grateful. Please do. But first, a drink."

"Let me pour you a cup."

He tilted the bottle and poured some sake into the cup in the old man's hand.

"You've certainly helped to alleviate the tedium."

Everything was quiet in the chest. Perhaps Tamae and the woman, both spurned, had hit it off.

"If you're ever bored, do come and visit. I just have to open this lid to start off some more boisterous merrymaking."

Indeed. The student smiled. The cycle of rowdy then quiet, rowdy then quiet, would carry on repeating itself. Time would stand still; nothing would change.

In Thy Shadow

妖翳記

(Yōeiki)

Hisao Jūran (1939)

久生 十蘭

Translation by Derek Lin

SHE WAS FACING away from me, squatting as she prodded something on the ground.

Curiosity got the better of me, and I closed the distance between us, only to find her tormenting a three-foot-long snake with a tree branch.

Stiffly, I made an introductory greeting, and she turned around. Pinning the snake's head under her straw sandal so it would not escape, she rose.

"Good day."

Her greeting was nonchalant, and she proceeded to scrutinize my face upon making it.

The beauty of her face sent a chill through my bones. It was like the face of one of those women who modelled for paintings, fully formed, well featured, and bearing the cool pallor of polished ivory.

It was hard to imagine that blood ran beneath that layer of skin. But it would also have been a mistake to call her beauty "aloof". It was inorganic, the kind that gave you a chill just to look at.

Just as I was about to close my mouth, she spoke, abruptly.

"Wait here until I come back. Step on the snake. You had better not let it get away."

Without waiting for an answer, she marched off in the direction of the main building.

I did as I was told, stepping obediently on the snake, waiting for her return.

The snake thrashed about under my foot, wriggling and slapping the hem of my trousers with its tail.

It was through this series of events that I found myself standing in the middle of a wide, spacious lawn with the sun beating down on my head. I waited, but she never came back.

And she was not going to. A careless melody drifted from the second storey of the building into the garden. She had started playing the piano.

I was but an honest student of modest means, there to tutor the lady in art and art history. Treading on snake heads was not part of the terms of my engagement, thus, it would not have been to my disadvantage had I refused the task. Yet something about the situation had made such a course of action untenable, and I found myself unable to do anything but obey the order and stand there till dusk.

– 2 –

I woke in a despairingly spacious room with high ceilings, done in the Western style.

It was my opinion that this room had served as a ballroom once upon a time. The floor was made of parquetry and several grand chandeliers hung from the ceiling.

This room, the sheer entirety of it, was my bedroom, and I slept on a tiny bed placed right in the middle of it.

I felt like I was floating in the middle of an ocean. The sheer vastness of everything else made me feel like I had shrunk by half. It made me uneasy, helplessly so. When night came, darkness fell and smothered me like a carpet the four corners of which rose and folded in, burying me in its midst. Sleep was unattainable out of fear.

Fuji was the mistress of the house. She lived in this ridiculously large mansion with nothing more than a minimal staff of attendants, all by herself.

It was an ancient mansion that dated to the Meiji Era. The house was filled with a fusty air one was hard pressed to put words to. The furnishings and trappings of the household were all from the days of the Rokumeikan, a time of dissipation and self-indulgent opulence by the government in an attempt to gain status in the eyes of foreign dignitaries. However, they had since fallen into a state of disrepair, were void of any signs of restoration, and bore the appearance of being beyond remedy.

Despite this, upon closer examination, one could still see that the chairs were upholstered with brocade and that the mantelpieces all looked like they were made of imported Italian marble. These signs were more than enough to hint at the opulence of life there years before.

The former lord of the manor was an envoy to Scandinavia, but it was said that he spent his lengthy tour of duty abroad drinking prodigiously and composing classical Chinese verse while seated cross-legged atop a long wooden bench. His verse was not so much an attempt at unravelling the intricacies of poetry as a way of coping with the many troubles stirring his heart, frustrations the nature of which he could not pinpoint.

He had assumed the post with the weight of his country's future heavy on his heart. It was discovered after his death, however, that the frustrations he felt were actually physiological discomforts brought on by the worsening of a syphilis-induced nervous disorder. (He died of cerebral syphilis.)

Fuji was born the year following the former master's return to Japan after he had resigned from his diplomatic duties. He had apparently wanted to bring her up as a strong, independent woman and so saw to it that her education was anything but conventional.

On one occasion, her father commanded Fuji to administer a beating to a gardener who happened to be passing by the edge of the lawn until she was pleased. It was unknown what Fuji had thought then, but when she went to her father's side, she struck him severely across the face with the whip he was holding out.

Caught unawares, her father fell from his chair and lay prone on the lawn, holding his face. He remained in that position for a while, not rising. It was said that as he buried his face in the grass, he wept tears of joy.

-3-

Every morning at about ten o'clock, I would trudge down the long corridor to the sunroom that was at the end of it.

My job was to sit in a chair in the shadow of a large potted palm there until eleven-thirty. The chair I sat in was a huge rattan affair large enough to swallow me whole. Occasionally, I was to clear my throat meaningfully or stare up at the ceiling. At eleven-thirty, I got up and trudged back to my room. And that would be my job for the day. I repeated it every morning like clockwork.

If you were to ask why I do this, it would go without saying that my purpose was to lecture Fuji on the topic of art history. However, that fortunate circumstance had yet, till then, to transpire even once. As a result, all I had done was wait idly for the time to pass, my only friend the rattan chair.

I was not particularly dissatisfied with this arrangement. Whichever the course of action, I would still have passed the time in boredom.

After lunch each day, I would set out to look for Fuji for permission to leave the premises. This was again a time-consuming task. Rarely, she would be in her own room reading or practising her penmanship with a copy book in front of her, but most of the time she would be hiding in some absurd, ridiculous corner by herself amusing herself with some outrageous game of her own mad devising.

I would search each of the numerous rooms from the upper level to the basement one by one, and after this painstaking endeavour, I would finally find her next to the boiler in the basement or behind a large shelf in the library.

There was a method to finding Fuji.

One had merely to examine the area of the floor near the windows. Upon careful examination of the same, one would find flies with their wings removed or spiders with their legs plucked, carelessly scattered. If they were still trembling or shaking their limbs, then it was safe to conclude that Fuji had just been there. The same principle applied whether it was a centipede or a small cabbage white butterfly. If one were to analyse the death throes of the insects and trace a path towards the ones with the most signs of life, one would eventually wind up at the place Fuji was.

But even after finding her, there was little satisfaction to be had.

- 4 -

In the afternoon of approximately my fifth day there, as I was standing blankly by the side of the tennis court, Fuji came at me with those marching steps that were her signature.

This was the second time I was seeing her since that incident with the garden snake. I hurriedly bowed. Fuji gave me a strange look as if she did not recognize me.

Then, without warning, almost abruptly, she said, "I have yet to give you a treat."

I had no idea what she was talking about. "What?"

"I make a really good French dish called *lapin chasseur*. I will make it for you. Do you like *lapin chasseur*?"

I had no idea what kind of dish a "*chasseur*" might be, but I had a premonition that if I said I hated it, I would not live to see the next morn. So I gave in.

"*Lapin*. . . . Yes, of course, I love it."

I accompanied my reply with a face that said I could not wait to sink my teeth into a *lapin chasseur*. At that, Fuji sniffed, apparently satisfied.

"I am going to start the preparations. Assist me."

Without waiting, she strode straight to the back of the greenhouse.

Not knowing where the rabbit hutch might be, I looked here and there before finally finding it. I went in, but with the sudden transition from sunlight into a dark, grey place I could not see a single thing. As I stood in the middle of the hutch not knowing what to do, I was surprised by a voice at my feet that said, “Here. Take this. Just like this, one hand on each ear.”

It was Fuji's voice. As I stuck my hands out awkwardly like a blind man, something warm and wet was thrust into them. I lifted it absently, and saw that it was a rabbit head hewn roughly at the neck.

In the hazy darkness of the warren, the head stared at me with betrayal crystallised in its widely flung open eyes, blood dripping from its neck. My instinctive reaction was to fling it away and I almost did with a yelp.

“If you swing it around so much, we'll lose all the blood, idiot!” scolded Fuji in an irritated voice. Through the hazy darkness, I saw her squatting at my feet, collecting the blood from the rabbit's head in a pot. She seemed to be enjoying it. There are many games in this world that are cruel, but a game as cruel as this, if it was a game at all, must be rare indeed. The sheer intensity of the situation almost made my legs give out.

It was only much later that I learnt that *lapin chasseur* was made with chunks of rabbit boiled in a mixture of fine red wine and rabbit blood, and was thus regarded as fine cuisine in France, but I did not have the benefit of that knowledge then.

– 5 –

Fuji would not eat any bird she did not prepare herself. As a result, I was often made to accompany and assist her in this regard.

While she slit throats and plucked feathers, I would hold down the chicken or the frog's legs.

Though the tasks were so gruesome one would usually want to avoid bearing witness to them, in a strange, mysterious way, performing them with Fuji rendered them not entirely unpleasant.

In fact, as I got used to them, I was eventually able to even enjoy them.

As time went by, Fuji's treatment of me improved and I started attending her after dinner for drinks or accompanying her when she went driving.

Fuji drank often, a trait she had inherited from her father. But she did not consume wine or cognac. Rather, she emptied half a litre of Nada vintage every night. When I drank with her, it was never enough for her to simply watch me drink at her command. She would drink until she got light-headed and stumbled back to her quarters hanging on my shoulder, singing songs she made up spontaneously.

Everything she did was superficial; she did not particularly care whether any one thing was done in the proper manner or not. Any idea that popped into her head was one she pursued to her heart's content, any whim or fancy one she entertained without reservation. She would go on a drive by herself in a Hispano-Suiza, get tired of it all of a sudden and leave it by the side of the road, or travel all the way to Atami to buy carnations, seedbed and all.

To the casual observer this might seem to be the behaviour of a mentally unbalanced person, but in fact it was once part of the everyday lifestyles of the most influential feudal lords. I had come to believe that Fuji's cruelty, then, was but a trait she had inherited from her bloodline, which she traced unbroken all the way back to the Sengoku period, the era of the Warring States.

A woman who did just as she pleased to the extent that Fuji did simply could not exist in the real world. She would ring a bell to summon me at three o'clock in the morning and proceed to ignore and avoid me for a full week right after. It only happened once, but I was once woken on the verge of slumber to attend her on a duck-hunting trip to Chiba.

My roller-coaster life lasted for a month, and it was a month of being buffeted and carried along by a wind that knew not how to abate. However, one month into this life, I was awakened at about eleven at night by the violent ringing of Fuji's bell. I rushed to her bedroom and stood before her door.

I knocked, but this time the skylark's voice that always greeted me was not to be heard. I pushed the door open and entered her room. There, scattered haphazardly all about, on the carpet and on the tall chairs, were articles of female clothing—chemises the colour of butter, stockings which resembled fishing nets, purplish pink culottes, and many, many more. To the uninitiated like me, there was no hope of understanding the items of female clothing arrayed before me like the aftermath of a floral explosion. And what of Fuji? She was sprawled on her bed sound asleep with the lights—every single bulb on the chandelier—on.

She lay there so languorously, stretched out on the sheets as if taking a long soak in a bath, that I was at a loss as to what to do. Finally, deciding that it was the only thing left to be done, I turned off the lights and retreated from the room.

– 6 –

The next morning, Tome, the elderly head housemaid, came to me as I sat idly in my room. "The lady wishes to begin her studies today and desires your presence in the sunroom at once," she said, articulating each word clearly, before withdrawing.

The foolishness of my morning ritual had caused me much frustration ever since the incident with the *lapin chasseur*, and having served the exclusive role of attending Fuji at her whims and fancies, I had forgotten entirely about the art history I had originally been hired to teach. I was stumped initially at the message, and it took a while for realisation to dawn upon me. When it did, I grabbed Hermann Lotze's lectures on the Parthenon and flew from my room.

Upon arriving at the sunroom, I was surprised to find Fuji already there, seated with a calm expression on her face. I nodded a greeting and took my seat in front of her. Fuji fixed me with a steely glare. "There is something I would like to ascertain. What is your role here?" Her tone cut right through me like a katana.

I did not comprehend the nature of her question, so I returned her glare with a blank gaze. This roused her ire and her brows twitched as she frowned.

"Are you not answering my question because you did not hear what I said? If that is the case, let me repeat myself. What are you to me? A friend? Or a lover?"

We had behaved with impropriety in each other's presence and even shared some rather lewd jokes, but it would have been untruthful to reply that we were lovers.

"I guess we would be something like friends." I must have grinned then. Fuji's glare was unfaltering.

"No," she said.

My heart quickened. "Then . . ."

Fuji's reply came like the autumn frost.

"You are my tutor."

I turned red and cast my gaze downwards. As if pressing the advantage in this verbal duel, she continued. "Did you not give your word that you would be here waiting from ten o'clock to eleven-thirty whether I came or not?"

I had no reply. All I managed was a soft, pitiful squeak, like the cry of an insect. "I didn't think you liked me much, so I thought . . ."

"Why did you not keep your promise? I like people who keep their promises, no matter how small or insignificant. Please do not think I meant that romantically. I am simply very serious on matters pertaining to obligations."

Somehow, I found myself unconvinced. But I knew better than to say so and so I responded in the most humble and respectful manner I could muster. Upon which, Fuji returned to her usual self. "You don't need to be so apologetic. Just don't do it again."

I heaved a sigh of relief and decided to make her laugh by scratching my head in an exaggerated manner. Fuji reached backwards and stretched. "Heh, heh. How was that? Were you scared? Looks like I got you today." She then brought her face uncomfortably close to mine.

"Did you think I was angry at you? That's not it. I'm sad. This was a reaction out of sadness. You probably don't know this, but I haven't had much luck with tutors, as rare as such people might be. Somehow, they all just end up disappearing and never coming back." As she said this she kept her gaze on my face, an eerie smile upturning her hard, porcelain cheeks.

"I can see why. You are a selfish, difficult, whimsical, do-as-you-please student. Anyone would run away."

At that, Fuji placed a hand on her cheek in an affected manner. "Really," she said, almost in a whisper.

Of course, I wanted to say. I was of a mind to expose her unglamorous position the previous night in an attempt to put her in her place, but the fright I had received unexpectedly a few moments before lingered in my breast, and I could not muster the lightness of mood necessary for the task. But I was not ready to give in.

"I thought I heard a bell last night at about eleven o'clock, but I guess it must have been my imagination," I said casually.

Fuji inclined her head to the side as if in thought, before replying, "I don't remember."

-7-

Several days hence, as I was making an exit through the gates of my university, Kinbara, a classmate, caught up with me.

"Hey, they say you've been going to the Kagatas'. Is it true?"

When I replied that I was, he laughed boorishly. "Be careful that they don't treat you too well. They might just smother you with their kindness!"

I ignored him, thinking that his usual envy was the cause for his strange, provocative words. He pouted comically.

"I'm serious. Those folks are strange. You need to be careful."

"What do you mean by 'strange'?" I snapped, annoyed.

Kinbara's eyes widened. "You mean you really haven't heard? Well, I guess it's not something the referral department's going to tell you."

That the nature of this news I had not heard about warranted such secrecy did not fail to intrigue me, so I got myself and Kinbara to Tiger in San-chome and presently learned that the two fellows who had undertaken the role of Fuji's personal tutor before me were deceased.

"Some say that one of them fell off a cliff during a trip to Yarigatake and that the other drowned. The details are a little murky, but the truth is that they're both dead."

This was certainly not a cause for alarm. Such coincidences were a dime a dozen.

Like myself, Kinbara tutored to pay for college, but he was a deeply jealous fellow. He never failed to envy the fact or put in a bad word about the family whenever someone had a better or more well-off student than he did. I was certain that this was just another instance of the same.

"It was probably a case of bad feng shui," I said, knowing it would provoke him, and left.

That night, I crept into bed at the cusp of midnight, as was my habit. I had taken some drink shortly before, and it was preventing me from getting to sleep. I smoked a cigarette and thrashed and wriggled in bed until a deep disquiet came over me, sending a chill from the tips of my toes up my spine like a bolt of lightning. I gave out a cry despite myself and shot upright in bed. I looked about the room, about the large space that held darkness and shadow, but all that was there was the still night air, and I saw nothing to scare me. I lay my head on my pillow again, but I could not still the stirring in my heart. What was the cause of that terrible fear that came upon me, that it aroused such terror?

I got up again, bending my knees and adopting the same posture as just before I had lit my cigarette. I squeezed my eyes shut and waited for the same image to flash once more across my retinas. Shadowy images flowed across the backs of my eyelids like members of a procession. One unanticipated image stood out amongst them, reflected clear and sharp in my mind's eye like a scene thrown up suddenly on a dark movie screen.

It was Fuji, on that fateful day in the sunroom when she had gazed up at me unblinkingly with that mocking smile of hers, her face a perfect ivory mask, and uttered the following words. "Somehow, they all just end up disappearing and never coming back."

Sitting on the bed, I folded my arms and rolled my eyes. "You know, I might just get killed," I muttered, matter-of-factly.

– 8 –

I returned from my errand, though my labours had not been fruitful.

I had inquired at the referral department and discovered the addresses of my two predecessors. Taking advantage of the fact that it was a Buddhist holiday, I splurged on two large boxes of incense. Bearing the boxes, I visited the addresses, pretending to be the Kagatas' secretary.

It was not under some flight of fancy that I had undertaken this course of action. Discovering the truth behind the deaths was to me a matter of top priority. If the rumours were baseless, then the suspicion and unease that plagued my days would be dispelled. If they were likely to be true, then I had to see to my own safety.

Fuji had been in a good mood lately, but that had not put me at ease. Rather, her good mood could also be read as a warning. There was something in her cheerful spirit of late that resembled a runaway train about to derail, and it worried me. That was not all. Every movement she made, every look she gave me planted a seed of suspicion in my mind. My nerves had been on edge that week and I had lost a fair amount of weight because of it. I could have simply fled from the Kagata estate, but when I thought of how stupid such an act would have been had it all turned out to be a rumour, I could not bring myself to run away.

After I had offered the incense before the ancestral tablet and paid my respects in a most proper fashion, I found a member of the family likely to take the bait and started talking about the deceased. I was able to uncover the facts only after pelting her with compliments for the deceased such as "What a genius he was!" and "What a capable youth he was!" until she was sobbing and then broaching the question, "Could you tell me more about how he died?"

One of them had fallen to his death while on a rock-climbing trip in the Japanese Alps. The other had drowned while swimming.

The families of both men had been vassals of the Kagatas in a bygone age. Perhaps they had meant to protect their former lord and master, but their accounts of the deaths were vague and ambiguous at the most important parts. I was unable to get anything concrete out of one family, but from the other, I managed to glean the fact that the rock-climbing trip was made "to accompany the lady". This, however, was of no help to me. Instead, it only served to further arouse my suspicions.

Thankful that I was not being called upon then, I lay on my bed facing the ceiling and contemplated.

Even if the details had been vague, I was now certain that the two men who had been Fuji's tutors had died under mysterious circumstances, one after the other. Moreover, one of them had died while Fuji was with him. On one hand, the two incidents might have been a mere coincidence, but on the other, there was enough reason to suspect that they were not.

Suppose that Fuji did have a hand in their deaths. What would have been her motive?

If Fuji did mean to kill me, I could easily guess at her reason. I had wounded her pride, where it hurt the most. I would be killed for revenge. I had erred, twice. Not only had I turned down her invitation, I had completely ignored her Romantic ideas. To Fuji, my rejection (despite the fact that it was not one) was unforgivable. If I had only arrived at the stipulated time that morning and sat in the shadow of that large potted palm, her appetite for Romanticism might have been sated, and that would have extenuated my crime somewhat. At the very least, it would have appeased her and saved me from her ire. But I had ignored her twice that morning, and that was the reason for Fuji's rage. And to that fire I had added the fuel of jesting about the previous night. "I thought I heard a bell last night..." I had begun, unaware then of my folly. Those very words were to be the nails in my coffin.

Those were the circumstances of my case. It was unlikely that they applied too to the other tutors. But what other reasons could there be?

Most of all, how could I have not seen from the start that the strange promise Fuji demanded was an expression of her pent-up admiration for the Romantic? If only I had seen that, how favourably for me everything would have worked out. It was premature of me to conclude without probing further that the promise had been born out of the silly whim of a feudal lord's daughter. But it was too late now. Even if I were to bare my heart and show Fuji the depths of my sincerity, she would not forgive me.

– 9 –

That morning, I stood at the edge of Shinsen Gorge in Nagano. The cliff that stretched out under my feet was so high it made my eyes glaze over. I was waiting for Fuji to come up behind me and tip me over.

It was not that I wanted to die by her hand in that careless fashion. The deepening worry and agitation inside me was getting to be too much to bear, and I simply had to know for sure, whatever the outcome was.

I no longer had the mental strength to keep my guard up. My heart had been aflame with the desire to know the truth for the past week. To this end, I had embarked on an experiment, with my own body as the test subject.

I stood at the very threshold of the cliff and waited. Presently, Fuji approached slowly. I heard voices from the suspension bridge below.

"Don't stand there. It's dangerous. Come over here," she called out to me.

– 10 –

My next experiment was to be more dangerous than that at Shinsen Gorge. I had recommended shooting to Fuji and assumed the task of raising the targets. Of course, I had a bullet-proof vest under my waistcoat. But I would not have lasted a second were I to be shot in the head or at close range.

I was aware of the recklessness of my ways, but my thirst for the truth was so deep I was now willing to overlook a certain amount of risk to my person. That I had conceived such a foolhardy plan was more than sufficient proof I was teetering on the brink of delirium.

If Fuji meant to kill me, there would be no better opportunity. The manner in which I weaved about in front of the targets inspired no confidence amongst those gathered, and there were at least three present who would testify to the accidental nature of the homicide. All she had to do was pull the trigger a fraction of a second before I was done flipping the targets.

However, in the end, Fuji did not shoot me. The muzzle of her weapon remained pointed at the ground until the targets were completely turned.

I returned to my room, moved a chair, and sat by the window. There was no mistake about it—Fuji did not shoot me either because she did not mean to kill me or because she knew of a better way in which to do it.

I was convinced that no better opportunity for Fuji to kill me existed than the one that had been presented that day. But if that were true, then what else could she have planned?

I furrowed my brow in contemplation. I wracked the recesses of my mind for all conceivable methods, until I arrived at one I had scarcely considered, for the mere thought of it invoked such fear in me I fell from my chair with a moan—

Poison!

***

I HAVE PREVIOUSLY written that Fuji entrusted to no one the preparation of the game she consumed. As a reward for my efforts in lending a hand to the slaughter, I, too, was allowed to partake of the feast by her grace; this had been the practice for a while. All the insidious deeds she could have been up to had she only had the inclination!

At the turn of the 18th century in Germany, a minor official by the name of Zweich poisoned a colleague by giving him a wild duck injected with colchicine. The truth of this matter was only made known by a confession made by Zweich on his deathbed.

My obsession with discovering how my two predecessors had died had excluded this line of thinking. The truth of the matter, however, was that what had initially appeared to be carelessness on my part was born out of the vague assumption that the act of poisoning a person in one's own home lacked the finesse one would expect from someone of Fuji's stature.

I finally understood the reason Fuji did not push me off the edge at Shinsen Gorge and why I had not been a victim of gunfire that other day. Someone as sagacious as Fuji would never condone a repeat performance of what had come before.

The mystery of Fuji's sudden kindness to me that day in the sunroom was thus solved as well. She wanted me to stay. She had been administering infinitesimal quantities of arsenic to me on a daily basis, killing me slowly but surely. There was no mistake about it.

It was a method that matched her sensibilities. Fuji was never one to take life in an instant, as evidenced by her morning ritual of insect-hunting. She took joy in the plucking of legs and pinching of wings, anything that prolonged the final moments of agony.

I was to be consumed by a regular dose of arsenic, to waste away into nothingness as the poison ate away at my metabolic system one minuscule bite at a time, and finally fade into oblivion.

- 11 -

It was the eighth day of my survival. Since the day I fell from my chair, I had been going to the physician for a medical examination every day. It was to discover any proclivity to steatosis in my kidney and liver—to pre-empt danger—that I had been doing this.

I hurried to the Shimizu Clinic of Internal Medicine. A month had passed since that incident in the sunroom. If one were to suppose that Fuji had begun her administration of the poison one day thence, then there was no doubt that drastic changes should be detected in my internal organs. In spite of this, the gauntlet of tests I underwent failed to discover any anomalies in my kidney, liver, vasomotor nerves, or the mucosal surfaces of my gastrointestinal system. In other words, the poison had yet to mount an offensive on my body. This was both a surprise and an unexpected stroke of good fortune, but I could not afford to be lulled into a false sense of security. The attack on my body was only a question of time. If not yesterday, today. If not today, tomorrow. If not tomorrow. The tests I took each morning were no longer for myself. They were for the dinners I had had the evenings before.

Each day, after examining me, the doctor would say, "You're fine, just fine." There was nothing in this world as maddening as the doctor's irksome tone. You're fine, just fine.

Each day, I waited. Each morning, with renewed hope, I dashed to the clinic. I counted the days, and they numbered eight.

Why had Fuji not begun her work? What was she waiting for? I could no longer endure this leisurely pace. The disappointment I experienced morning after morning was more than I could bear, and I grew immensely irritable. I felt a strong compulsion to wreak destruction on all within my reach.

– 12 –

That afternoon, I sat at the edge of a fountain. At my feet were a handful of seasonal flowers. The white clouds overhead could be seen in the water.

I came here every day to cool off. What I needed most during this trying time was to suppress any strong emotion and to remain as calm as possible. I let the breeze caress my bare head as I thought about Fuji. For five days, she had not let me join her mantis games. The slaughter in the rabbit hutch and her hunt for insects were now solitary pastimes for her. I could not comprehend why she had started to mistreat me so.

In my mind, a female mantis crawls out from behind a commode. From above a bench, a male leaps to the ground. They meet on a Persian rug and hold their heads against each other. The female strikes the shoulders of the male with her long legs. He retreats. She gives chase. He flees towards the back of the bench. She corners him there. She pulls him towards her with her long legs and starts to devour him. His front legs are gone. With only his hind legs, he makes a run for it. The female pounces and continues her feast, this time from the back. Slowly, the male's body disappears into her mouth. Slowly, one morsel a time.

For five whole days Fuji had withheld from me moments of pleasure like no other: the ecstasy of her devouring my arm, the frisson of her gnawing on my torso. As I fingered the anemone petals in idle contemplation, a most repugnant thought crept into my mind, sending a chill down my spine. The female mantis fed on the male not out of anger, but out of love. It had always been about love. My two predecessors had been loved by Fuji, and so they had been killed.

Yet, I . . . I survived. I lived.

Fuji did not mean to kill me. She did not love me enough to. At last, I saw the truth.

Fuji had devoured them, and only them, for real. With me, she only went through the motions. This, what she was doing to me, was just a little too much. It was just a little too much.

I knelt, my head against the rim of the fountain pool, and cried.

– 13 –

To me, to kill someone was to show your love for them. I did not want to die, but if Fuji loved me so much that she were to kill me, then my life was a small price to pay for her affection.

I went to Fuji's side each day to beg, like a child pleading for candy.

That evening, as I entered Fuji's room, I found her seated cross-legged on the floor shaving the fur off a cat with an electric shaver. She looked keen to render it bald. I lay on my side next to her and tugged at her sleeve, which was draped across the floor.

"O Fuji, O Miss Mantis. Won't you kill me? I would very much like to die by your hand."

With a puff, Fuji blew away some cat fur that she was close to inhaling.

"Are you at it again? Why do you want to die so badly? You're strange."

"I'm not kidding. I'm serious. Don't just pretend at eating me. Eat me, for real."

"That's too much trouble."

I found my affection and unease too much to bear.

"Is it really so much trouble? Is it really? You can kill me like you would a rabbit or a shrimp. I don't really mind how. Just kill me please, I beg of you. Why won't you kill me?"

With her left hand holding down the neck of the cat, Fuji turned to face me and smiled like a thousand summer days. "I guess I could strangle you."

It was like a dream come true.

"Strangling's fine. Anything's fine, as long as it's not for show. You have to strangle me for real!"

Fuji released the cat and turned to face me, but I could see that she had changed her mind.

"I guess not. It sounds boring. Why don't you fetch me an Utamaro from the attic? It should be in the chest on top. Tome has the key."

I left Fuji's side grudgingly. I got the key from downstairs and proceeded to the attic. I quickly found what I had been sent to find. As I was about to leave the room with it under my arm, I spotted something which stopped me in my tracks.

It was a thick, strong rope, trusty by all appearances, hanging straight down from a beam. I was seized by a suddenness of emotion which gave way to an outcry. "This, this is it!"

In that instant I had my epiphany, the proverbial revelation from the heavens. There was no need for Fuji to taint her own hands. All she had to do was hint. Beguile. Leave a trail of bread crumbs to her final trap. My two predecessors had not died in the mountains or at sea. They had met their ends here, beneath this beam. They, too, must have been driven to the edge, driven to their very deaths, at this spot. Indeed, had they not stood, as I did then, at the very same spot beneath that beam? And not without reason: we three were bound by the same fetter, and Fuji was her name. And now, we were about to be bound by the same piece of rope.

At last, Fuji had displayed her love for me. I approached the rope and tried it on my neck. It was sturdy and supple.

And it was thus I whispered, "I can finally die now."

Spider

蜘蛛
(Kumo)

Endō Shūsaku (1959)

遠藤 周作

Translation by Rossa O'Muireartaigh

IT HAPPENED IN June two years ago. It was a Sunday evening. Silent, misty rain had been falling all day. I'd work to finish up and had to spend the whole of my Sunday, starting from early, stuck at my desk. Every time I'd look up from my work I'd see raindrops gently streaming down the glass of the window that looked out onto the garden. It was six o'clock by the time I managed to finish. I opened my diary and saw that I had to leave at eight o'clock for a restaurant called Hakujian in Yotsuya.

I was to attend a small gathering my uncle was involved in organizing. It wasn't a particularly important gathering, just a frivolous bunch of curiosity-seekers made up of businessmen, doctors, and others who, like my uncle, had a lot of time to spare. Once a month they'd gather, have a meal and then go visit something of interest or furtively watch some louche movie.

I myself, in fact, had nothing to do with the group. I was only going that evening at the invitation of my uncle. They were having some sort of "ghost stories night" where people who had seen ghosts or encountered spirits were being invited to tell their tales.

Alas for me, I had a tale to tell them. It happened the previous December when I went to Atami to meet up with M., a fellow writer. While we were there, we both experienced something that felt like a cold shiver going down our backs. Neither M. nor I believe in ghost mysteries and all that, but when two people in the same place encounter something slightly out of the ordinary, it does of course unnerve one a bit. I did think it weird what we felt, but I still don't believe in ghosts. Whatever it was it had a scientific cause and we were merely hallucinating.

My uncle had phoned me to ask me to speak to the group that evening about this experience. I had already written about it in a magazine, so it was annoying to have to repeat the same story all over again. It was not going to be an enjoyable evening.

At around half-eight I made my way by taxi through the still-falling misty rain towards Yotsuya. We got held up at Mitsuke on account of subway construction, and I recall that it took us a long time to get to Hakujian, which would normally be just five minutes away.

Hakujian is a traditional high-class Japanese-style establishment built by the tea ceremony master Takahashi Yoshio. It isn't very well known, but it boasts a delightful garden and serves great *shōjinryōri* vegetarian cuisine.

Upon my arrival the waitress showed me into the tatami room where the group had gathered. The ghost story session had already begun.

Such stories should normally be told in the wee hours, but some of the members were probably too busy to wait around till then. So as soon as it was evening, the guest speakers were called upon to recount their experiences. The room was darkened, illuminated only by a single lamp with a gaudy crimson shade that was placed at the center of a large table. The speaker's eyes and nose were tinged with make-up to create a spooky look—probably my uncle's idea—something which I must say I found ridiculous.

"You've come," said my uncle in a whisper from his seat near the corridor. "Sit down here so I can introduce you to everyone afterwards."

The members were mostly middle-aged or older. They crowded around the large table, some kneeling, some smoking cigarettes, as they listened attentively to the guest speaker's tale. *What a bunch of wasters!* I thought to myself as I put a cigarette in my mouth and lit it. It all looked so ridiculous, these people of status wasting their time with such silliness.

The man recounting his experiences so earnestly in front of the bright red lampshade was a senior executive of a company. He was telling us all about a time, about five years before, when he was staying at an inn in front of Yamagata Station. His 8-tatami room on the second floor was separated from the neighboring room by sliding *fusuma* doors. In the middle of the night, he suddenly awakened and saw an old woman near the window illuminated in the blue-white moonlight. She was staring at him. As he watched, she crept as far as the *fusuma* and disappeared.

"I thought it was just a bad dream." The little man addressed us in hushed tones as though he was still frightened by the memory. "I dozed off, but when I opened my eyes the same old woman was there again sitting on a tatami mat in the light of the moon."

He was doing his best to tell the story, but it seemed a little contrived to me. Listening to him, I didn't feel one bit scared. I wondered if the others were as bored as I was. Many shifted their knees constantly; others stared at him blankly.

Country hotel room—the middle of the night—the ghost of an old woman who'd hanged herself in the same room appears. Heard it before. Boring! I thought to myself.

Putting out my cigarette, I found myself looking round at the expressions of the people gathered. I suddenly noticed one remarkably pale face. It belonged to a young man in a corner of the room near the garden. He had very fine features and was sitting there with both hands on his knees. He was staring over at me and seemed to be clearly conscious of my presence. I instinctively turned away.

"Who's that?" I discreetly asked my uncle in a low voice.

"One of the members must have brought him. It's his first time," he said with a slightly puzzled expression, then shook his head.

The story of the Yamagata inn finished. Next up was a plump doctor called Abe from the Institute of Infectious Diseases in Meguro. He sat down in front of the table.

"I'm a doctor, but I'm not a psychoanalyst so I have never studied dreams."

With this proviso, Dr. Abe launched into his account of an incident that had happened to him about four years previous. He had read a book about a new school of psychology postulating that dreams are a harbinger of future events that will happen to the dreamer. After reading the book, the doctor set out to amuse himself by writing down in a notebook any dreams he remembered whenever he awoke in the middle of the night.

One night he dreamt he was at the deathbed of a woman with tuberculosis. She wasn't his patient, but the hospital was his, although he couldn't make out which room they were in. He was there alone with this emaciated patient, grasping her hand, keeping watch as she breathed her last. The dream ended and he woke up.

"I didn't think anything of it at the time. I just wrote the details and date into my notebook as I always did."

Dr. Abe was not a good speaker. His delivery was slow and halting, his voice monotonous.

Three months later he was on night duty when, in the middle of the night, a nurse came to alert him about a girl with pharyngolaryngeal tuberculosis in a private room on the second floor. She had been admitted quite some time before, but her breathing had suddenly become irregular. There was no time to call whoever was looking after her. Dr. Abe entered her room and found the girl's eyes to be closed, her pallid arms hanging limply from the bed. As soon as the nurse gave him the instruments he needed to inject camphor he knew the situation was hopeless.

"Call the family, please."

The nurse ran off to the telephone cabinet. Dr. Abe took the girl's hand. Her pulse was fading fast. Only he and she remained in the room.

"Suddenly I remembered that dream I had and felt afraid."

He instantly let go of the girl's hand. Not that he needed to hold it any longer—she was dead.

Just then her white hand, which had fallen lifelessly from the bed a moment before, began to move. This was no rigor mortis. It slowly searched out Dr. Abe's hand as if it were alive, inching forward like an insect.

Dr. Abe bounded out of the room into the corridor, colliding with the nurse. When the two of them looked back into the room, they could see under the bright light the girl's arms folded over her chest and her body stretched out straight on the bed.

"As a doctor, I am a man of science, but to this day I cannot explain the strange things that happened that evening."

Dr. Abe looked up from the red lampshade and fell silent, gazing at a single point on the table. This was a better story than the last one, but the doctor wasn't able to tell it well. It didn't scare me. I always doubted such ghost stories and couldn't bring myself to believe his tale.

I lit a second cigarette. When I looked up, the young man with the pale face was still staring at me. This time it made me feel quite uncomfortable. I turned away.

"You'll be speaking after the next one. I'll introduce you to everyone then," my uncle whispered to me.

When it was my turn, I told them about what had happened to me in Atami as tersely as I could and then promptly bowed my goodbyes and left the room. I had done what my uncle had asked me to do. I didn't want to spend any more time with this crowd with their endless time to kill. I still had another manuscript to submit the next day.

"Are you off already?"

My uncle had followed me into the corridor to see me out. He didn't look very pleased.

"Yes."

I put my arms into my raincoat, which the waitress was holding for me. I bowed to my uncle in an ill humor.

When I went outside, the misty rain was still falling without sound, almost invisibly. Many cars were passing by along the wide Yotsuya-Mitsuke street, splashing mud and water as they went. I felt I'd wasted too much of the evening at that stupid meeting. I had to get back home quickly and get to work at my desk.

Every taxi that passed was full, as is typical of rainy days, when getting a taxi can be nigh on impossible. A few times I put out my hand to hail one but to no avail. I stood with the collar of my raincoat turned up, getting wet from the rain.

Just then a Datsun taxi stopped in front of me. I could see the silhouette of a passenger moving behind the misted glass. I'd have no luck with this one either. I decided to give up trying for a taxi and started across the road for the train station. But then the window of the Datsun opened, and the passenger peered out. It was the pale young man who had been staring at me from across the room at Hakujian.

"Where are you going?" He had a high-pitched voice like a woman's. "Are you heading home?"

I told him I was going to Seijō on the Odakyū subway line.

"I'm going to Kitami, so let's share this taxi, shall we?"

I forgot all about my discomfort with his previous impolite behavior and nodded a few times in gratitude.

The taxi headed on in the rain, through Gondawara and the Gaien gardens. When I'd first got in, I'd noticed a horrible smell—like a sudden whiff of rusty copper. Human blood has the same kind of smell. I assumed it was the stench of gasoline or machine oil in the humid rain.

"That was some meeting," I said. I didn't know what to talk about with this young man, hence my cryptically cynical comment.

"It was very interesting," he replied. He may have been talking about my story. But as I nodded my thanks I began to wish I wasn't sitting there with him.

"You're welcome. Actually I felt it was a bit silly while telling it."

The rain intensified some. It sounded like the right-side window was being bombarded with pebbles. The driver silently held tight to the steering wheel as we drove through Jingu-Gaien.

I got a whiff of that odor again. It arose whenever the young man shifted his body slightly. Even with his pale complexion, I hadn't expected a young man as well groomed as he, with such fine features, to have a body odor like this.

"Was it your first time with the group?"

"Yes." The young man shifted again. "I know one of the members."

"Yes, well, it was a bit boring, wasn't it? All ghost-story soirees are like that." I felt I needed to explain myself so I added, "It might be scary for the person involved, but the people listening aren't going to feel the same thing."

"Hmm."

There was that rusting copper smell again.

"The story about the inn in Yamagata was a bit silly. I actually yawned during it. But the Institute of Infectious Diseases—that was interesting what the doctor had to say." As he spoke, his pale face stared straight ahead, and his voice was very low. He spoke without intonation or feeling. What was he thinking about as he gazed at the dashboard?

I forgot the train of the conversation. I needed a smoke, so I took out a cigarette and went to light it. "Wait!" the young man suddenly shouted. "Sorry, but I just hate the smell of cigarettes."

After that, the two of us sat in a frosty silence that lasted for some time. It was then that I noticed something odd. Well, I don't know if it was odd, but the fingers of his hands, those white hands that he held so primly on his knees, were extremely long and skinny, like the legs of a long-legged spider, and their hairiness also astonished me. Slender black hairs grew densely between the joints of his white fingers. But then again, when I think back, perhaps it wasn't so strange, as jittery urban types often have hands like that.

The long silence was broken only by the driver turning the wheel and overtaking the other cars. *Driving at that speed in the rain is pretty dangerous*, I mused.

Well, here indeed was a strange young man. Giving me a lift but not talking to me. Detesting me smoking. And his voice with its flat tone devoid of all intonation. And that odor he emitted whenever he moved.

(What was he looking at?)

With both hands on his knees, his pale face looked forward, just staring at something. I looked curiously to see what it was.

It was the rear-view mirror! He had been staring in the rear-view mirror for more than twenty minutes.

"I'm getting fed up with these kinds of meetings." I joylessly repeated what I had been saying in a sorry attempt to spark some conversation.

"It was here."

"What?" I could hardly hear what he said so I shifted closer to him.

"It was here," he repeated in his low, flat voice. "About two months ago. It was evening, and the rain was falling just like tonight."

The taxi went up a narrow road from Kamitōri towards Seijō. We were now in an area of woods and fields with only the odd old farmhouse and not a soul to be found on this country road lashed with rain.

"I was coming through here in a taxi, coming from Shibuya. When we got here there was a woman standing in the middle of the road waving her arms. The driver stopped immediately."

The young man went on recounting how the young woman had tapped on the window and had politely asked if they could give her a lift as far as Seijō. She had been waiting for some time but no car had passed. She was about thirty and wore a wrap under her raincoat and carried a black handbag. She looked like the kind of woman you'd find working in a bar somewhere.

"Did you give her a lift?" He had aroused my curiosity.

"Yes."

"Well, lucky you. Was she pretty?"

"Well, yes. But," he continued staring into the rear mirror speaking in his lifeless voice, "just one half of her."

"One half of her?"

When the woman had gotten into the car, she'd propped her umbrella against the door and had taken off her raincoat carefully so no raindrops would wet the young man's clothes.

The taxi that evening was a Renault. The interior light was turned down to stop the battery going flat. The woman and the young man had started chatting about how hard it was to get a taxi on a rainy night.

"So there we were driving along this road toward Seijō. It was around this time in the evening. Then the car skidded at the corner just up here."

The taxi had suddenly started sliding sideways on the wet road losing its hold for an instant. There was a squeal, and they just avoided going into the fields on the other side. It was then that the woman had grabbed the young man's knees and unwittingly looked up at him.

Her face was covered with red-black blisters down one side. They were like small dots across her forehead and eyelids but much bigger on her cheeks.

"It made me shudder to see them. The light inside the car had been dimmed, so I only saw the side of the face without the blisters when she got in. I took another look at the other side of her face, the side that was all swelled up and red."

The young man was telling all this in his usual rhythm-less drone. I just assumed he was merely trying to tell me some clichéd horror story. I had trashed the Hakujian meeting, so this had made him want to try out his own favorite scary yarn on me. I wanted to laugh.

"The swelling on her face—was it a burn?"

"No, it wasn't that."

"I see. Was it a skin disorder?"

"It was a spider."

"A spider?"

At that moment the young man smiled slowly for the first time. It was a sickening, sneering smile.

"Have you ever heard of the Kusune spider?"

"No."

"It's a spider with long grey legs. It lives in southern China and Taiwan, but sometimes you can find them in the mountain villages of Kyushu. But, I tell you, I never knew it existed in Setagaya in Tokyo."

"So what about this spider?"

"Sometimes," he said in his low voice, still staring into the rearview mirror, "this spider lays eggs in human skin."

At night in Taiwan and southern China when people are asleep, the Kusune spider plops down from the ceiling like a drop of black water. It slowly crawls around your face and hands and feet. When it finds the right place, it sinks its poisonous fangs into your skin. It sucks your blood and then, using the hole it has made in your skin, it inserts a needle growing from its ventral end to deposit eggs underneath your skin. You don't feel any of the itchiness you would with a flea bite, and the hole it makes is tiny, something like what lice would make, so the victim sleeps right through it. Larvae then emerge from the eggs, and, nourished by blood in the victim's skin, they start to grow.

"The woman said she first assumed it was an ordinary skin disease. But none of the hospitals could cure her. Eventually the dermatology department at Tokyo University identified the fang marks of the rare Kusune spider.

I gulped slightly, overcome by a sense of disgust, and said nothing. I felt millions of spider eggs growing under my skin and saw the larva wriggling around, taking constant sips of my blood. Wriggling and growing. Just thinking about it made me shudder.

"Is that a true story?"

"Yes." The hint of a smile appeared on his lips once more. "The woman showed me."

In the car's dim light, the woman apologized for her ugliness and then pressed one of the boils that blotched her blistered face. A small blot of blood lay on her finger, and within it wriggled a spiderling.

"I saw it clearly. With my very own eyes. A young spider with legs still growing, moving around in the drop of blood on the woman's finger."

The car moved on in the darkness. I looked out the right-hand window and tried to erase from my mind the young man's awful story. The powerful smell suddenly assailed my nose again. When I turned around, the young man's face was right at my neck.

"I'm sorry. The car skidded."

The car hadn't skidded. He'd just told me a blatant lie. Why had he done that? When his face had been close to me and I had got that smell, I had felt something weird, like the time I'd felt a cold shiver going down my back. The young man was staring at me with empty eyes.

"I'm getting out here."

"Here? But aren't you going to Kitami?"

"No. I just remembered I have to go see a relative who lives near here."

I had no time to say anything. The car stopped, he bowed his head with impeccable good manners, and then disappeared into the rainy, hazy darkness. I heaved a sigh and wiped a bit of sweat off my forehead. I began puzzling over why he had told me a lie.

"Well," the driver started to speak to me as he turned the steering wheel, "he was bit of a creep, that guy. I saw, just now, through the mirror here, he, eh, he tried to bite your neck. Like he was trying to suck your blood or something."

"Can you turn up the light a minute?"

I felt sick and put my hand on my neck. The driver was turning up the light so I tried to calm down. The light came up, and then I noticed it. It was there where the young man had been sitting.

A long-legged, grey spider scurrying away from the light.

The Talisman

お守り

(Omamori)

Yamakawa Masao (1960)

山川 方夫

Translation by Karen Sandness

"HEY, YOU DON'T need any dynamite, do you?" my friend Sekiguchi blurted out all of a sudden. We were drinking in a small, second-floor restaurant, having retired there after running into each other on the Ginza for the first time in four or five years.

Sekiguchi and I had gone to school together until high school. He was employed at a construction company, so it wouldn't have been all that difficult for him to lay his hands on some dynamite, but that utterance was a bit outlandish even for someone who had always been an oddball.

"Not really," I said. "Even if I got hold of some, I wouldn't have any use for it, would I?"

"I have some with me right now," Sekiguchi said.

That had to be a joke, of course. I laughed and poured some sake into his cup. "Stop trying to scare me. First of all, dynamite explodes pretty easily, right? It's dangerous, right? Why would you be carrying it around?"

That's when Sekiguchi started telling me his story.

These days I live in an apartment in a housing project with my wife. We applied for it the year before last, got married last spring because we couldn't wait, and were finally selected for an apartment in the fall. We felt as if we'd died and gone to heaven.

There was a lawn of newly laid sod, scraggly cherry trees that looked as if they'd just been planted—everything looked fresh, and we felt that this was the perfect atmosphere for newlyweds. Anyway, till then we'd been living at my dad's house, in a single six-mat room in a large, traditional Japanese-style family home, so you can imagine how we longed for a place where we could shut ourselves off from other people's view and other people's noise and have a room that we could lock. In that sense, we certainly fulfilled our dream.

But about six months after we'd settled into our brand-new apartment, I began to feel a strange edginess or anxiety, a vague fear that I couldn't pin down, as if I couldn't find myself. It wasn't anyone's fault, maybe just some sort of neurosis. It's not as if that guy did anything particularly wrong. Still, I'm sure that that guy Kurose triggered my current situation.

It happened one evening when I came home late from a banquet. The buses had stopped running, and I took a taxi as far as the entrance to the housing complex. I strolled over to my building, enjoying the nighttime breeze, trying to sober up a little.

Then, to my surprise, I noticed a man walking in front of me. From the back, he looked exactly like me. He wore the same kind of felt hat, was dangling a lunch box from his left hand, and walked with a stagger, as if drunk. With the thick fog that evening, I felt as if I were looking at my own shadow.

But he was no shadow. He was walking unsteadily in front of me. "Wow, he sure looks like me," I thought, and that's what prompted me to follow him. Then I saw that he lived in Building E, just like me. He headed up the same stairs in Building E that I always took. Even in a housing complex or apartment building, I ought to have recognized the faces of the people who went up and down the same staircase as I. But I didn't know that man at all. I thought it was odd, but the man continued up the stairs as if he was accustomed to doing so. He stopped on the third floor and knocked on the door in the right alcove.

I stopped in my tracks. That door was the door to my apartment. But there were more surprises in store. The door opened, and he disappeared into the apartment, like any weary husband arriving home.

For a moment, I wondered if the man was my wife's lover. It made sense. Intending to catch them in the act, I tiptoed up the stairs. Standing in front of the entrance, I inclined my ear to the door and listened.

Then I got a strange sense—well, I really don't know how to make you understand this, but I realized that I was wrong. He wasn't my wife's lover. What I mean is, he was me.

Don't worry. I'm not crazy or anything like that. But at that moment, I certainly felt as if I had gone mad. Inside the apartment, my wife was calling my name, just as she always did: "Jirō! Jirō!" She was laughing as she talked about my sister, who had dropped in to visit that day, and somehow, my own weary voice was mumbling comments at appropriate points. Evidently, she was in the kitchen, just like always, preparing a light supper, while "I" seemed to be picking up an evening paper. I was dumbfounded. At any rate, there was actually another "me." If that was the case, who the hell was this "me" who was standing there staring like an idiot? Which of us was the real "me"? If that other fellow was the real "me," where was MY home?

I was pretty sure that I had already sobered up, but thinking back, I may still have been a bit drunk. I seemed to have lost the conviction that I was the real "me." I no longer had any confidence that the man in the room was a fake "me" or that there had been some sort of mistake. The only reason that I opened the door was that I simply didn't know where else this "I" should go.

"Who is it?" my wife said. I was caught short and had no idea what to say. I entered the room hesitantly and said, "It's me."

You should have seen what happened next. My wife came running out and screamed, took a terrified look at the man behind her and cried out again. She threw her arms around me, moving her lips soundlessly, and then burst into tears. The other "me" peeked out from inside the apartment, his face red with embarrassment.

His name was Kurose Jirō. Ever since then, I've been afraid of the sight of his face and the sound of his name.

Sekiguchi's face assumed a thoughtful expression. He picked up the sake flask and filled his own cup.

"Another 'you,' huh?" I laughed. "What an amazing doppelgänger." I glanced up at him, but he didn't respond. Without cracking a smile, he continued his story.

Kurose apologized profusely, explaining that I lived in E305 and he lived in D305. I saw what had happened when he handed me his business card. He had mistaken my building for his and gone up into my apartment. My sister's name is Kuniko. But Kurose, a civil engineer, has a cousin named Kuniko. My name is Jirō, and so is his, although written with different kanji. He and his wife live alone. Sure, I can tell myself that it's all a coincidence, but our situations certainly are similar.

As he left, Kurose said to my wife, "You know, I thought you were acting awfully girlish today, because, after all, my wife and I have been married for four years." He acted as if this was a compliment, but I couldn't even pretend to be pleased about it. The fact that my wife and that man hadn't noticed their mistake until I opened the door deeply disturbed me.

"But I went straight to the kitchen after I opened the door," my wife explained. "That man immediately lay down and started reading the paper, so it never occurred to me that he might not be you."

When I scolded my wife, she glanced nervously around the room and added, "It's certainly not just the apartment. They're a couple exactly like us. He completely mistook me for his wife. It kind of scares me."

I thought about saying something, but I didn't. It wouldn't have been a big deal if it had been an ordinary case of mistaken identity or accidentally going to the wrong apartment. That happens all the time. What made me uneasy was that Kurose had mistaken our life for his own.

My beloved wife had gone and mistaken Kurose for me. Did all of us husbands look so much alike as we came home to the housing complex after work?

I understood that we all live in apartments built according to identical standards, because it is, after all, a housing complex. But a thought occurred to me. What if our lives had become standardized without our realizing it?

Do you know anything about living in a housing complex? It's very conformist. The people in a housing complex all live pretty much the same kinds of lives, in terms of their qualifications or their needs, and they're about the same age, too. But it goes beyond those external traits. The conformity somehow extends to the core of their being. At least that's how it seems to me.

For example, suppose my wife and I are having a fight. When that happens, I can distinctly hear the sound of another couple having the same type of quarrel floating in through the window from somewhere else in the complex. This seems so absurd that we stop fighting. Aside from that effect, realizing that the people living here usually quarreled on a certain day at a certain time and that we were no exception, made our fights seem less significant. They were nothing more than a hysterical manifestation that came upon us periodically. Just think of it. It's really weird.

You go to the toilet, and then you hear someone flushing at exactly the same spot in the room directly above you. This kind of synchronicity happened day after day... The kind of coincidences that I had never given much thought to before gradually came to bother me quite a bit.

I began to wonder if our identical environments and identical daily routines would lead us to developing identical physiologies and identical emotions. If that were true, then we'd be just like countless toy soldiers displayed in the toy department of a department store, just like an endless array of standardized marionettes.

I wondered if there was anything that was just mine, something that no one else had, something that was really my possession, a domain of my very own, and if so, where it was. Wouldn't I become unable to distinguish myself from anyone else, just like a single bean in a pile of beans that are being mashed into paste?

What really set me off was something my wife said. One night, after a little foreplay, she said, "It's strange. You know, every time I go to the bathroom, without fail, I hear the sound of a toilet above and below me. We're all the same, aren't we?"

The moment she said that, I drew my hands away from her. I could just imagine it. All of us husbands in the housing complex assuming the same position and initiating the same actions at night as if responding to a silent command . . .

From then on, I lost interest in that sort of thing, too. When I heard my wife cry out, I felt as if I could hear all the wives of the housing complex crying out simultaneously in a grand chorus in the dark. I found myself unconsciously grimacing. Ugh, what conformity!

Anyway, even though we believed that we had something no one else had, it seemed that each of us was a standardized person exhibiting standardized reactions to our standardized lives. Weren't we just deluded in thinking that we had something of our own when each of us actually conformed to some kind of invisible discipline and was manipulated into leading our everyday lives?

I couldn't stand it. I wasn't a doll. I wasn't a puppet. How could I value my own life unless I had the confidence that I was myself and no one else? Could I love my wife? Could I believe that I was loved by my wife?

I flashed a grin at Sekiguchi and then stopped. He was staring at me with absolute seriousness.

Finally, a faint smile appeared briefly on his face.

Come to think of it, it had always been difficult to make Sekiguchi smile.

"I'm completely serious," he said.

You know, for me, Kurose seemed like a representative of all the countless husbands in the housing complex, the toy soldiers, the countless middle managers who were like me. He represented all the other "me's."

As you can maybe imagine, after that foggy evening, I didn't want to speak to that guy. The way we resembled each other irritated me, and even he seemed to be always clutching his briefcase to his chest and avoiding my gaze. He walked as if he was trying to sneak away. Of course, we never exchanged pleasantries.

There's no doubt that he made me hate all of us who were nothing but toy solders, all of us who had become standardized. I kept trying to repudiate all the countless, standardized "me's."

I hated him. I wasn't him. I wasn't just "one of those middle managers who looks like me." I wasn't one of many "me's." I was ME, and I most certainly wasn't HIM.

And yet, how were we different? Where was the clear proof that we were different?

I kept telling myself, "I'm not just some arbitrary item. I'm me, a specific person named Sekiguchi Jirō, an individual, irreplaceable person.

But what was the basis for distinguishing me from anyone else? Did we differ only in our names? A name is just a code word. What proof was there that we weren't they, that we weren't some random so-and-so in the housing complex?

I had to make something. I needed to. In other words, I thought that I had to get hold of something that clearly distinguished me from all those countless Kurose Jirō-types in the housing complex. I had to gain a firm grasp of what there was about me that wasn't true of anyone else, or, to put it another way, it may have been a matter of taking myself back and regaining my mental stability.

Then finally, about ten days ago, I finally got hold of a certain talisman, Of course, I kept it secret from my wife, because after all, this was strictly my problem. The talisman I found was this. . . .

Sekiguchi reached for the thick leather bag that he had placed behind him and took out something that was wrapped in oil paper, tied tightly with a thin string, and the right thickness to be grasped in one hand.

"It's dynamite. The real thing. . . ."

He untied the string with nimble fingers to give me my first look at real dynamite—four steel tubes, twenty centimeters in length, bound tightly with wire. When I took them in my hand, they seemed rather heavy.

"This is my talisman!" Sekiguchi said. "No matter what people might say, they'll probably never step outside their standardized lives. But I, I could blow you away at any time if I felt like it. In pondering the fact that I possessed this secret power, I realized that I had finally found something to support me. In other words, this is my uniqueness."

"Wow."

Sekiguchi looked fondly at the dark, slightly shiny, thin cylinders, almost as if he were caressing them.

"But I don't want it," I said. "I really don't."

"Oh? That's too bad. I don't want it anymore either. I need to look for some other talisman."

"That's for sure. Even assuming that you've been straight with me, something so dangerous. . . ."

Sekiguchi held up his hand to silence me. "Don't misunderstand me. You're really lucky." He smiled. "The reason I don't want it anymore is that I may no longer be able to say that it's something unique about me." He paused briefly and continued. "Did you listen to the radio this evening?

"No," I replied.

A smile that was more a grimace spread across Sekiguchi's face. "Well, this evening, some dynamite suddenly exploded inside a bus. Three passengers were killed instantly. The rest survived but with severe injuries or burns. It happened right near my housing complex."

"What do you mean?" I immediately sobered up.

Carefully returning the oil paper package to his briefcase, Sekiguchi averted his eyes as he answered, "Well, you see, it's clear that the other guy always walked around carefully clutching his briefcase to his chest. He was avoiding me. I suppose he hated me, too. He needed a talisman, too."

"What are you talking about?" I asked.

Sekiguchi rolled over onto the tatami mat and, in a voice that sounded like a distant sigh, explained, "Well, according to the radio report, an investigation showed that the dynamite was in the briefcase of one of the passengers who was killed instantly, a civil engineer named Kurose Jirō."

The Arm

片腕

(Kataude)

Kawabata Yasunari (1963)

川端康成

Translation by Mark Gibeau

"I WILL LEND you the arm for one night." She removed her right arm at the shoulder and, using her left hand, placed it on my lap.

"Thank you," I said, looking down at my knees. Her arm felt warm against my legs.

"Oh, and let me put this ring on too," she said. "It will be a sign—to show that it's mine." Smiling, she held out her left hand. "Would you?" It was difficult for her to remove the ring herself, now that she only had her left arm.

"Isn't this an engagement ring?"

"No, it belonged to my mother. I wear it as a keepsake." The platinum ring was set with several small diamonds.

"I suppose it does look like an engagement ring but I don't care. I wear it anyway," she said. "Ever since I started wearing it, I feel lonely when I take it off. It's as though I'm leaving my mother."

I pulled the ring free and, standing the arm on my knees, pushed it onto the ring finger of her right hand. "Is this finger OK?" I asked.

"Yes," she nodded. "Oh, I nearly forgot. Why go through all the trouble of taking the arm if the elbow and fingers don't move? That would be no better than having a wooden arm. Here, I'll make it move." Taking the arm from my hands she brushed her lips gently against the elbow and each of the joints of her fingers.

"Now it will move."

"Thank you." I took the arm back from her. "Does the arm talk? Will it speak to me?"

"The arm is only an arm. I would be frightened if it started speaking after you returned it! Yet, you may try. . . . At the very least it may listen to you, if you are gentle with it."

"I will be gentle."

"Go on then." She brushed her right arm with the fingers of her left, as though imbuing it with a bit of her soul. "You belong to this gentleman now. But only for one night." She looked up at me and seemed to be struggling to hold back tears.

"Once you get it home you might want to try putting my right arm on in place of your own. . . . You may, if you like."

"Oh. Thank you."

I concealed her right arm beneath my raincoat and walked out into the fog-drenched city night. I thought it would be too risky to take a streetcar or a taxi. If the arm, separated from her body, suddenly started to cry or called out it would cause a commotion. I grasped the round base of her arm in my right hand and leaned it against the left side of my chest. Though the arm was hidden, I couldn't help pressing my left hand against the raincoat every few minutes to feel it underneath. I suppose this was less to ensure that the arm was safe than it was to affirm that my joy was real.

She had removed her arm at my favorite spot, at the full, soft roundness where the base of the arm met the end of the shoulder. It had the soft curve of a slender, beautiful Western woman—rare among Japanese. Yet she possessed it. It shone with a faint, innocent light, like a globe. It was a pure, elegant curve. When a woman loses her innocence this delicate purity clouds, the shape weakens and grows flaccid. Even in the prettiest of girls, this exquisite roundness lingers only briefly. Yet she possessed it.

The alluring curve of the shoulder conveyed all the delightful charm of her body. Like the swell of her small breasts, just enough to fill the palm of my hand, with a firmness, a softness that beckons me to suckle shyly. Gazing at the curve of her shoulder I imagined her legs as she walked. She lifted her legs as though they were the slender limbs of a small bird, or a butterfly, flitting from blossom to blossom. She was filled with a delicate melody that reached even to the very tip of her tongue as she kissed.

It was the season for sleeveless blouses and her shoulders had only just made their debut. The color of her skin showed that her shoulders were unaccustomed to direct exposure to elements. Their paleness retained the luster of a bud concealed in the spring damp, not yet ravaged by the harsh summer heat. I bought a magnolia bud at the florist that morning and placed it in a glass vase. The curve of her shoulder reminded me of the large, white bud.

Her blouse revealed just the right amount of her shoulder. It was not sleeveless, but rather the fabric was sewn in such a way that it seemed to be pulled back, to bunch up around the base of her neck. Her shoulder seemed to glow faintly against the deep blue of the blouse, a blue so dark as to be nearly black. Women with rounded shoulders often have a curve in their backs. The slight bend of her back, together with her round, sloping shoulders brought to mind the image of a gentle, rippling wave. Standing behind her at a slight angle, I saw the line of soft skin running across her shoulders and up her long, slender neck. This line was broken only by the black of her hair, tied up at the nape of her neck, a glittering shadow against which the curve of her shoulders glowed softly.

She had removed the arm at this soft roundness of the shoulder. No doubt she had guessed my thoughts when she lent me the arm.

I cradled the arm protectively in my raincoat. It was slightly cold to the touch. My heart raced, and I knew the excitement was making my hands grow warm, yet I hoped the heat would not spread to her arm. I wanted it to remain precisely as it was, to retain its placid cool. The faint chill of the arm in my hands made me even more aware of its fragile beauty—like breast of a maiden, unsullied by the touch of man.

The night mist grew thicker still, and it seemed that it must soon turn to rain. As I was wearing no hat, my hair grew damp. A radio could be heard from behind the door of the pharmacy. The voice reported that three passenger planes were unable to land because of the fog and had been circling the airport for thirty minutes. The voice continued, urging families to be alert. On nights like this, clocks will lose time on account of the damp, it said. On nights like this, winding clocks too tightly the damp will cause the springs to grow brittle, the voice said. I looked up into the sky, wondering if I would be able to make out the lights of the circling planes, but I couldn't see them. There was no sky. The dripping fog even crawled inside my ears, making a wet sound like hundreds of worms slithering off into the distance.

Wondering if there would be any more warnings I stopped in front of the pharmacy door. Announcing that lions, tigers, leopards and other wild beasts in the zoo were howling in frustration at the mist they switched to a live broadcast from the zoo. The sound of animal cries rumbled from behind the door, like the trembling of the earth. The radio said that pregnant women and the melancholy would do well to rest quietly on nights like this. On nights like this, the radio said, ladies should avoid spraying perfume directly onto their bare skin as the scent will soak in and will be impossible to remove.

I resumed walking at the sound of the roaring animals, but the warning about the perfume pursued me into the night. The sound of the beasts had scared me. Afraid that the arm might become infected with my fear, I walked quickly from the sound of the radio. I thought of her, left with only one arm after lending me her other, on this night. Though she was neither pregnant nor melancholy I thought it would be best if she too did as the radio suggested and rested quietly in bed.

When crossing the street I held my left hand pressed against my raincoat, over the arm. I heard the sound of a car horn. Something twisted against my ribs, and I gave a start. Frightened by the noise, the fingers of the arm had grabbed my side.

"Don't be afraid," I said. "The car is far away. It's only using its horn because it's difficult to see in this fog."

Cradling the precious arm, I looked carefully up and down each street several times before crossing. I didn't really think the horn was directed at me, but as I looked in the direction of the car, I couldn't see anyone else. Only the headlights of the car were visible, a blurry, diffuse light, tinged a light purple. It was a very strange color for headlights, and after I crossed the road, I stopped to watch the car pass. A young woman in a vermillion dress was driving. She turned to me and appeared to dip her head in a slight bow. My first instinct was to turn and flee, thinking it was her, coming to take the arm back. Then I realized that she wouldn't be able to drive a car with only her left arm. I wondered if the woman driving the car hadn't seen through me. Could she know that I was carrying the arm? Perhaps there was a bond between the arm and other women. I resolved to avoid other women as I made my way back to my apartment. The rear lamps on the woman's car were also tinged a faint shade of purple. The car itself remained invisible. Shrouded by the grey mist, the faint lamps emitted a pale purple glow as they floated off into the distance.

"Perhaps she's just out for a drive. Driving just for the sake of driving, unable to stop. Maybe she will just keep driving until she disappears entirely," I muttered. "I wonder what's in the back seat of the car. . . ."

There didn't seem to be anything in the back seat. That seemed strangely ominous and I wondered if it was the arm that was making me feel so uneasy. The woman's car must also be carrying the night's damp mist. Something about the woman made the fog, pierced by the car's light, turn a faint shade of purple. If the woman's body was not the source of the purple light what else could it be? There was something sad and empty about a woman driving alone on a night like this. Or maybe it was because of the arm that I felt this way. Had the woman nodded in greeting to the arm? Perhaps, on nights like this, the angels and fairies roamed, watching over women and keeping them safe. Perhaps she hadn't been driving a car at all but rather riding on a cloud of purple light. That was hardly sad and empty. She had seen into my secret and departed.

I made it back to my apartment building without encountering anyone else. I stopped at the entrance, listening for any sounds from within. A firefly flew over my head and vanished. Realizing that the flash had been far too big and far too bright for a firefly, I quickly jumped back four or five paces. Again I saw two or three more quick flashes of light like those of a firefly. They vanished even before they could be swallowed by the mist. Had some spirit or will-o'-the-wisp raced back to my apartment before me? Did it now lie in wait for me? However, I soon saw that it was simply a small cloud of moths, hovering near the lamp. Their wings reflected the light over the door, flashing like fireflies. They were larger than fireflies but small for moths—small enough to be mistaken for fireflies.

I shunned the elevator, instead silently climbing the narrow flights of stairs to the third floor. My right hand remained concealed beneath the raincoat and, not being left-handed, I struggled with the lock. My fingers trembled in my excitement, not unlike nervous thrill of one about to commit a crime, I thought. I sensed a presence in my room. It was just my room, as solitary as ever. Yet, perhaps this solitude meant something was there. After all, tonight, for the first time, I was not alone. I had brought her arm home with me. It must be my own, accumulated solitude that filled the room, intimidating me.

At last I managed to get the door open. "After you," I said, removing the arm from under my raincoat. "Welcome. This is my home. I'll turn on the lights."

"Has something frightened you?" the arm seemed to ask. "Is someone there?"

"What? You think someone is here?"

"There is an odor."

"An odor? It's probably my scent. Look at that! Isn't that my shadow—large and faint in the darkness? Perhaps my shadow was awaiting my return."

"It is a sweet scent."

"Ah, that's the magnolia," I said brightly, relieved that it wasn't the musty, unclean odor of my solitude. It was fortunate that I had set out the magnolia today, the day I was receiving such a lovely visitor. My eyes adjusted to the darkness and, thanks to my familiarity with the room, I was able to make out where things were in the dark.

"Please, let me turn on the light," the arm said unexpectedly. "After all, I've never visited your apartment before."

"Please do. That would be nice. It will be the first time that anyone other than myself has switched the light on in this room."

I held her arm up so the tips of her fingers could reach the switch beside the door. All five lights in the apartment—on the ceiling, atop the table, next to the bed, in the kitchen, by the washroom—came on simultaneously. I wondered if my apartment had always been this bright. I looked around as though seeing it for the first time.

In the glass vase the petals of the magnolia had opened wide into a large flower. It had only been a bud that morning. Though it had only just opened, petals were strewn across the top of the table. Fascinated, I found myself gazing at the fallen petals more than the white flower itself. I picked up a couple of petals, and, as I looked at them, the arm on the table began extending and contracting its fingers, moving around the table like an inchworm, gathering up the fallen petals. I took the petals from the palm of the hand and threw them in the dustbin.

"The fragrance of the flower so strong. It stings my skin. Help me . . ." the arm cried out.

"Ah, I'm afraid you had a very difficult journey. You must be exhausted. Please rest a while," I said, laying the arm on the bed and sitting down next to it. I stroked the arm gently.

"How wonderful. It's so pretty." I supposed the arm was referring to the quilt—a three-colored floral pattern set against a sky blue background. It was perhaps a bit too colorful for a solitary bachelor.

"So this is where I will be sleeping tonight. I won't make a sound."

"Really?"

"I'll crawl right up next to you, but I'll be so quiet you won't even know I'm there." The arm squeezed my hand gently. I looked down at the fingernails, colored a pale China pink, glittering prettily. The nails extended beyond the tip of the fingers.

Next to my thick, squat nails, these fingernails seemed strangely alluring. They were almost too beautiful to belong to a mere human being. Could it be that the tips of these fingers were her attempt to transcend the human? Or were they a pursuit of the essence of the feminine? Old, hackneyed metaphors comparing fingernails to "the iridescence of a seashell" or "the luster of a fluttering flower petal" came to mind. Yet these nails resembled no flower or shell I could recall. The nails at the tips of her fingers were the nails at the tips of her fingers and nothing else. They were more translucent than any delicate seashell or any tiny, fragile flower petal. Most of all they made me think of tragic dew. They were the nails of a woman who labors tirelessly, through the day and the night, refining her tragic beauty. They pierced my solitude and droplets of this solitude fell from her fingertips. Transformed, perhaps, into tragic dew.

I placed her little finger on the index finger of my free hand. Gazing down at it, I gently stroked the long, slender nail with my thumb. I brushed the flesh concealed beneath the peak of the fingernail. Her finger gave a slight jump and pulled back.

"Did it tickle?" I asked the arm. "It's a bit ticklish, isn't it?"

The words slipped carelessly from my mouth. With that one remark I told the arm that I knew women with long nails were ticklish at their fingertips. In short, I let the arm know that I was very well acquainted with women—with other women.

It was one of these women, older than the one who lent me her arm, who told me that fingertips were ticklish. Well, not just "older" but more accustomed to being with men. She said that women with long fingernails were used to picking things up with their nails. Since they rarely touched anything with their fingertips even a light touch would tickle them.

"Is that so?" I had said, surprised at the unexpected discovery.

"Even if I'm just cooking or eating," she had continued, "if something touches the tips of my fingers—I can't help it. It feels dirty somehow and a shudder runs through my whole body. I know it sounds funny, but it's true."

I wondered whether it was the food or her fingertips that became dirty at the touch. I suppose sensation of anything touching her fingertips made her shiver at the defilement. Sheltering behind her long fingernails, a single droplet of pure tragic dew lingered at the tip of her finger.

Naturally, at the time I wanted to reach out and touch the tips of her fingers. The lure was strong but that alone I did not do. My solitude would not allow it. She was inured to the touch of a man. She the sort of woman who could be touched almost anywhere without feeling the slightest bit ticklish.

I imagined that she who had lent me the arm would be ticklish all over. I wouldn't need to feel guilty with her. Tickling her fingers might even be an act of playful affection. But she hadn't lent me her arm as a plaything. I mustn't allow the tragic to become comic.

"The window is open," I said, suddenly noticing. The window itself was closed, but the curtains were open.

"Will something spy on us?" The arm asked.

"If anything will spy, it will be a person."

"Even if someone peeks in they won't be able to see me. If anyone spies on me, it would be none other than you yourself."

"Myself . . . ? What is my self? Where is it?"

"Your self is far away." The arm spoke in a soothing, almost singsong voice. "It is in search of their distant selves that people walk."

"Will I ever find it?"

"It is very far away," the arm repeated.

I suddenly felt as though an immeasurable distance separated the arm and its she who had lent it to me. Would the arm ever manage to find its way back to that remote body? Would I be able overcome the vast distance and return the arm to her? Is she resting peacefully now, her trust in me as tranquil as that of the arm? Did she feel odd without her right arm? Were her dreams filled with ill omens? Hadn't she struggled to hold back her tears when parting with the arm? The arm had been brought to my apartment, but she had never visited here.

The window was wet and cloudy with the damp. The film of moisture was like the skin of a toad's stomach stretched thin across the surface of the glass. The mist looked like a fine rain frozen in midair; all sense of perspective vanishing from the night beyond the window, enshrouded in a limitless distance. The roofs of the houses vanished, the car horns silent.

"I'll close the window," I said, moving to pull the curtains shut. The curtains were also damp. My face stared back at me from the glass of the window. Did I look younger than usual? However, I did not stop my hand from pulling the curtain closed. My face vanished.

I suddenly recalled a scene I had once witnessed. It was a window on the ninth floor of a certain hotel. Two young girls, dressed in red skirts, had climbed onto a window seat and were playing. As they looked alike and were dressed in identical clothes I supposed that they were probably twins. They were Westerners. They were pounding on the glass with their tiny fists, banging against it with their shoulders, pushing and shoving one another. I could see that their mother was knitting, her back to the window. If that large, single pane of glass should break or give way the two girls would plunge nine stories to their deaths. I was the only one aware of their peril; the girls and their mother were oblivious to the danger. The thick glass of the window was strong. There had been no danger.

I pulled the curtain shut and turned around. "They're very pretty," the arm said. The curtains were of the same fabric and design as the quilt.

"You really think so? They've grown a bit faded from the sun. They're falling apart, really." I sat on the bed and placed the arm on my lap. "Now *this* is true beauty. There's nothing so beautiful in all the world."

I placed the palm of my right hand in hers and grasped the base of the arm with my left hand. Very slowly I bent the arm at the elbow and then extended it again, so it was perfectly straight. I repeated the movement.

"Now you're being mischievous," the arm said kindly, as though there was a smile in her voice. "Are you having fun? All this bending and straightening?

"Me? Mischievous? This has got nothing to do with fun." This time the arm truly did smile. The smile fluttered, a flash of light across the skin. It looked exactly like her glowing, smiling cheeks.

I knew because I had seen her smile before. Both her elbows had been planted on the table, the fingers of one hand placed lightly on top of the other hand, her chin, or maybe her cheek, resting on her hands. I suppose it wasn't a very elegant pose for a young woman. At the same time the words "plant," "place," and "rest" aren't really appropriate. They fail to convey the delicate tenderness of the pose. The roundness of her shoulders, the fingers on her hand, her chin, her cheek, her ear, her long slender neck, even her hair—they all became one. They were an elegant harmony. Completely absorbed in her meal, she sometimes lifted her still-bent pinky and index finger the merest fraction of an inch from her deftly manipulated knife and fork. With her, the placing of food between her small lips, chewing, swallowing—these did not seem like the acts of a human being eating. Hand, face and throat were engaged in the performance of a delightful song. Her smile had flashed even across the skin of her arm.

As I bent and straightened the elbow the thin fibers of the muscles grew taut, delicate waves breathing beneath the surface. It was this effect, along with the intricate play of light and shadow, shifting and flowing across the smooth, white skin that made the arm appear to smile. I had seen it earlier, when I brushed the hidden tips of her fingers and the arm started with a jerk, bending at the elbow. The light flashed from the arm, striking my eyes. That's why I was bending her arm now. It certainly wasn't just to be mischievous. I unbent the arm and placed it on my lap. Gazing down at the now motionless arm I could still see the vibrant play of light and shadow upon it.

"Since you mention mischief and fun, did you know that I received permission to put you on? To swap you with my right arm?"

"I know," her right arm replied.

"But even so, I'm not really being mischievous. I . . . For some reason I'm afraid."

"Is that so?"

"May I really do it? Put you on?

"You may."

I paused. Something in the arm's voice struck me. "Say it again. . . . Say 'you may' one more time."

"You may. You may."

I remembered. It was her voice, almost—the voice of a woman who had resolved to give herself to me. She hadn't been as beautiful as the one who had lent me her arm. Perhaps there had been an odd, strained note to it as well.

"You may," she had said, staring up at me, her eyes unblinking. I brushed her eyelids gently, trying to close them. Her voice trembled when she spoke.

"*Jesus wept. Then said the Jews, 'Behold how he loved her.'*"

I paused. That was wrong. "Her" should have been "him"—the dead Lazarus. Had she learned it wrong or had she deliberately replaced "him" with "her"?

Her sudden, strange pronouncement, so inappropriate to the situation, took me aback. I held my breath as I gazed down at her, half expecting to see tears trickle from behind her closed lids. She started to rise. I shoved her back down.

"Ouch!" She said, holding one hand to the back of her head. "That hurt."

There was a tiny bloodstain on the white pillow. I pushed her hair aside, searching. A single droplet of blood welled from her skin. I placed my mouth over it.

"I'm fine. I bleed at the smallest thing." She took her hairpins out. One of them had pricked her scalp. Her shoulders seemed almost to tremble, but she suppressed it.

While I understand the feelings of a woman who gives herself to another, there is also something about it that I cannot comprehend. I cannot help but wonder what a woman thinks. What does it mean for her to give herself away? Why would she want this? Why would she seek it? Even with the knowledge that women's bodies are all made in this way I cannot bring myself to believe it. Old as I am, it remains a mystery to me. What is more, a woman's body, the desire to give herself away—one could argue that it is different for each and every person. On the other hand, one could also say it is similar for each person or even that it is identical for everyone. What a mystery it all is. Perhaps I only marvel at it because I am consumed by a longing far too immature for my age. Perhaps it is due to disappointments beyond my years. Could it be a defect or lameness in my soul?

In this case, her suffering was not the suffering all women experience when they give themselves away. With her it was just this one time. The silver cord is severed, the golden bowl broken.

"You may," the arm had said. That's what brought back all the memories. Yet did her voice and the arm's voice truly resemble one another? Perhaps they just sounded similar because they had used the same words. Even though the arm had spoken the same words, since it had been separated from its body, didn't that mean the arm had greater freedom than the other woman? As the arm had truly been given away wasn't it completely liberated from self-restraint, responsibility and regret? It could do anything. Yet, what if I did as she said and swapped her arm for mine? I couldn't help thinking that she would be assailed by an uncanny sense of oppression or distress.

I continued to gaze down at the arm upon my lap. There was a dim shadow of light on the inside of the elbow. I thought I might be able to drink it up. I bent the arm very slightly, pooling the shadow of light and, lifting her arm I pressed it to my lips, sipping.

"That tickles! You're being naughty again." The arm clasped my neck, as though trying to escape my lips.

"And I was having such a nice drink, too. . . ." I said.

"What did you drink?"

I remained silent.

"What did you drink?"

"The scent of light, maybe. From your skin."

The mist outside grew thicker still, and the damp seemed to have penetrated even to the leaves of the magnolia. I wondered what the radio was saying. I stood and started toward the portable radio sitting on the table but then changed my mind. It would be too much, listening to the radio with the arm about my neck like this. Instead, I imagined what the radio would be saying. *The pernicious damp is not only causing tree branches to get wet, it has soaked the wings and legs of small birds. These birds are liable to slip and fall from trees and are unable to fly. When driving through parks please be careful to avoid hitting any small birds. If a warm wind blows, the mist may change color. Colored mists are poisonous. If the mist turns purple or peach-colored please avoid going outside and fasten all doors securely.*

I held the curtain between my thumb and forefinger and peered outside. "Will it turn purple or peach?" I muttered to myself. The fog seemed to press in against the window, pushing with an immense, hollow weight. Another, thinner darkness seemed to be swirling about in the darkness of the night. Perhaps the wind had begun to stir. It was as though something terrible seethed beyond the infinite distance of the fog.

I suddenly recalled the woman in the vermillion dress, driving past me as I carried the arm home, floating in the mist, a faint purple glow in front and behind. It had been a purple mist. I suddenly felt as though a massive purple eye was bearing down upon me from out of the mist. Panicked, I let the curtain drop.

"Shall we sleep? Perhaps we should sleep too."

It seemed that in all the world not a soul remained awake. It was terrifying to be awake on a night like this.

I took the arm from my neck and placed it on the table so I could change into my new nightclothes, a light cotton *yukata.* The arm watched me closely as I changed. I felt myself blush under its gaze. Never before had a woman watched me undress in this room.

I picked up the arm and climbed into bed. Turning to face the arm, I clutched it to my chest, gently gripping its fingers. The arm lay perfectly still.

I could just make out a scattered sound, like drizzling rain. The fog hadn't turned to rain—it was fainter than that. Rather, it seemed that the mist had coalesced into tiny, falling droplets.

Though I knew the arm would grow warmer as it lay beneath the covers, my hand on its fingers, I was warmer still. For some reason this filled me with a profound sense of peace.

"Are you asleep?"

"No," the arm replied.

"You were so still. I thought you must be asleep."

I opened the front of my *yukata* and pressed the arm against my chest. I felt my chest sting slightly at the difference in temperature. On a night like this, where the muggy heat seemed to conceal a biting cold in its depths, the touch of the arm felt good against the skin of my chest.

The lights in the room were still burning. I had forgotten to turn them off when I got into bed.

"That's right, the lights . . ." I got up, and her arm slid from my chest.

"Oh," I picked up the arm. "Would you turn the lights off for me?"

"Do you sleep in the dark," I asked, walking to the door, "or with the lights on?"

The arm didn't respond.

The arm must know. Why didn't it respond? I didn't know her sleeping habits. I imagined her sleeping with the lights on. Then I imagined her sleeping in the dark. She would probably sleep with the lights on tonight, the night she lost her right arm. Suddenly I too thought it would be a great pity to turn out the lights. I wanted to gaze at the arm longer. I wanted to stay awake while the arm slept, but the fingers of the arm stretched out to grasp the switch by the door.

Feeling my way through the darkness, I returned to the bed and lay down, cradling the arm against my chest to sleep. I lay very still and waited silently for the arm to fall asleep. Perhaps the arm thought I was being inattentive, or perhaps it was afraid of the dark. The palm, pressed against the side of my chest, lifted itself up and, walking on its fingers, climbed on top of my chest. Bending at the elbow, the arm wrapped itself about my chest, as though in an embrace.

A sweet pulse ran through the arm. The wrist sat just above my heart, the arm's pulsing and the beating of my heart echoing one another. The arm's pulse was slower at first, but soon the two beats matched one another perfectly. I could only feel my own heart pounding. Whether one had sped up or the other had slowed down, I couldn't tell.

Was this the moment? Perhaps I had been allowed this brief moment, when the pulsing of her wrist and the beating of my heart were in perfect harmony, precisely so that I could take her right arm and switch it with my own. No, it might just be a sign that the arm had fallen asleep. I once heard a woman say that true joy was not to be found in wild, drunken ecstasy, but rather in the comfort and peace of sleeping beside her lover. No woman had ever slept beside me as peacefully as the arm did now.

The pulsing wrist on my chest made me acutely aware of the beating of my own heart. In the time between each beat something seemed to race across an immeasurable distance at terrible speed, only to return again. As I listened to the pounding of my heart the distance seemed to grow greater and greater still. No matter how far it went, though it were to go even to the infinite reaches of space, there was nothing at its destination. It did not simply reach something and then return. Rather, the next pulsing beat called it back. I should have been frightened, but there was no fear. Still, I searched for the light switch near the head of my bed.

However, I rolled the covers back gently before turning on the light. Oblivious, the arm slept on. A pale glimmer of white light encircled my naked chest. The soft light glittered faintly in the darkness, like the warm rays of a tiny sun in the moments before it crested my chest.

I turned on the light. Taking the arm from my chest, I placed one hand at the base of the arm and held its fingers with the other and straightened it. In the dim glow of the ten-watt bulb the shadows of light and the curves of the arm appeared to grow softer. I gazed down at the arm, following the flickering play of light and shadow as I turned it this way and that, examining it from end to end. The supple roundness of the base of the arm tapered until it reached soft flesh of the upper arm only to narrow again at the delicate curve of the elbow. I spied a faint dimple on the inner side of the elbow. From there the arm narrowed to the roundness of the wrist. I gazed down at the back of the hand, its palm, and its fingers.

"I think I'll keep it," I muttered, not realizing I had spoken aloud. Captivated by the arm's beauty, I wasn't even aware that I had taken my own right arm from my shoulder, attaching hers in its place.

"Aah . . ." A quiet gasp. Not knowing whether it was her voice or mine, a tremor rippled through my shoulder, and with it came the realization that I had swapped the arms.

Her arm—my arm, now—trembled and clutched at the air. I bent the arm and brought it up to my face. "Does it hurt? Are you in pain?"

"No, it's not that. It's not that," the arm said. At these rushed, fragmented words a shuddering bolt of lightning seared through my body. I bit down gently on the fingers of the arm.

I could not speak. What words could describe this ecstasy? The mere touch of her fingers against my tongue was inexpressible.

"It's fine," the arm replied. The trembling, of course, had stopped. "She said this would happen. Yet . . ."

That's when I suddenly realized that I couldn't feel the fingers. I felt the fingers in my mouth, but the fingers of her right hand—that is, my right hand—couldn't feel my lips or teeth. Frantic, I shook the arm in the air, but there was no sensation of the arm being shaken. There was some kind of barrier, a resistance between my shoulder and her arm.

"The blood's not flowing," I cried. "Will it flow? Won't it?"

I sat up, seized by a sudden terror. My arm lay discarded on the bed beside me. I glanced at it. Separated from my body, the arm was repulsive. But I was more concerned about its pulse. Had it stopped? The warm pulse of her arm continued to beat on, but my right arm looked as though it was growing cold and stiff. Using the arm I had attached to me shoulder, I picked up my right arm. I was able to grasp the arm, but I couldn't feel myself holding it.

"Is there a pulse?" I asked the arm. "It's not growing cold, is it?"

"Just a tiny bit. . . . It's just a tiny bit cooler than I," her arm replied. "But that's because I've grown warmer."

The arm referred to itself as "I"; it used the first person pronoun. I realized this was the first time the arm had used "I" since being attached it to my shoulder.

"The pulse hasn't vanished?" I asked again.

"Come now, can it be that you really don't believe?"

"Believe what?"

"You exchanged our arms yourself, did you not?"

"But, the blood, will it flow?"

"*Woman, whom seekest thou?* Do you know the passage?"

"Yes, I know the passage. *Woman, why weepest thou? Whom seekest thou?*"

"When I wake up from a dream in the middle of the night I often whisper those words."

The "I" here was clearly referring to the owner of that precious arm, the arm now attached to my right shoulder. The passage from the Bible seemed to be spoken in an ageless voice, from some eternal place.

"I wonder if she's having nightmares, if she's having trouble sleeping . . ." I said, thinking of the one who lent me her arm. "This mist—it's as though it exists solely to let packs of demons wander about. But even a demon would feel this damp and start coughing."

"This will block out the sound of any demons coughing, then," her arm said and, without letting go of my right arm, covered my right ear. I hadn't moved her arm—my arm. It had moved on its own. No, we had reached a point where such distinctions no longer held.

"My pulse, it's the sound of my pulse. . . ."

Since her arm had been holding my arm when it lifted itself to my head, my right arm was now pressed against my ear, filling it with the sound of my arm's pulse. It was still warm and, as the arm had said, it was just a tiny bit cooler than my ear or her fingers.

"I'll scare the demons away for you," it said, teasing. The long, slender nail of her pinky gently scratched the inside of my ear. I shook my head, trying to get away. My left hand—the hand that really was mine—grabbed my right wrist, which is to say her right wrist. Pulling my head back, I glimpsed her pinky.

Her hand gripped my right arm—the one I had removed from my shoulder—with her thumb and three fingers. As though the pinky alone had been let out to play, it was bent back so the tip of the nail brushed lightly against my right arm. Only the supple fingers of a young woman would be capable of such contortions. It would be impossible for a man like me, with my stiff and clumsy fingers. The knuckle was bent at a right angle, the first joint bent at another right angle and the second as well. With the ring finger on the fourth side, the pinky formed a square.

This square window was positioned such that I could peer through it. It was far too small to be called a window; I suppose it would be more accurate to call it a peephole or perhaps a lens. Yet, for some reason, it seemed like a window to me. It was the sort of window a violet might use to gaze outside. The delicate finger was so white it seemed almost to glow. I leaned forward, bringing my eye closer to the frame of window, the lens. I closed my other eye.

"Is it a picture show?" the arm asked. "Do you see anything?"

"There's my gloomy room, a dim, ten-watt bulb. . . ." Suddenly I broke off, "No! I *can* see!" I said, almost shouting

"What do you see?"

"It's gone."

"What did you see?"

"It was a color, a light, blurry, faint purple . . . In the purple light there were tiny gold and red rings as the size of millet seeds, lots of them, spinning around and flying about."

"You're just tired."

She placed my right arm on the bed and gently stroked my eyelids with her fingers.

"The tiny red and gold rings formed giant cogwheels. I wonder if some of them were spinning. . . . Did I see something moving inside the cogwheels? Was something appearing and disappearing?"

I couldn't say if I had seen either the cogwheels or something inside the cogwheels. Had I seen them or did it only seem that I had seen them? It was a fleeting vision and it slipped through my memory. Unable to recall the vision I asked, "What vision did you want to show me?

"No. I have come here to erase visions."

"The dreams of days past, I suppose, of longing, and sadness."

Her fingers and palm stopped moving and came to rest atop my eyelids.

"When you let your hair down, does it reach your to shoulders and arms?" I asked without thinking, the question slipping out.

"Yes, it does," the arm answered. "When I take a bath, I wash my hair with hot water, but when I rinse it I always use cold water at the end. I don't know why. It's just a habit of mine. I keep rinsing it until the hair grows icy cold. I like the way it feels, when the cold hair brushes against my shoulders and arms, and my breasts as well."

The arm was referring, of course, to *her* breasts, those of the mother of the arm. Perhaps the separation of the arm from its body had also separated the arm from her sense of modesty or shyness. As one who had likely never suffered anyone to touch her breasts, I doubted very much that *she* would have been so bold as to describe the sensation of cold, wet hair on her naked chest.

Her arm was my arm now. I cupped the enchanting, soft, round base of the arm gently in my left hand. I imagined the small roundness of her breasts in the palm of my hand. They had not yet grown over-large. The roundness of her shoulder transformed into the soft curve of her breast.

Her hand rested lightly atop my closed eyes. Her palm and fingers clung gently to my eyelids, their heat seeping through my eyelids. The inside of my lids grew warm and damp. The warm dampness spread, sinking into my eyes.

"The blood flows," I whispered. "The blood flows."

There was no shout of surprise this time. It was not like when I suddenly realized I had switched her right arm with mine. There was no shudder or trembling in my shoulder or in her arm. When did my blood start to flow into her arm and her blood begin to flow into me? When had the barrier, the resistance at the base of her arm vanished? At that moment, as I lay there, the blood of a pure, innocent woman flowed into me. My blood, the corrupt blood of a man, flowed into her arm. What would happen when I gave the arm back, when it was returned to her shoulder? What if it couldn't be reattached? What would I do?

"I would never betray her so," I muttered.

"Don't worry," the arm whispered.

There was no dramatic sensation to mark the flow of blood out from my shoulder, the flow of blood in from her arm, the commingling of our blood. The palm of my left hand, cupping her right shoulder and the roundness of her shoulder, which was now my shoulder, simply knew. Without becoming consciously aware of it, the arm and I simply knew. This knowledge that pulled me, melting, into a deep, almost enchanted sleep.

I slept.

A pale purple mist gathered about me, I drifted along on large, gentle swells. Only where I bobbed in the water did tiny, green ripples sparkle across the broad waves. My dank, lonely bachelor's apartment had vanished. I seemed to be resting my left hand on her right arm. Her fingers seemed to be clutching the magnolia petals. I couldn't see them, but their fragrance filled my nostrils. Hadn't I thrown all the petals in the dustbin? When—and why—had she gotten them out again? Why had the petals fallen so soon? On the very first day that the white flower had blossomed, why did the petals fall? They shouldn't have fallen yet. Off in the distance the woman in vermillion clothes drove her car, circling me, gliding smoothly by. It was as though she was watching over us as we dreamed, over the arm and me.

I must have been sleeping very lightly to have had such dreams, but never before had I experienced such a warm, sweet sleep. Being an insomniac, I usually have to endure hours of tossing and turning, before I finally fall asleep. This kind of peaceful sleep, like that of a small child, was an utterly new experience for me.

I felt a gentle touch, as though her elegant, slender fingernails were scratching my palm, playfully. This faint sensation drew me further and deeper into sleep. I vanished.

"Oh!" The sound of my own cry caused me to jerk awake. I rolled out of bed, nearly falling. I stumbled three or four paces.

I was suddenly wide-awake. I felt something disgusting pressed against the side of my chest. My arm!

I braced my unsteady legs as I caught sight of my right arm, which had fallen from the bed. My breath caught in my throat, and a sudden wave of panic sent the blood rushing to my ears. A shudder ran through my entire body. I gazed at the arm for only an instant. The next moment I tore her arm from my shoulder and replaced it with my own. It was as though I was a murderer in the grip of a diabolical seizure.

I fell to my knees and rested my chest against the bed. My heart pounded crazily. I massaged my chest with my right arm, the arm I had just attached. As the palpitations subsided I felt a profound sadness well up from deep within myself.

"Her arm. . . ?" I raised my head.

The arm lay palm up at the foot of the bed, discarded in the confusion of blankets I had kicked aside in my panic. Its outstretched fingers were motionless, a faint, white glow in the dim light.

"Aah."

Frantically I gathered up the arm and clutched it fiercely to my chest. I embraced it as one might hold a cherished child, frail and sickly, as life slips away. I placed a finger between my lips. If only her dew would well up from the tip of the finger. . . .

Expunged by Yakumo
八雲が殺した
(Yakumo ga koroshita)

Akae Baku (1981)

赤江 瀑

Translation by Nancy H. Ross

AMONG A COLLECTION of ghost stories written by Koizumi Yakumo[1] is one entitled "In a Cup of Tea." It is commonly believed that most of Yakumo's ghost stories and strange tales had other sources and that he based them on stories he selected from popular books and collections of ghost stories that had been published in the Edo era (1603-1868). Thus some people believe that they can not be considered original fiction. Nevertheless, the fact remains that as literature Yakumo's *Kwaidan* is held in high regard today.

Along with other stories such as "Yuki-onna" and "The Story of Mimi-nashi-Hōichi," the very short "In a Cup of Tea" is well known, so perhaps there is no need to summarize it here. But it has a peculiar connection to the troubles of Murasako Otoko, so first I'll set down the original story that became the source of "In a Cup of Tea." This story was first published in 1891 in the *New Collection of Things Written and Heard.*[2]

The Face of a Young Man Appears in a Cup at a Teashop

On the fourth day of the New Year in 1684, Lord Nakagawa Sado and his retainers set out to offer the customary greetings. After calling on Hotta Kosaburō they stopped at a teahouse in Hakusan in Hongō to rest. A retainer by the name of Sekinai had just begun to drink some water when he saw the face of a beautiful young man reflected in it. Thinking it eerie, he threw the water out and got more, but each time he did so the face reappeared. So finally he simply gulped the water down. That evening a young man came to Sekinai's lodgings stating that he was Shikibu Heinai and that they had met for the first time

1. Lafcadio Hearn (1850-1904)

2. 新著聞集.

earlier that day. Sekinai was surprised and said he had no recollection of any such meeting. His suspicions aroused, he asked Heinai how he had gotten past the front gate. Thinking Heinai might be an apparition, Sekinai drew his sword and lunged at Heinai, who ran off. Sekinai followed in vigorous pursuit, but Heinai vanished at the wall bordering the neighboring property. Sekinai reported these events to the other retainers, but no one had seen or heard anything.

The following night three samurai came to see Sekinai. They identified themselves as Matsuoka Heizō, Okamura Heiroku and Tsuchibashi Bunzō, vassals of Shikibu Heinai. They demanded to know why Sekinai had not only rebuffed but attacked one who had come to visit merely because he was fond of him. They reported that Heinai was recuperating from his wound at a hot spring. He was quite upset and would return on the sixteenth of the month to settle the score, they said menacingly. Sekinai drew his short sword and attacked. The men dashed to the boundary of the neighboring property, where Heinai had escaped the night before, and disappeared over the wall, never to return.

Yakumo clearly based his story on this one, and of course he used the same characters when writing in "In a Cup of Tea." That is to say, the overall story is the same, but the nuances of Yakumo's story differ from the original in several respects.

I'd first like to address that issue while providing a simple outline of the original story. Lord Nakagawa Sado and his party have stopped at a teahouse to take a break while making the rounds to offer greetings at the New Year. Sekinai, a young servant, is surprised to see the face of a handsome young man reflected in the cup he is about to drink from. He throws the water out and gets more, but no matter how many times he does so, the face reappears. Although he finds it eerie, in the end he gulps the water down.

Yakumo described the scene thus:

... once more the strange face appeared—this time with a mocking smile. But Sekinai did not allow himself to be frightened. "Whoever you are," he muttered, "you shall delude me no further!"—then he swallowed the tea, face and all, and went his way, wondering whether he had swallowed a ghost.

But that evening a young man unfamiliar to Sekinai comes to his lodgings and introduces himself as Shikibu Heinai, saying he had met Sekinai for the first time that day. Sekinai is puzzled as he has no recollection of Heinai nor are they acquainted.

Yakumo wrote:

And Sekinai was astonished to find before him the same sinister, handsome face of which he had seen, and swallowed, the apparition in a cup of tea. It was smiling now, as the phantom had smiled; but the steady gaze of the eyes, above the smiling lips, was at once a challenge and an insult.

"No, I do not recognize you," returned Sekinai, angry but cool;—"and perhaps you will now be good enough to inform me how you obtained admission to this house?"

"Ah, you do not recognize me!" exclaimed the visitor, in a tone of irony, drawing a little nearer as he spoke. "No, you do not recognize me! Yet you took upon yourself this morning to do me a deadly injury!..."

Sekinai instantly seized the tantō[3] *at his girdle, and made a fierce thrust at the throat of the man. But the blade seemed to touch no substance. Simultaneously and soundlessly the intruder leaped sideward to the chamber-wall, and through it!... He had traversed it only as the light of a candle passes through lantern-paper.*

3. Short sword

The following night three men visit Sekinai. Their names have been changed slightly, but the scene unfolds as follows:

"Our names are Matsuoka Bungo, Tsuchibashi Bungo, and Okamura Heiroku. We are retainers of the noble Shikibu Heinai. When our master last night deigned to pay you a visit, you struck him with a sword. He was much hurt, and has been obliged to go to the hot springs, where his wound is now being treated. But on the sixteenth day of the coming month he will return; and he will then fitly repay you for the injury done him. . . ."

Without waiting to hear more, Sekinai leaped out, sword in hand, and slashed right and left, at the strangers. But the three men sprang to the wall of the adjoining building, and flitted up the wall like shadows, and . . .

Yakumo left off here, and after leaving one blank line concluded the story with the following:

Here the old narrative breaks off; the rest of the story existed only in some brain that has been dust for a century.

I am able to imagine several possible endings; but none of them would satisfy an Occidental imagination. I prefer to let the reader attempt to decide for himself the probable consequence of swallowing a Soul.

I have quoted from the story at some length, but in any case, while adhering to the original, Koizumi Yakumo's "In a Cup of Tea" thus states that the original story was unfinished and leaves the ending to the reader's imagination.

Murasako Otoko read this story years ago when she was a student. At that time she was interested in what Yakumo wrote at the end as well as at the beginning of the story. Yakumo's "In a Cup of Tea" begins with this preface:

Have you ever attempted to mount some old tower stairway, spiring up through darkness, and in the heart of that darkness found yourself at the cobwebbed edge of nothing? Or have you fol-

lowed some coast path, cut along the face of a cliff, only to discover yourself, at a turn, on the jagged verge of a break? The emotional worth of such experience—from a literary point of view—is proved by the force of the sensations aroused, and by the vividness with which they are remembered. Now there have been curiously preserved, in old Japanese story—books, certain fragments of fiction that produce an almost similar emotional experience. . . . Perhaps the writer was lazy; perhaps he had a quarrel with the publisher; perhaps he was suddenly called away from his little table, and never came back; perhaps death stopped the writing-brush in the very middle of a sentence. But no mortal man can ever tell us exactly why these things were left unfinished. . . . I select a typical example.

After reading Yakumo's preface to the story and the lines at the end, Otoko took an interest in this Japanese story that Yakumo referred to as a "fragment of fiction" that had been "left unfinished," and she wanted to read the original.

While perusing two or three books written by researchers on Yakumo, she found that the original story was the "The Face of a Young Man Appears in a Cup at a Teashop" from the *New Collection of Things Written and Heard.* So Otoko was able to read the original as well, but after doing so she was puzzled.

Or rather, she had some questions. Why did Yakumo call this a "fragment of fiction"? Otoko didn't think the original had been "left unfinished" nor did she think "the writer was lazy." Nor did she think he "left his little table" and "never came back" after having "a quarrel with the publisher" or something of that sort. Neither did she think, of course, that it was a story that had ended when "death stopped the writing brush."

Because it was included in a book that collected the anonymous sources of popular tales it was not of particular literary value, but at least the original stood on its own, and she felt that the story was completed by the final "never to return."

Yakumo's "In a Cup of Tea" was longer and vividly depicted the background to the story. But even if you took into account the differences in nuance from the standpoint of Yakumo's theme, she felt his story was far less well done than the original.

Otoko loved fiction in her student days, and the thing she was least able to accept was that the most important part of the story, which amounted to just one sentence, had been eliminated from Yakumo's "In a Cup of Tea." It could be argued that the story had value precisely because of that sentence and that it was thus complete. That is to say, the story's most essential part had been omitted.

There was no reason to believe Yakumo had overlooked that part. Otoko could only conclude he had intentionally deleted it. By doing so, perhaps Yakumo intended to substantially alter the style of the original and give it more depth as a ghost story. One might suppose he had taken pains to write the story in that particular fashion. But precisely because she could infer that, Otoko had doubts about that conclusion.

Yakumo's works have all been translated into Japanese, and anyone can read them today, but they were originally written for Western readers and published overseas. So at the time Otoko thought perhaps this discrepancy could be accounted for by differences in the way Westerners and Japanese thought about things. Nevertheless, because the critical element represented by that sentence in the original was missing from Yakumo's "In a Cup of Tea," she felt it was far inferior to the original story. If anything should be considered incomplete it was certainly Yakumo's work, she thought.

When comparing the preceding excerpts from the two stories, it is obvious that Yakumo eliminated part of the scene in which the three retainers of Shikibu Heinai visited the protagonist and complained bitterly. In Yakumo's "In a Cup of Tea" the key sentence should have been included in that part, which was rewritten as a conversation.

Specifically, he omitted the italicized portion of the following: "They demanded to know why Sekinai had not only rebuffed but attacked *one who had come to visit merely because he was fond of him.*"

Murasako Otoko simply could not understand why Yakumo had disregarded this part. Precisely because it is included, the mystery of the face seen in the cup can be explained, thus adding even more horror and dread to the eeriness of the story. *That's the very essence of the story's horror!* Otoko thought. *It's precisely because of that essence that it's so unfathomably frightening! Oh, why did he do it?*

For a while after reading the story that served as the source of "In a Cup of Tea," Murasako Otoko was preoccupied by this question, and every time she thought about it she squirmed with irritation. Occasionally she suddenly felt so frustrated with the long-dead writer that she wanted to stamp her foot.

But that was long ago when she was young and impressionable.

– 2 –

Murasako Otoko's husband died the year before last, and her only son left home last year. She'll turn 50 this year.

Her son isn't really her son. Five or six years after they got married Otoko and her husband discovered that they couldn't have children. After that they adopted the son of an acquaintance and raised him as their own, so he isn't actually related. But Otoko felt she had raised him with care just as if he were her own son, and she believed her late husband must have felt the same way. She was aware that Takao had given them the usual joys and hardships of child-rearing, and that was enough for her.

From the start she and her husband had discussed it and agreed that they wouldn't expect their son to take care of them in their old age. So when Takao decided to get married and leave home, Otoko didn't get too upset or put up much of a fuss. She was resigned to the fact that the time had come to let her son go. They weren't supposed to have had a son in the first place, so she decided to think of it as reverting to the life she had been originally intended to lead.

But Otoko sometimes felt somewhat relieved that her husband had not lived to see Takao get married, and she wondered if perhaps it was because he had managed to avoid experiencing the sort of loneliness and emptiness that she had.

Otoko didn't feel old, but after losing her husband and then her son she was terribly lonesome, and there seemed to be no way to suppress that feeling.

Fortunately, she was able to live in comfort by taking over the management of the rental properties her husband had left her. Takao, who had moved away after getting married, sometimes telephoned.

She was alone, but Otoko got used to her new life and bounced back, reminding herself that it wasn't as if she were wandering the streets or in similarly desperate straits.

The peach blossoms had begun to bloom.

On his way home from a business trip, Takao stopped by for the first time since he'd gotten married.

"Can you stay over?"

"No, I have to catch the bullet train home this evening."

"Oh. So you don't have much time."

"No, I just stopped by because I was worried about you here all by yourself. I thought we could have dinner together."

"In that case you should have called ahead, but there's no time to complain about that. I guess I'll just have to go to the grocery store."

"You don't need to do that. Let's eat out. That's what I had in mind actually."

"But you went out of your way to come home. . . ."

"So let's make the most of the time. If we eat near the station we can have a leisurely dinner until it's time for me to catch my train. Go get changed."

Otoko hurried to get dressed. She hadn't seen her son for a while and regretted they'd have so little time together, but she was happy that he wanted to spend as much of that short time with her as possible.

He had shown up out of the blue, seeming brusque yet kind at the same time. Soon he'd be off again. He'd always had something of that quality about him. When they had lived together she'd had the feeling that Takao was distant and unreachable. Yet whenever she had reached out for him she had found he was surprisingly close.

Tears welled up in Otoko's eyes as she recalled the past.

She'd brought her son up until he'd left the nest. From now on he could fly off anywhere. She would no longer reach out for him, so he could live as he liked. That's what she'd decided. But when he appeared out the blue like this and she saw his face and heard his voice her resolve wavered and she dreamed of things she shouldn't have.

Seeing her son for the first time since he'd gotten married, he seemed somehow more grown-up and muscular.

"Is everything going OK?" she asked.

"Don't worry."

"I'm not. Not having to worry about you any more is a load off my mind."

"Good. You need to think about yourself, not me."

"What do you mean?"

"Are you going to go on alone like this?"

"What do you mean 'go on'?"

"With your life."

"I am going on with my life."

"I mean for the rest of your life. You're still young."

Otoko burst out laughing. "Are you trying to get me to remarry?" she asked.

"So, you won't?"

"Of course not."

"Well, I suppose anyone who'd ever seen you and Dad together would know that."

"So if you already know that, then don't worry yourself unnecessarily. When you moved out didn't I tell you not to think of me as being alone? Dad is always with me. Since Dad died I've never once thought my life with him was over. Finding a guy like that and getting married to him—I just feel lucky to have been born. Even if he's no longer here, the bond between us will never be broken. That's the kind of person Dad was."

"OK, OK. I take it back. I figured you'd say that."

Takao rolled his eyes and laughed.

That day Takao took Otoko to a cheery restaurant with a sunny central courtyard.

"I didn't realize there was such a nice restaurant here."

"Really? It's been here three or four years. Don't you remember? I brought home some fancy ice cream desserts from here once."

"Oh, I remember. They were like something out of some kind of dreamland. We said they were so pretty it seemed a shame to eat them. Those?"

"Yeah. That's their specialty."

"Really."

"It's all right to go on about Dad, but he should have brought you to places like this now and then."

"He took me lots of places. You just don't know about it."

Otoko was in high spirits. *What a nice day, completely unexpected,* she thought to herself again.

The dishes on which the meal was served were exquisite, and the food was delicious. The colorful dishes and food perfectly suited the comfortably large table and the relaxed atmosphere.

And it was fun to watch the unconcerned way Takao ate. The pleasant sound their knives and forks made, the clear sparkle of the water in their glasses, the savory smell of the grilled meat—Otoko thoroughly delighted in sharing a meal with her son.

"Oh, I just remembered. I have to make a phone call." Takao got up from the table.

Otoko slowly picked up her wine glass as she watched him head off. His movements were so brisk, and he looked so dependable. Seen through the glistening glass, the swaying of the deep red liquid was beautiful. Just then Otoko stopped. She held the glass aloft as she was about to bring it to her lips. Her gaze fixed on its graceful roundness. A white light was reflected in it. When she looked closely, she found that it was the reflection of a person.

Otoko turned to look behind her. A man was sitting by himself at a table on the terrace a short distance away. The brightness of his white suit as the sun shone on it was being reflected in Otoko's wine glass. Against the white light his youthful face looked fresh and clean.

Otoko looked back at her glass and gazed at the white light in the red liquid for a while. As the liquid swayed, the image in the light broke up and then formed again.

How pretty!

Seen through the transparent glass the image seemed to be floating in the deep red liquid. Otoko slowly drank the wine down in several swallows while admiring the play of the light. The wine steward came to refill her glass.

Just then Takao came back.

"Your wife?"

"No way. The office. Why should I call my wife?"

"Now, now. Don't act big. You have to be good to her."

"I know, I know. Anyway, eat up. Look, you haven't finished your wine."

Takao began energetically wielding his knife and fork again.

Otoko looked from Takao back to her wine glass. The white light was gone.

Startled, she turned around and looked behind her. The man who had been sitting at the table on the terrace was no longer there.

When she saw Takao off at the station and headed into the city the sun was beginning to set.

A few days later, the name Koizumi Yakumo, a name Murasako Otoko had not thought of in nearly thirty years, popped into her head.

– 3 –

On nights when she couldn't get to sleep Otoko would have a drink or two. It had become a habit, but that night after Takao left she didn't need a drink. She was already quite drunk.

She didn't feel like doing anything, so she went to bed early in the evening, leaving her clothes strewn about. She fell asleep right away. Sleeping was her greatest pleasure because it was the only time she could see her husband. He was waiting for her, not as some invisible illusion but as her real flesh and blood husband. There the two of them lived together, just as they always had. So every night before she fell asleep Otoko prayed that she wouldn't wake up. After spending the day with Takao she wanted to see her husband as soon as possible and tell him about Takao's visit. With all there was to tell him about Takao, she was sure they'd spend the whole night laughing and crying and never run out of things to talk about.

Being drunk added to her feeling of anticipation.

When Otoko woke up the next morning, she sat unmoving on her futon for a while, feeling slightly groggy.

How can that be? It can't be that you didn't come, can it?

No, he must have come and we met and chatted as usual, but I just don't remember because I was a little too drunk.

Otoko had a splitting headache from the drunkenness of the night before.

She didn't see her husband in her dreams the next night or the night after that either.

Each morning when she woke up she was puzzled, and with a serious expression she restlessly ransacked her memories of the night before, searching for him. She conducted a thorough examination, determined not to overlook even the most trifling recollection.

What happened? Why?

Something was different. Not only could she not see her husband, the scenery of her recollections had changed in some peculiar fashion. No, *scenery* wasn't the right word.

It was certain that her husband wasn't in her recollections, but someone else was. Or so it seemed to Otoko. Thinking of it that way, she was sure she must have dreamed that night, the night before and the night before that—the night after she saw Takao.

But her husband hadn't appeared in her dreams, so she searched and searched for him, seeking the dream she should have been seeing, waiting for it all night long. Otoko was forced to conclude that not only had she been unable to see her husband, she must not have dreamed at all.

But she had. She had dreamed, but her husband wasn't in her dreams, and to Otoko dreams without her husband were pointless and not worth dreaming. So she'd forgotten all about them.

She was intent on finding her husband in her dreams, and she awoke each morning feeling empty. After three nights of that emptiness, Otoko had to concede that something unusual had taken place in the world of her dreams.

When she stopped and went over her recollections again, she realized that the face of someone other than her husband had appeared in her dreams—the faint outline of the face of a man she didn't know. When she became aware that that face had unmistakably been in her dreams at some point for the previous three nights Otoko suddenly felt an irritating unpleasantness.

Why did the face of a stranger appear in her dreams instead of her husband, whom she was supposed to meet but couldn't?

On the third morning, while making her bed and feeling that irritating unpleasantness, Otoko suddenly stopped. A face flashed across her mind. Could it have been *him*, the man in the dazzling white suit who'd been sitting at the table on the sunny terrace at the restaurant three days before?

But... Otoko thought.

She couldn't remember his face clearly except that he was a young, fresh-faced man in his late 20s. She had only a vague impression she had retained after turning around to glance at him. She couldn't even remember whether he'd been having lunch or tea.

Otoko had turned to look at him then not because she was paying particular attention to him but because she had been mesmerized by the brilliance of the white light reflected on the surface of her wine. Otoko's interest was focused entirely on the beauty of the form of the light that sparkled in the glass of red wine she held. She had merely become fascinated by that white light and instinctively looked for its source. And the man in the white suit had just happened to be there. So she hadn't observed his face carefully, but nevertheless when it occurred to her that it must have been him, Otoko stifled a small cry.

The wine glass, the human form reflected in the red liquid.

Yes. I had the feeling I was drinking a certain delicious, beguiling liquor then. The color and form of the sparkling rays of light... It seemed a shame to drink it, and I wanted to gaze at it forever. While enjoying that luxurious feeling, I drank it down. . . .

Amid those recollections, Otoko let out a small cry.

Yes, she thought, *I drank that wine*. And as that realization occurred to her, Otoko suddenly recalled a short story in a book she'd read years before. From among her distant memories, like a living being parting the waves as it swam swiftly toward her, Otoko suddenly recalled Koizumi Yakumo.

She was surprised and flustered. That momentary bizarre association that flashed across her mind simultaneously set off a strange chain reaction. Otoko felt as if memories from the recent and distant past were gathering and closing in on her.

She had as yet no inkling of the even stranger events that were to begin that night.

-4-

On the fourth night Otoko saw the man's face clearly.

He was a fresh-faced young man with strong features. His loose-limbed build was pleasing, and everything about him—the way he moved, his choice of words, his voice—was mannerly and imbued with a sense of cleanliness and decency. Otoko chatted with him eagerly. He was an engaging conversation partner. He nodded enthusiastically, interjected short replies and laughed in a pleasant voice, sometimes looking serious, sometimes smiling.

The whiteness of his white suit and shirt was blinding. Otoko repeatedly shielded her eyes with her hand, squinting and blinking as if looking into the summer sun.

She had no recollection of what they talked about, but when she woke up the next morning, a clear impression of the young man remained. It was an awakening unlike any Otoko had experienced—exhilarating, gay and strangely refreshing.

My! What was that all about? There certainly are some incredible things in this world! Otoko thought.

Of course, what really surprised Otoko that morning was that she had recalled Koizumi Yakumo's "In a Cup of Tea." A man drank down a cupful of water in which a face that certainly shouldn't have appeared *had* appeared, and then the person to whom the face belonged had come to visit him.

That's it. That young man must have come to visit me, Otoko thought.

She recalled with a sort of wistfulness her youthful self, who had so intensely bemoaned the fact that Yakumo had not included the most important part of the original story in "In a Cup of Tea."

"They demanded to know why Sekinai had not only rebuffed but attacked *one who had come to visit merely because he was fond of him.*"

So, the face in the cup of water was not just some strange, ghostly apparition. It had come because it had taken a liking to Sekinai. The young samurai had appeared because he had fallen in love and was intent on conveying his feelings to Sekinai. Sekinai had gulped the water down. He had ingested the face on which the young samurai's feelings of love had appeared. The samurai's love had been fulfilled. His feelings had been favorably received. So he had gone to visit Sekinai, jumping for joy. Therein lay the misunderstanding between the one who had done the drinking and the one who had been drunk down.

Then the vassals had come to convey their master's resentment and demand that Sekinai account for having suddenly attacked with cries of "Phantom! Ghost!" and for having wounded their lord without the slightest demonstration of consideration for the poignancy of his single-minded devotion. Sekinai had attacked the vassals as well, and they had disappeared "never to return." The story ended with those words. So inside the man who had swallowed the face, the young samurai's attachment had turned from feelings of love to resentment that would reside in him for the rest of his life, becoming part of him, all because he had drunk down the face that had displayed such ardor.

"Never to return." It was those words that completed the tale and provided a splendid ending. There was no need to *come back.* Something truly frightening would someday occur inside Sekinai's body because he had drunk the water.

That's what Otoko used to think.

But Yakumo had eliminated this important and truly brilliant conclusion from "In a Cup of Tea."

What a stupid man Yakumo was. He didn't know a thing about fiction. And he shamelessly labeled the original an "unfinished story" when in fact it was Yakumo himself who made it unfinished while failing to appreciate the substance and essence of the original and ripping them out! Otoko had been positively indignant.

"*. . . because he was fond of him . . .*" Those words were recalled to Otoko's mind in a way that made her heart leap in a strangely agreeable manner.

Even if it was purely a coincidence and had nothing to do with Yakumo, it was pleasant to think that that young man had appeared in her dream because he was thinking of her and had feelings for her. What could be more delightful than that?

Yes, God must have sent him to take the place of Takao, to be my son in my dreams. I should think of him as my son, live with him as if he were my son. That's what God is telling me.

Otoko actually had that feeling.

On the other hand, maybe it wasn't God. Was it you? Otoko asked herself.

Perhaps her husband had done this for her.

Now I get it. It was you, wasn't it? That's why you stayed away, wasn't it? You sent that young man. You're suggesting I make him my surrogate son. You're hiding, watching to see whether or not we'll get along. It's a test, isn't it? Don't worry.

He'll pass. That young man will make a wonderful substitute for Takao. Too wonderful. If you and that young man were both here. . . . Oh, how I've longed for a life like that.

You found him for me, didn't you? A son who can lead that kind of life with me. Right? You're just going to pop up and surprise us one day with a smug look on your face. Did you think I wouldn't realize what was going on? It's OK. You can come out now. Don't be shy. I'll thank you many times over. Thank you, thank you so much.

Otoko was sobbing. Just the three of them. She wept to think that such a life could go on forever. She'd never need anything else.

I never thought a day like this would come. Otoko cried out for joy, feeling happy just to be alive.

The young man came to her every night in her dreams. Each time they met they became better acquainted. They fell into a rhythm, opened up to each other and became closer with each passing day. Otoko was thoroughly enamored of the son in her dreams.

She could hardly wait for night to come.

Today's the day my husband will show up. He'll certainly appear tomorrow. The pleasure of waiting for that day made her heart leap.

Time passed.

Every morning the hooks on the curtain rods squeaked as sunlight flooded Otoko's bedroom. But one day the room was silent, although it was nearly noon.

Otoko sat limply on her futon in the middle of her dim bedroom, unmoving. She couldn't think straight. No matter how hard she tried, she couldn't understand what had happened, and she didn't have the energy to go back and figure out where the dream of the night before had begun or where it had ended. All she knew was that the young man in her dream was no longer her son. Where had that ferocious, lustful, brutish animal been lurking inside that pure, fresh-faced young man?

Throughout her naked body Otoko could still sense all the sordid tricks of pleasure that the young man had employed. When did that happen? Before she knew it she was at his mercy, pinned beneath his naked body. Where had he been hiding that sensual, vigorous, untiring body—that body that had wantonly made a fool of her, rendered her helpless?

Her countless recollections of the young man's body came flooding back to Otoko in graphic detail. She couldn't understand why such a thing had happened. She simply sat there dazed, staring through unseeing eyes.

It was the same the next night, and the next night and the night after that. The young man greedily devoured Otoko like some sort of beast and made her beast-like as well.

Otoko called her husband's name. She shouted until she was hoarse. She continued to cry out even after she was hoarse. But her husband didn't appear. Only *he* did.

Otoko decided she must not fall asleep. If only she didn't sleep she wouldn't have to see him. But she fell asleep anyway.

Did sleep summon Otoko or did she hurry off to sleep? She didn't know.

Amid her dreams Otoko sometimes noticed that her body was growing visibly younger, and as the days passed that youthfulness gave her a healthy glow.

As she was being assaulted by the young man, Otoko suddenly thought of the man who abruptly thrust his sword in anger at the ghost with the beautiful face—the weird, implausible, incomprehensible ghost. Sekinai had drawn his sword and attacked solely because it was a ghost. He needed no other reason. He attacked simply because it was a ghost, because it was eerie. It was murderous intent, plain and simple. That's what it was—or perhaps what it should be called.

In "In a Cup of Tea" Yakumo described the reprisal taken against the man who acted on that murderous intent.

"*... because he was fond of him ...*" Yakumo had no need for any such aroma of personal feeling. All he needed was a simple confrontation between a ghost and one who was not a ghost.

Otoko didn't know why she thought about things like that, but she couldn't get Sekinai's murderous intent out of her mind.

No, it really should be a love story, she thought.

And within Sekinai's murderous intent must have been the shock of a man who had been the object of this unreasonable love. That's why he had attacked so ferociously. Otoko thought about this and that, but in the end she always ended up back at *murderous intent.*

A glass brimming with red liquid shimmered before her eyes. Amid her rambling thoughts it occurred to Otoko that that flesh-and-blood devil had been lurking in that wine, that that beautiful liquor was beginning to turn into a demon inside her body.

The days came and went as she considered this.

– 5 –

Summer was approaching. It was impossible to walk about town without a parasol. As she crossed the street Murasako Otoko casually rested the shaft of her parasol on her shoulder. A young man was walking amid the crowd of people ahead of her. His sporty white suit looked as cool as if it might smell of peppermint.

No one noticed Otoko begin to tremble strangely.

The young man was waiting at the next corner for the signal to change.

Cars were passing in an endless stream.

Otoko suddenly let go of her parasol.

She was right behind him.

A Sinister Spectre

不安の立像

(Fuan no ritsuzō)

Morohoshi Daijirō (1973)

諸星 大二郎

Translation by Mark MacWilliams

NOTE TO THE READER:

Japanese books normally have the binding on the right side of the front cover, and are read from right to left. In manga this can cause a problem because the artist designs his layout with that sweep in mind. We have left this manga in the standard right-to-left format. Before you turn the page, please turn the book upside down!

Thank you.

A SINISTER SPECTRE
不安の立像

WHEN'S THE FIRST TIME I SAW IT ANYWAY?
(MAN, THAT GUY REALLY LIKES HIS NEWS-PAPER EVEN ON THIS PACKED TRAIN)
DOORS ARE CLOSING. THE TRAIN IS NOW READY FOR DEPARTURE.
(IT WON'T STOP AT ANY MORE OF THESE LITTLE STA-TIONS...)
IN THE MIDDLE OF ALL THESE DUMB SHEEP.

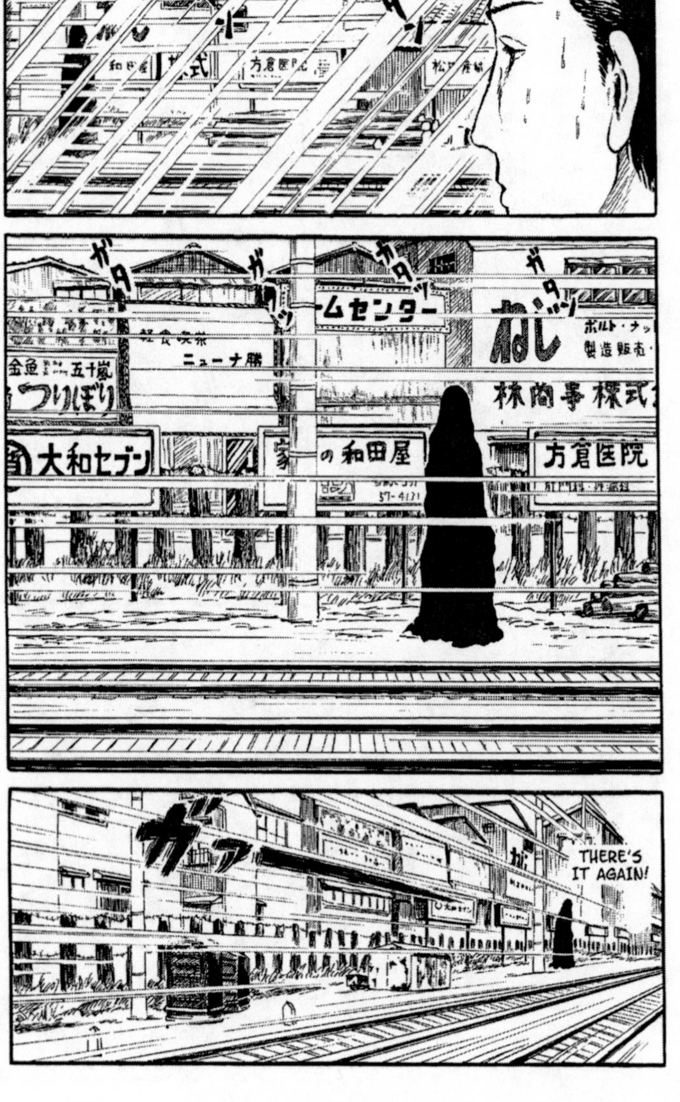
THERE'S IT AGAIN!

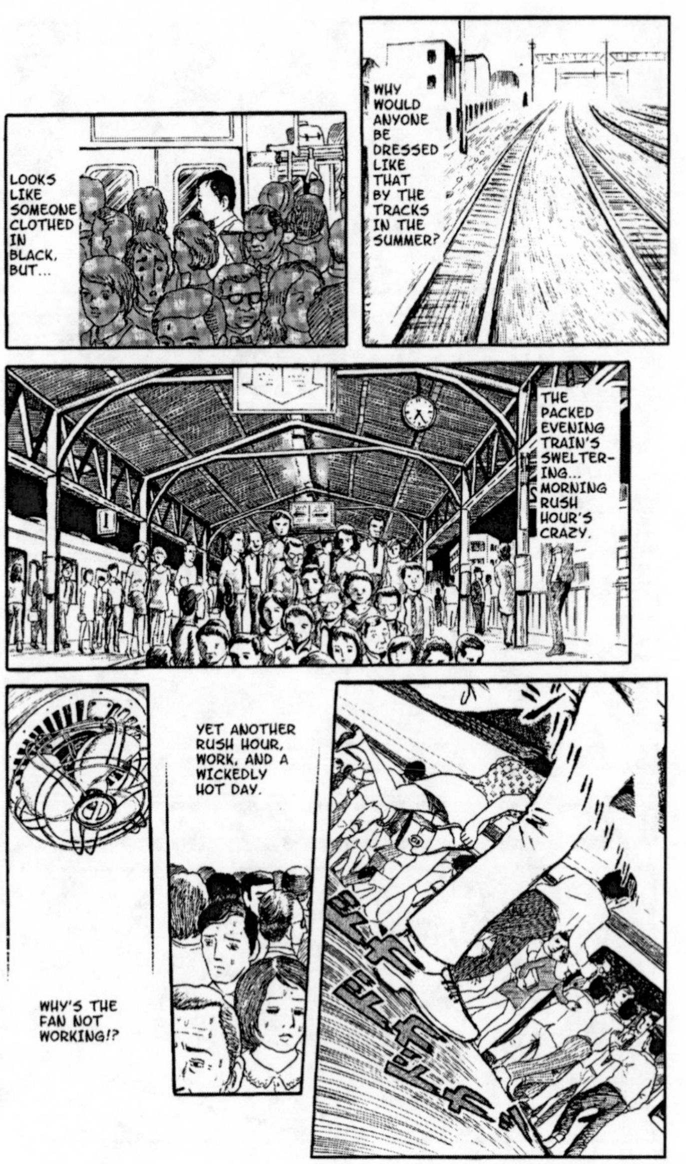
WHY WOULD ANYONE BE DRESSED LIKE THAT BY THE TRACKS IN THE SUMMER?
LOOKS LIKE SOMEONE CLOTHED IN BLACK, BUT...
THE PACKED EVENING TRAIN'S SWELTER-ING... MORNING RUSH HOUR'S CRAZY.
YET ANOTHER RUSH HOUR, WORK, AND A WICKEDLY HOT DAY.
WHY'S THE FAN NOT WORKING!?

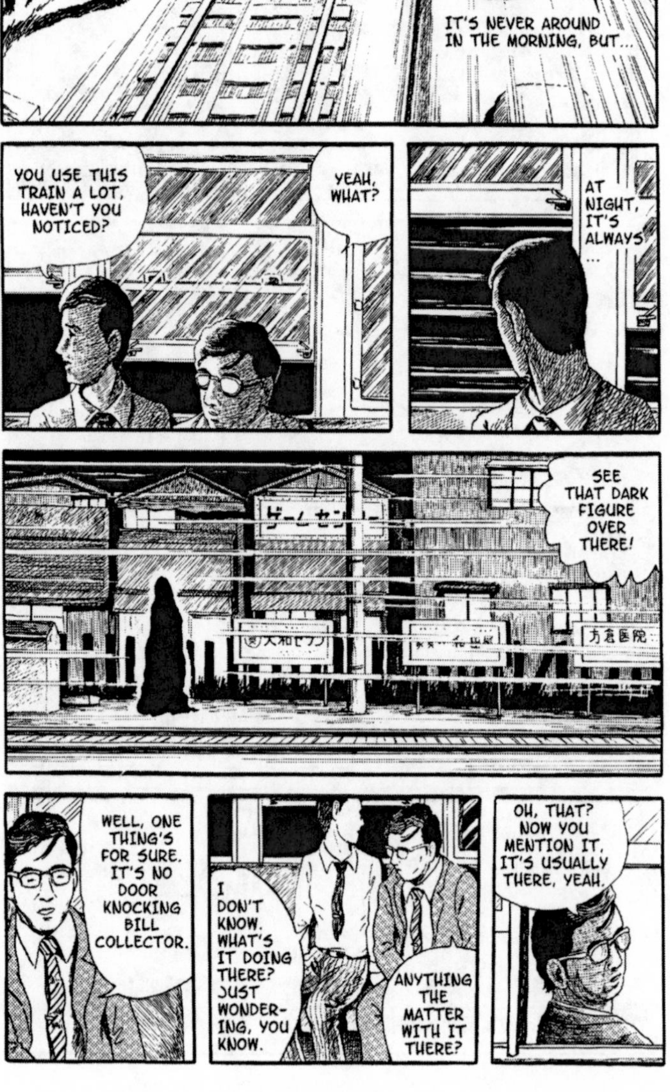
IT'S NEVER AROUND IN THE MORNING, BUT...
AT NIGHT, IT'S ALWAYS ...
YOU USE THIS TRAIN A LOT, HAVEN'T YOU NOTICED?
YEAH, WHAT?
SEE THAT DARK FIGURE OVER THERE!
OH, THAT? NOW YOU MENTION IT, IT'S USUALLY THERE, YEAH.
ANYTHING THE MATTER WITH IT THERE?
I DON'T KNOW. WHAT'S IT DOING THERE? JUST WONDERING, YOU KNOW.
WELL, ONE THING'S FOR SURE. IT'S NO DOOR KNOCKING BILL COLLECTOR.

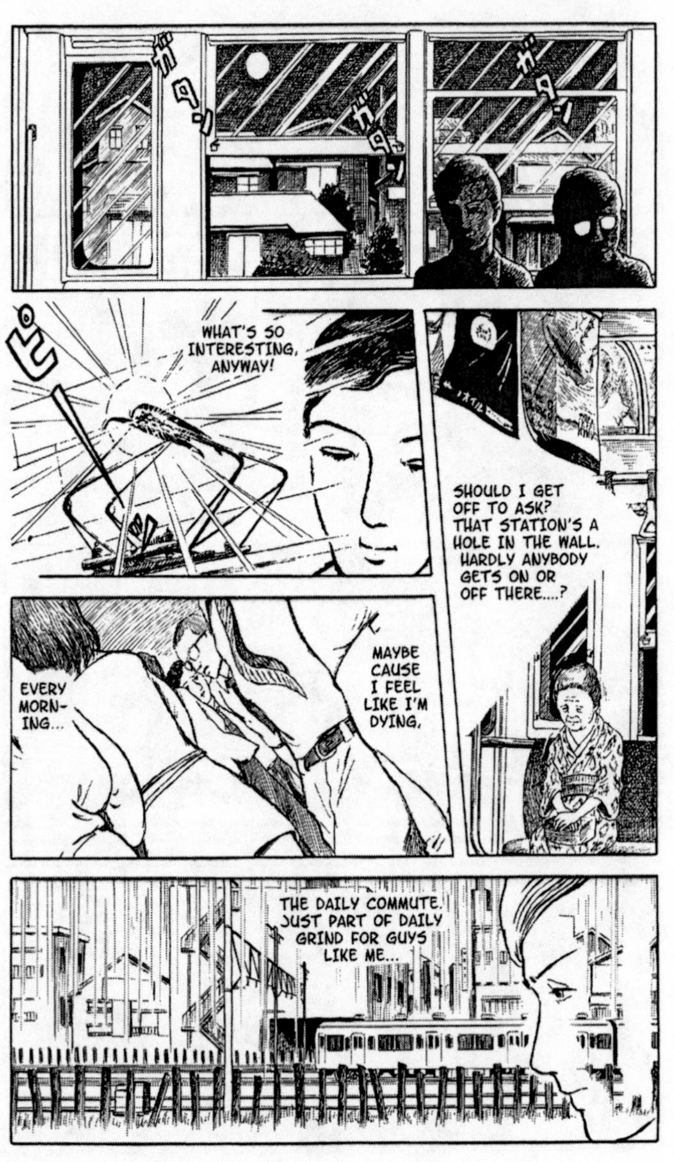
ガタン
ガタン
ガタン
SHOULD I GET OFF TO ASK? THAT STATION'S A HOLE IN THE WALL. HARDLY ANYBODY GETS ON OR OFF THERE....?
WHAT'S SO INTERESTING, ANYWAY!
EVERY MORNING...
MAYBE CAUSE I FEEL LIKE I'M DYING.
THE DAILY COMMUTE. JUST PART OF DAILY GRIND FOR GUYS LIKE ME...

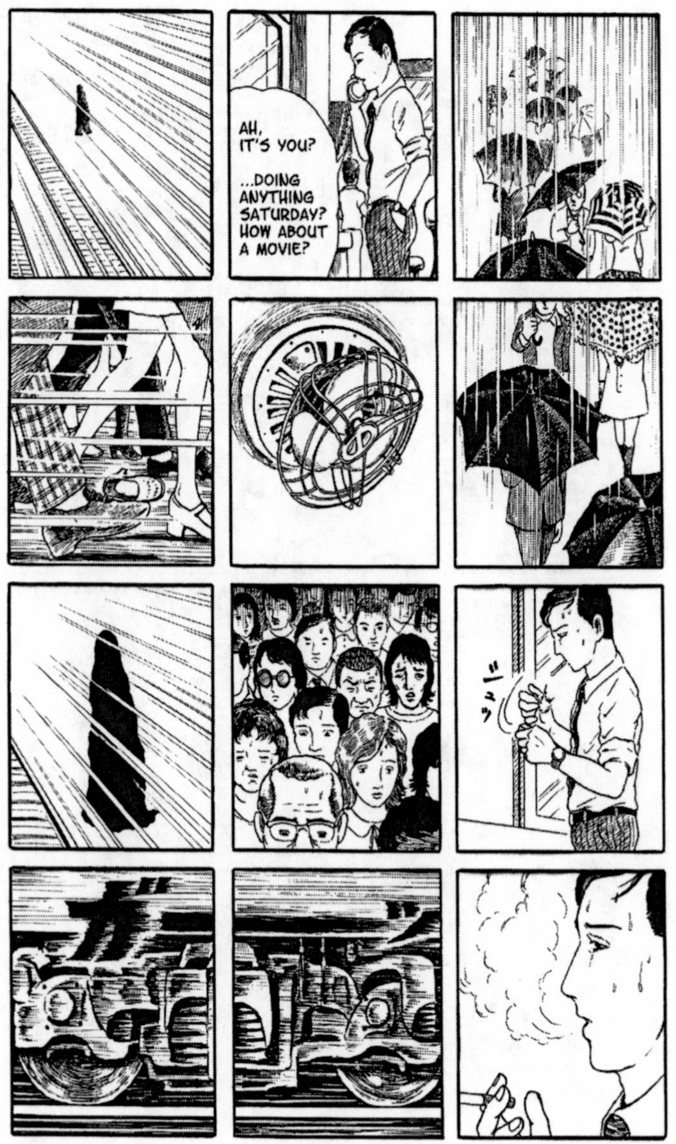
AH,
IT'S YOU?
...DOING
ANYTHING
SATURDAY?
HOW ABOUT
A MOVIE?

WHAT'S UP? ....WHY' RE WE GETTING OFF HERE?....
HEY, I THOUGHT WE'RE HEADING HOME. WE LEFT HALFWAY THROUGH OF THE MOVIE AND...
JUST FOR A BIT.
AAH, EXCUSE ME... THAT DARK FIGURE STANDING OVER THERE... KNOW WHAT IT IS?
IT'S HERE!
2

GEE, UH... IT'S BEEN AROUND, EVEN BEFORE I WORKED HERE, I THINK.
DON'T KNOW REALLY. HAVEN'T PAID MUCH ATTENTION, I GUESS. CAN I HELP YOU...
NO, NO, IT'S NOTHING REALLY...
OKAY, SUIT YOUR-SELF.
EH? GOTTA PROBLEM WITH THAT BLACK THING OVER THERE?

HAVEN'T NOTICED TILL NOW, BUT YOU'RE RIGHT, SOMETHING'S THERE ALRIGHT
HEY, IT'S NOT AROUND UNTIL EVENINGS
AFTER THE LAST TRAIN, IT VANISHES, I THINK.
DOESN'T CAUSE ANY PROBLEMS SO WE IGNORE IT.
WHY'RE YOU ASKING ANYWAY?
NO BIG DEAL, SORRY TO BOTHER YOU...
WHAT'S THE STORY ANYWAY?
WHAT'S SO INTERESTING ABOUT A SHADOW? DONE SOMETHING TO YOU?
I'LL BE RIGHT BACK...

HEY...
ピクッ
IT MOVED... YUP, IT'S HUMAN?
HELLO? JUST A MINUTE...
ローラン
サササッ

クラブ ローラン
麻雀
あさひや
HE'S A BIT JUMPY. SEEMS SHY. IS IT REALLY HUMAN?
WHAT ARE YOU DOING RUNNING AROUND ASKING ABOUT...
IT'S UN-NERV-ING.
WHAT'S WRONG ANY-WAY?
AREN'T YOU A BIT CON-CERNED? WITH SOMETHING SO WEIRD IN THE MIDDLE OF TOKYO...
SO SOME-THING'S HERE. OK BY ME. IT'S NOT CAUSING ANY PROBLEMS. SO WHAT? IT'S FINE!
株式会社浅倉水道
ガー

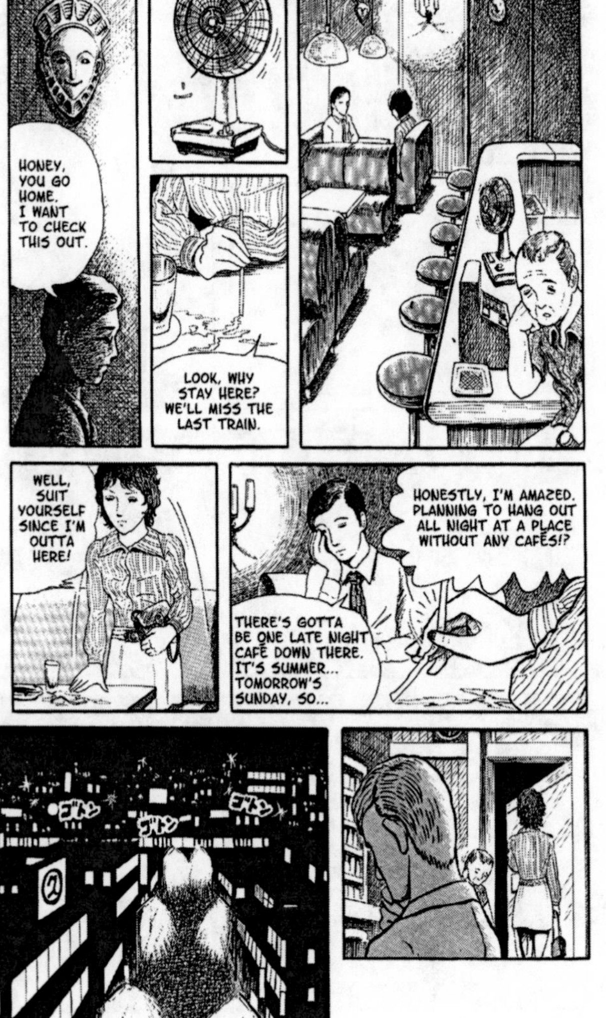
LOOK, WHY STAY HERE? WE'LL MISS THE LAST TRAIN.
HONEY, YOU GO HOME. I WANT TO CHECK THIS OUT.
HONESTLY, I'M AMAZED. PLANNING TO HANG OUT ALL NIGHT AT A PLACE WITHOUT ANY CAFÉS!?
THERE'S GOTTA BE ONE LATE NIGHT CAFÉ DOWN THERE. IT'S SUMMER... TOMORROW'S SUNDAY, SO...
WELL, SUIT YOURSELF SINCE I'M OUTTA HERE!

TODAY'S LAST TRAIN IS NOW DEPARTING ON TRACK NUMBER TWO. ALL ABOARD.
ガタタン
ガタン
ガタン
ガタン
ガタン
ガタ
ガタ
ガタ
ガタ

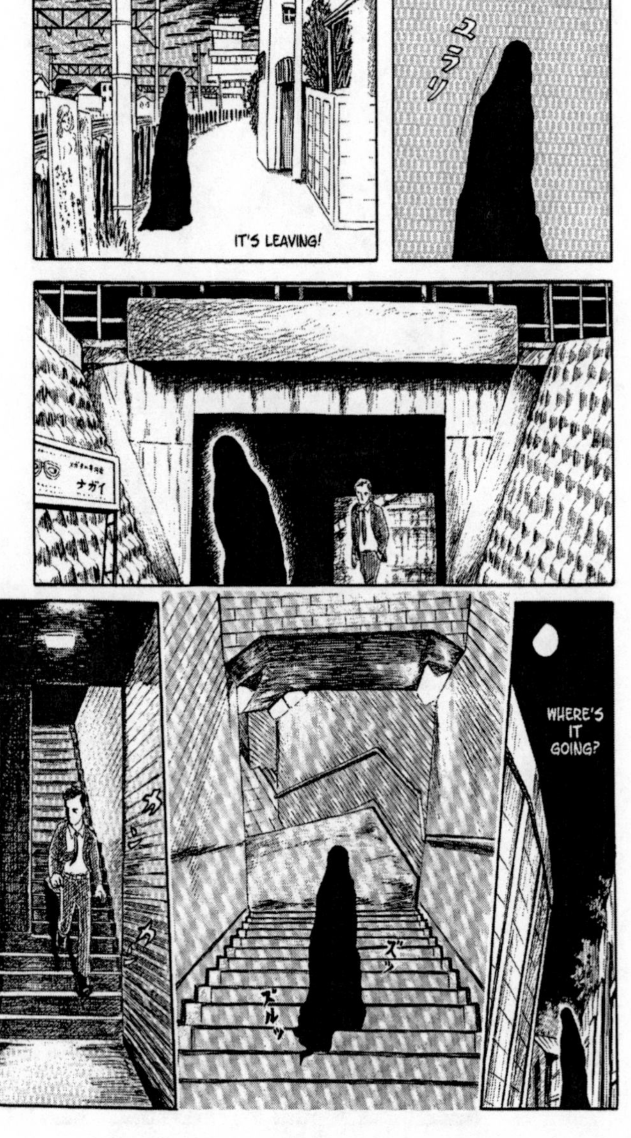
ユラッ
IT'S LEAVING!
ナガイ
WHERE'S IT GOING?
ズッ
ズルッ

ビクッ
ズルッ

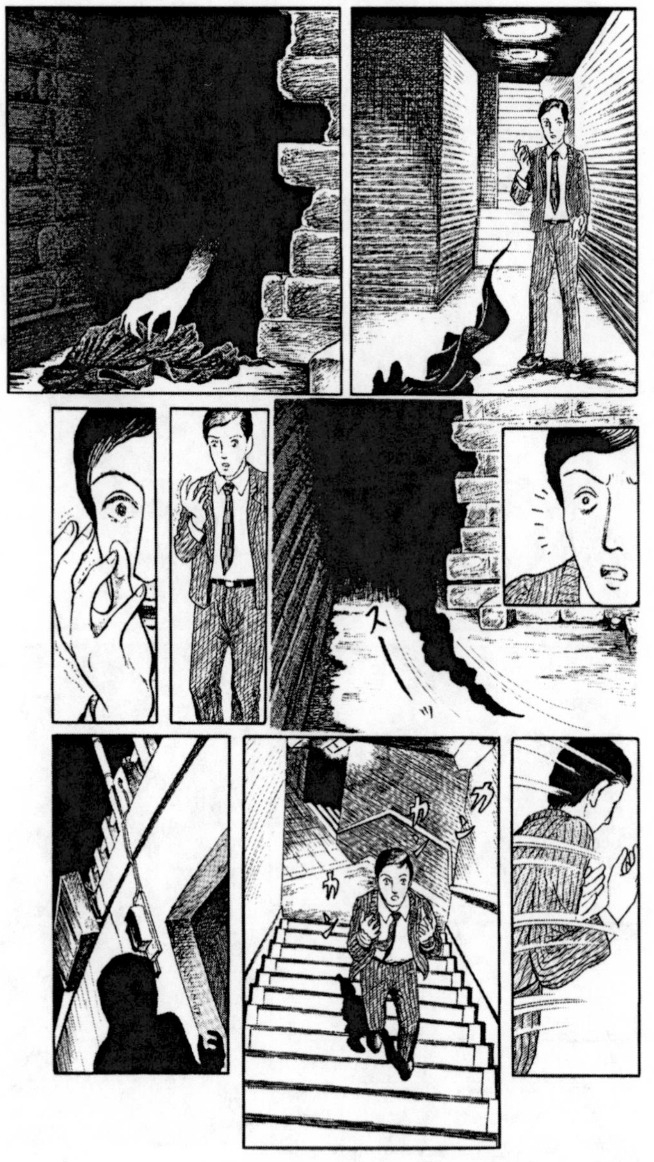
スーッ
カッ
カッ

MY GIRL-FRIEND AND BUDDIES ARE PROBABLY RIGHT.
I GLIMPSED SOMETHING WEIRD UNDER THAT CLOTH...
THAT SURE WASN'T A GUY FROM THE COLLECTION AGENCY...
I TOUCHED IT... WHAT AN ODD, IN-DESCRIBABLE FEELING.
SOMETHING WRONG WITH THE CONSTRUCTION THERE?
IT'S HALF FINISHED AND EMPTY, A DEAD END...
NEXT MORNING I CHECKED THAT SUBWAY STAIRWELL, BUT...
AFTERWARD I STILL SAW THE SHADOW NEXT TO THE TRACKS.

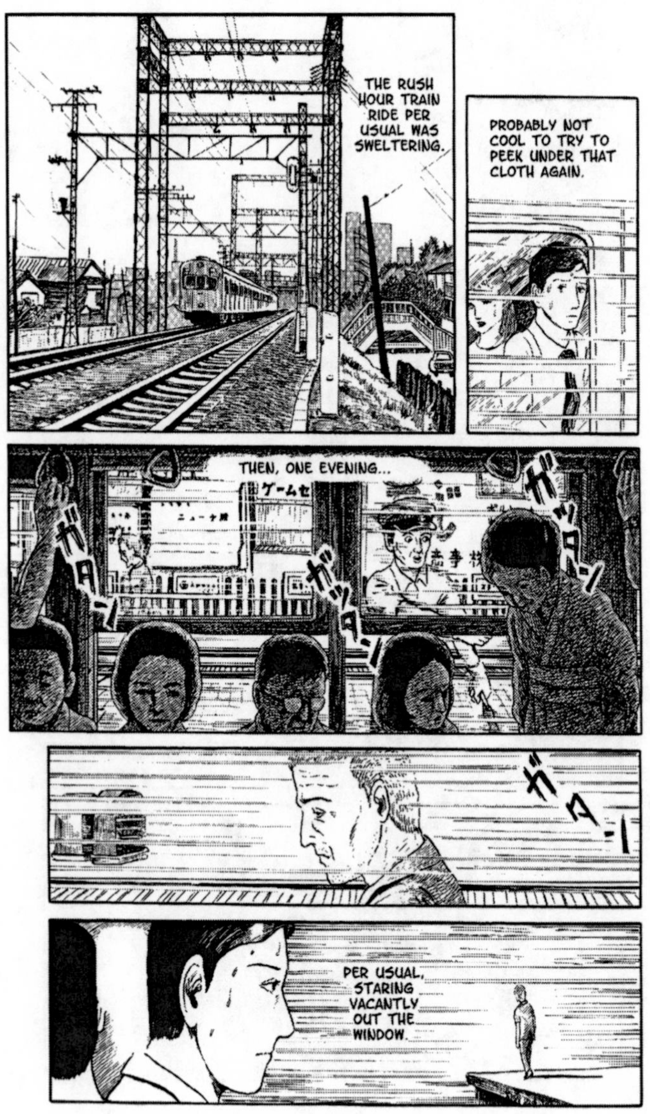
PROBABLY NOT COOL TO TRY TO PEEK UNDER THAT CLOTH AGAIN.
THE RUSH HOUR TRAIN RIDE PER USUAL WAS SWELTERING.
THEN, ONE EVENING...
ゲームセ
PER USUAL, STARING VACANTLY OUT THE WINDOW.

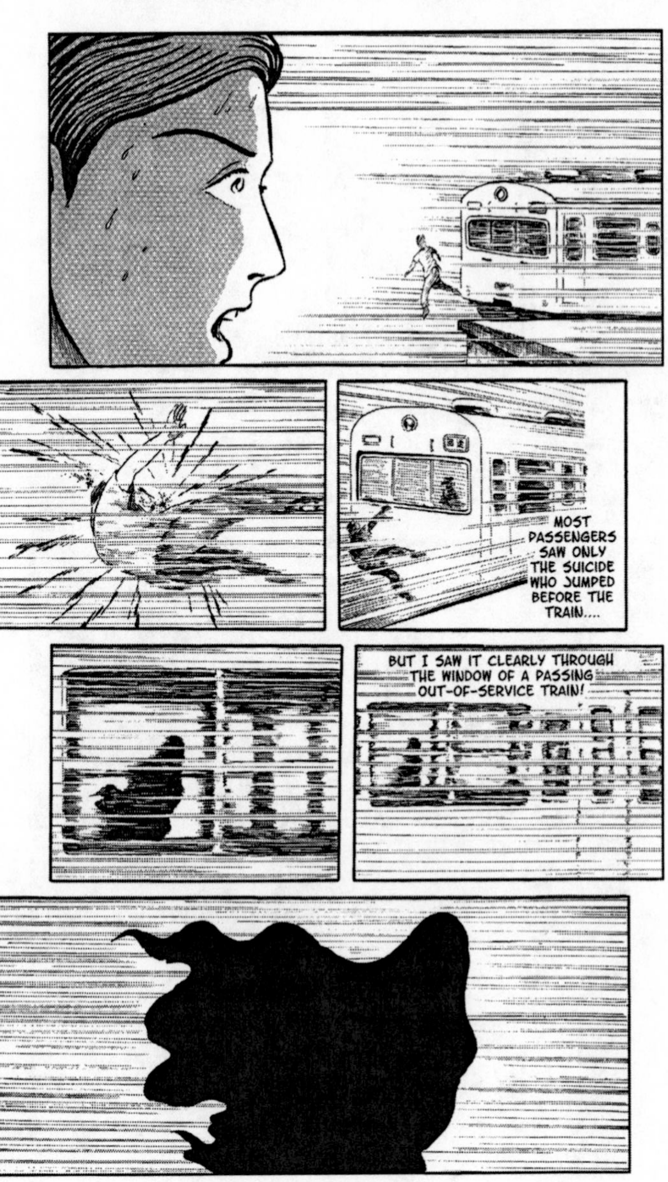
MOST PASSENGERS SAW ONLY THE SUICIDE WHO JUMPED BEFORE THE TRAIN....
BUT I SAW IT CLEARLY THROUGH THE WINDOW OF A PASSING OUT-OF-SERVICE TRAIN!

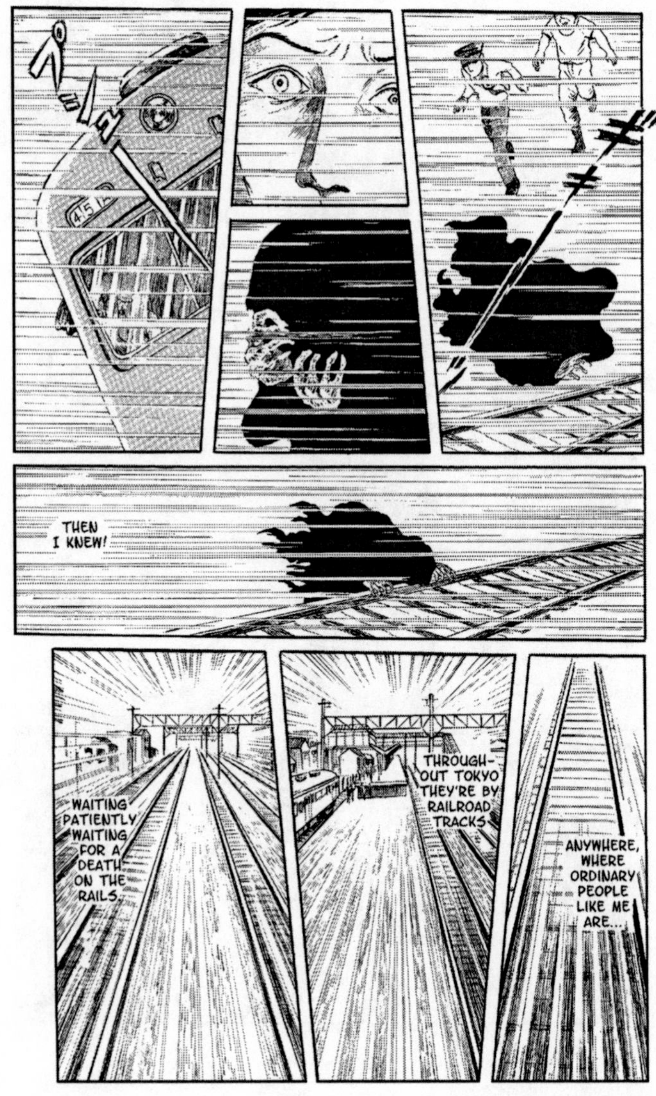
THEN I KNEW!
WAITING PATIENTLY WAITING FOR A DEATH ON THE RAILS.
THROUGH-OUT TOKYO THEY'RE BY RAILROAD TRACKS
ANYWHERE, WHERE ORDINARY PEOPLE LIKE ME ARE...

JUST TO
GOBBLE UP
A LITTLE
PIECE OF
FLESH
OR TO LICK
THE BLOOD
FROM THE
TIES.
PERVERSELY
HUNGRILY
WAITING
TO QUENCH
A LITTLE
OF THEIR
THIRST.
WAITING
ON AND
ON...

CAN'T HELP BUT WONDER IF THERE'S A CORRIDOR BEYOND MY SIGHT.
WHERE DOES THAT DARKNESS LEAD TO? WINDING DEEPER DOWN INTO THE DARK....
DEEP WITHIN THAT SUBWAY PASSAGE....
ズッ
THE SHADOW OF OUR OWN BLACK HEARTS?
ズルッ
OR IS THAT DARKNESS ...
ズッ
.....GHOULS...

AS ALWAYS, THAT SPECTRE WAITS BY THE TRACKS.
BUT I DON'T STARE VACANTLY OUTSIDE ANYMORE.
READING SPORTS IS MY DAILY ROUTINE NOW.
IT'LL BE COOLER IN THE FALL.
AND MY DAILY COMMUTE'S NOW A LITTLE MORE COMFORTABLE.

Thank you.

Please turn the book back right-side up now.

Contributors

Dorothy Gambrell ("A Sinister Spectre")

DOROTHY GAMBRELL, WHO localized "A Sinister Spectre," has neither a career nor hobbies. She has spent the last ten years self-publishing cartoons at catandgirl.com

Mark Gibeau ("The Arm")

I AM A lecturer in Japanese language, literature and culture at The Australian National University in . . . Australia. My interest in Japanese literature was first sparked by the Abe Kōbō story "The Magic Chalk" in Van Gessel's wonderful anthology of short stories, *The Shōwa Anthology*—an interest that (much to my own surprise) ultimately led me to graduate school and a Ph.D. dissertation on Abe Kōbō. In addition to teaching, trying to improve my literary translation and slowly converting my dissertation into a book, I am interested in Okinawan literature and the work of Medoruma Shun in particular.

Higashi Masao ("Introduction: Earthquakes, Lightning, Fire, and Father")

HIGASHI MASAO IS a noted anthologist, literary critic, and the editor of Japan's first magazine specializing in *kaidan* (strange tales) fiction, named *Yoo* (幽).

In 1982 he founded Japan's only magazine for research into strange and uncanny literature, *Fantastic Literature Magazine* (幻想文学, Gensō bungaku), published by Atelier Octa, serving as editor for twenty-one years until the magazine folded in 2003.

It was an invaluable publication not only for its content, but also because it discovered and nurtured a host of new authors, researchers and critics in the field.

Recently he has concentrated on compiling anthologies, producing criticism of fantastic and horror literature, and researching the *kaidan* genre, active in a wide range of projects. As a critic he has suggested new styles and interpretations in the field, including the growing "Horror Japanesque" movement and the "palm-of-the-hand *kaidan*" consisting of uncanny stories told in no more than eight hundred characters. He is well-known as a researcher of the uniquely Japanese *hyaku monogatari* tradition, with numerous books and anthologies published.

He serves on the selections committees for various literary prizes in the kaidan genre, and since 2004 has written the Genyō (幻妖) book blog on uncanny and fantastic literature cooperatively with online bookseller bk1, at http://blog.bk1.jp/genyo/

Seth Jacobowitz
("Doctor Mera's Mysterious Crimes")

SETH JACOBOWITZ IS currently an assistant professor of Humanities at San Francisco State University. He received his B.A. in English literature from Columbia University, and his M.A. in Asian Studies and Ph.D. in East Asian Literature from Cornell University. He was a Fulbright Fellow to Nagoya University, a Japan Foundation Fellow at Waseda University, and a Postdoctoral Fellow at the Reischauer Institute of Japanese Studies at Harvard University. His published translations include *The Edogawa Rampo Reader* (Kurodahan Press, 2008).

Derek Lin
("In Thy Shadow")

DEREK LIN TEACHES elementary Japanese to middle school children in Singapore. In his spare time, he plans road trips across Japan. He has a Bachelor's in Literature from Tsukuba University. This is his first published work.

Mark MacWilliams
("A Sinister Spectre")

MARK MACWILLIAMS IS a professor of Religious Studies at St. Lawrence University, Canton, NY, where he teaches East Asian religions. His current area of research is religion and visual culture. His manga-related publications include "Revisioning Japanese Religiosity: Osamu Tezuka's *Hi no tori* (*The Phoenix*)," in *Global Goes Local: Popular Culture in Asia* (University of British Columbia Press, 2002), and *Japanese Visual Culture: Explorations in Manga and Anime* (M.E. Sharpe, 2008).

Miri Nakamura
("Introduction: Earthquakes, Lightning, Fire, and Father")

MIRI NAKAMURA IS Assistant Professor of Japanese Literature and Language at Wesleyan University. She specializes in Japanese fantastic fiction, and she is currently working on a book on the rise of the uncanny in modern Japan. She has translated several academic works, which can be found in *Robot Ghosts and Wired Dreams* (University of Minnesota Press, 2007) and *Pacific Rim Modernisms* (University of Toronto Press, 2009).

Rossa O'Muireartaigh ("Spider")

ROSSA O'MUIREARTAIGH IS a freelance Japanese to English translator. He has previously studied Asian philosophy at Nagoya University in Japan. He has also lectured in Japanese studies at Dublin City University, Ireland and in Japanese translation at Newcastle University in England. He has written various academic papers on translation, drama, and religious studies. Married with one adorable daughter, he is currently enjoying a change of scenery residing in Malta.

Nancy H. Ross ("Expunged by Yakumo")

Nancy H. Ross worked as a reporter and editor before coming to Japan in 1993. She was the winner of the Distinguished Translation Award in the 4th Shizuoka International Translation Competition in 2003 and the 2008 Kurodahan Press Translation Prize. She lives in Hiroshima Prefecture with her charming cats Koharu and Ayame.

Kathleen Taji ("The Face")

A THIRD-GENERATION JAPANESE American, Kathleen Taji has been involved in several literary translation projects with Kurodahan Press beginning with the four-volume Lairs of the Hidden Gods anthology where her translated works include "Import of Tremors" by Yamada Masaki, "Terror Rate" by Konaka Chiaki, "The Road" by Aramata Hiroshi, "C-City" by Kobayashi Yasumi, "Quest of the Nameless City" by Tachihara Tōya, and "City of the

Dreaming God" by Yufuku Senowo. She also translated the novel Queen of K'n-Yan by Asamatsu Ken, and is presently working on the translation of the SF novel Crystal Silence by Fujisaki Shingo. She lives in the suburbs of Los Angeles with her two African parrots and her desert tortoise, Miz Pamie.

Ginny Tapley Takemori
("The Midsummer Emissary")

GINNY TAPLEY TAKEMORI started out translating Spanish and Catalan, and went on to work as a literary agent specializing in foreign rights (with Ute Körner in Barcelona) and as an editor with Kodansha International in Tokyo, before returning to translation, this time from Japanese. She holds a BA (Hons) in Japanese from SOAS (London University) and is currently studying for an MA with the University of Sheffield. Now based in Tsukuba, Japan, she has long enjoyed roaming other worlds, and hopes to similarly touch the hearts and minds of readers with her own translations of fiction and nonfiction.

Steven P. Venti
("A Bizarre Reunion")

STEVEN P. VENTI was born in 1953 and grew up in the town of Braintree on Boston's south shore. Upon graduating from the University of California at Santa Barbara with a B.A. in music composition, he came to Japan in 1984 and began translating full-time in 1995 after ten years of teaching. He completed an M.A. in Advanced Japanese Studies through a distance learning program at the University of Sheffield in 1998 and in September 2002 founded BHK Limited, a company specializing in Japanese-to-English translation services.

Robert Weinberg
("Secrets of the Metropolis")

ROBERT WEINBERG IS the author of sixteen novels, two short story collections, and sixteen non-fiction books. He has also edited over 150 anthologies. He is best known for his trilogy, the *Masquerade of the Red Death*, and his non-fiction book, *Horror of the Twentieth Century*. Bob is a two-time winner of the Bram Stoker Award; a two-time winner of the World Fantasy Award; and a winner of the Lifetime Achievement Award from the Horror Writers Association. www.robertweinberg.net

"The Fox-Woman Kuzunoha Leaving Her Child"

Print by Yoshitoshi Tsukioka, courtesy of the John Stevenson Collection

In East Asia, foxes (kitsune) are mysterious, magical creatures, and may be friendly or (more often) malicious and dangerous.

A tenth-century nobleman, Abe no Yasuna, was reciting poems in the gardens of the Inari temple outside Kyoto when men ran by, hunting a fox. The fox stopped in front of Abe, appealing for help, and Abe hid it in his robes. Soon after, Abe met and married a beautiful young girl named Kuzunoha. She bore him a son and they lived happily together for three years. She then died of a fever, appearing in a dream to tell him not to mourn her as she was not human but the vixen whose life he had saved. In this print, her shadow reveals her true nature to her child, who grew up to become Abe no Seimei.

Yoshitoshi Tsukioka (芳年月岡), aka Yoshitoshi Taiso (芳年大蘇) (1839–1892), is generally recognized as the last master of ukiyo-e woodblock printing, as well as one of its great innovators. His career spanned the Meiji Restoration, covering from the feudal era to modernizing Japan, and while Yoshitoshi was interested in new ideas from the West he was concerned with the erosion of traditional Japanese culture, including traditional woodblock printing.

His life is perhaps best summed up by John Stevenson, in his book *Yoshitoshi's One Hundred Aspects of the Moon* (Hotei Publishing, 2001):

> Yoshitoshi's courage, vision and force of character gave ukiyo-e another generation of life, and illuminated it with one last burst of glory.

The cover is from his *New Forms of Thirty-Six Ghosts* (1889–1892), a series of 36 prints now recognized as one of his greatest achievements, together with the one hundred prints in his masterpiece, the *One Hundred Aspects of the Moon* (1885–1892) series.

AHAN PRESS

CPSIA information can be obtained at www.ICGtesting.com
Printed in the USA
LVOW052000120213

319790LV00001B/9/P